S0-BFB-413

Daniel Seery is a writer from Dublin. His work has appeared in local and national publications including *The Stinging Fly* and *REA Journal* and he has worked on a number of public arts commissions. In 2012 he was the resident writer in the Axis Centre Ballymun. He has also written and directed a play, *The One We Left Behind*, which ran in The Irish Writers' Centre in May 2012 and in the Helix in August 2012.

First published in 2014 by
Liberties Press
140 Terenure Road North | Terenure | Dublin 6W
Tel: +353 (1) 405 5701
www.libertiespress.com | info@libertiespress.com
Trade enquiries to Gill & Macmillan Distribution
Hume Avenue | Park West | Dublin 12
T: +353 (1) 500 9534 | F: +353 (1) 500 9595 | E: sales@gillmacmillan.ie

Distributed in the UK by
Turnaround Publisher Services
Unit 3 | Olympia Trading Estate | Coburg Road | London N22 6TZ
T: +44 (0) 20 8829 3000 | E: orders@turnaround-uk.com

Distributed in the United States by
IPM | 22841 Quicksilver Dr | Dulles, VA 20166
T: +1 (703) 661-1586 | F: +1 (703) 661-1547 | E: ipmmail@presswarehouse.com

Copyright © Daniel Seery, 2014
The author asserts his moral rights.

ISBN: 978-1-909718-23-4
2 4 6 8 10 9 7 5 3 1

A CIP record for this title is available from the British Library.

Cover design by Liberties Press
Internal design by Liberties Press

This book is sold subject to the condition that it shall not, by way
of trade or otherwise, be lent, resold, hired out or otherwise circulated, without the publisher's prior consent, in any form other than that in
which it is published and without a similar condition including this
condition being imposed on the subsequent publisher.
No part of this publication may be reproduced or transmitted in
any form or by any means, electronic or mechanical, including
photocopying, recording or storage in any information or retrieval
system, without the prior permission of the publisher in writing.

The publishers gratefully acknowledge
financial assistance from the Arts Council.

*All characters in this book are fictitious, and any resemblance to
actual persons, living or dead, is purely coincidental.*

A Model Partner

Daniel Seery

For Sonia

Chapter 1

It was March when Tom Stacey met the woman from Donaghmede who couldn't stop crying. The date had been set up by an agency, Happy Couples, a business owned by two middle-aged women, both silver-haired, both wearers of glasses, Anna slightly more dumpy than Martha but without the facial hair which Martha tries to hide under sludgy-looking foundation. Their office, a single room above a dental surgery near the Artane Roundabout, is the cramped type, yellowed blinds on the window, desks side by side, two sturdy grey filing cabinets and a wooden unit where thin documents slouch and bend on each shelf.

They are believers in love, Martha and Anna, devout followers. And a couple of years ago Tom would have never set foot in a place like this but in some ways Tom is a believer himself, a believer in last chances. He would never admit this to himself, never clasp his hands together and rock back and forth urging himself on with a mantra.

Last shot Tommy boy, last one in the bag.

But there's only so long that emptiness can stay unfilled and at the time he joined the agency Tom was starting to worry about what was going to fill his emptiness.

So he walked in off the street and he took the single chair that was neither in front of Martha's desk nor in front of Anna's but somewhere in between and which made Tom feel exposed and a little unsure of where to look. He rested his hands on his lap and waited for their guidance.

They sat with identical straight-backed poses, heads angled to the right and that little half-smile that comes on people when they are dealing with those who they pity.

'We know what it's like,' Martha said.

'We've been there before,' Anna added in an identical tone.

'It can be difficult to meet new people.'

Martha offered an exaggerated slump of the shoulders and a put-on sad face or what Anna would later refer to as a 'frownie face'.

They settled on the woman from Donaghmede. The crier. It was to be his first date with the agency and the ladies congratulated each other on the find and then congratulated Tom on what was to be his perfect match. Tom was shown her picture. She was pretty in a stylised, conventional way, her hair layered in varying shades of brown, her eyebrows the barest of lines, large blue eyes and thin face. Two weeks later, in real-life physical form she would resemble this photograph only slightly and Tom would think of those travel guides that are on a special stand in his local library, the ones where all the photographs have been taken on a bright sunny day, and he would think how different a place can look with an overcast sky in the middle of winter.

He met her in a pub on Capel Street, a place with large arch windows and a recently constructed dining area. Cutlery rested on white paper napkins and the menus were laminated and sandwiched between glass salt shakers and grubby bottles of tomato ketchup. He arrived first and requested the table nearest the door, moving his chair so that when he sat down he was directly facing the exit. She arrived ten minutes late. She shed her first tears after the starter and by the time the main course landed on the table she could hardly speak. She would inhale rapidly a number of times at the start of each sentence and make a stammering noise at the back of her throat, in some ways like a Cortina his grandfather once owned, a car which would choke over and over on cold mornings before the engine would eventually catch and grumble to life.

She said she was a primary school teacher and that she was depressed, going as far as to call herself a 'puddle'.

'I'm a puddle,' she blubbered. 'Nobody wants to be anywhere near a puddle.'

This would stay with Tom long after the date ended. A puddle. There is something deeply sad about puddles, he would think to himself.

'Try not to worry about it,' Tom had said. 'Things will get better. They always get better.'

At one point he almost touched her hand. It looked so delicate and soft resting on the table. He reached across but lost his nerve at the last moment, instead jilting his hand to the right, sending the sauce bottle into a precarious wobble.

They didn't agree to a second meet that evening but Tom did ask Martha a few weeks later how the woman was getting on. Martha gave a flight-attendant type smile and said that 'Everyone is entitled to their privacy and if a particular client decides they do not want to see another particular client then it is best for all concerned to leave it in the past.'

Tom didn't press any further.

His second date wasn't as bad as the first but Tom laughed a little too loud at her jokes and asked her if she was okay too many times. As the night wore on she became standoffish and the noise of chewing became more audible and the clink of cutlery on plates all too uncomfortable in the silence. There have been plenty of dates since then, all as unsuccessful, and Tom is beginning to wonder if this dating agency is the best way to go.

'Tom,' Martha says when he enters the office. She folds her arms and sits forward. 'How are you keeping?'

He notices the strain of her smile, the half-glance to her colleague. Anna stands and retrieves a file from the cabinet behind her while Tom takes a seat.

'How did it go last night with . . .' Anna rifles through the files for a couple of seconds, stops and scrolls her finger downward. 'Ah, with Joyce. The lady from, um, Cabra Park.'

'The Spark from the Park!' Martha suddenly shouts and claps her hands together.

They both howl.

Tom waits for them to finish.

'We didn't really get on,' he says and recalls the woman from the previous night, attractive, pallid skin and shoulder-length mousey hair that she had a habit of fidgeting with. The date was uneasy. She kept her head down for most of it, refusing to look him in the face, played with the food on her plate. It gave him plenty of time to notice the skinniness of her arms, the six tiny holes along the edge of her ear, relics of a more extreme lifestyle of piercings and God knows what else.

Tom tried his best to make the date a success. Twenty-one failed dates can do that; they can drive a person to make an effort. He talked about this and that, the food and service, the traffic in Dublin and the price of drink. This received little response so he talked about the book he was reading, a book about love and beauty that he had found in a second-hand bookshop. She didn't seem interested in the changing nature of beauty, in the societal benefits that come with being beautiful or his claims that in the sixteenth century people believed that ugliness and deformity were signs of inherent evil.

'Imagine that. Thinking that you are evil just because you have a mono-brow or something,' he joked.

She didn't laugh and she didn't even look up when he revealed that some people have a fear of ugliness.

'Cacophobia,' he said and nodded, waiting for a reaction. She continued to play with her food. 'Where venustraphobia,' he muttered, 'is the fear of beautiful women. I'd imagine that's much more common.'

As the evening wore on Tom couldn't help but see fragility behind her quiet beauty. He didn't ask her if she would like to go for a drink afterward and she walked off without offering him a kiss on the cheek. Her departure was so quiet that he wasn't even sure she had said goodbye to him.

'God, I thought you two would have made a nice match,' Martha says.

'Me too,' Anna agrees. 'But don't worry. There are plenty more fish in the books.' She flicks through her folder. 'There are certain things that make two people incompatible. But all you need is to find the one person that is compatible. That's the good thing Tom. You only need one woman and you only need to find her once.'

Tom has heard this before. She speaks and he drifts, becomes distracted by the disorganisation of the desks, the uneven nature of the furniture, a picture on the wall that is clearly askew. Not mildly askew. Completely askew.

Christ, they might as well have hung it upside down.

There is a stain on Anna's sleeve, red, roughly the shape of Madagascar, an island which has been the focus of a series of documentaries he has enjoyed recently. He couldn't say for sure but it is most probably tomato ketchup and it most probably smells of vinegar and it will probably stay on that sleeve even after the blouse has been washed. He follows the mark as she talks.

'And I know that sometimes it's hard to keep the head up. But just remember. It only has to work once,' Anna makes notes on a page in the folder.

That smell, Tom thinks.

That stain.

The blob of sauce falling from the bottle.

The slurp as the air replaces the wet gloop.

Splat as it lands.

Splat as it drips.

Splat.

'Splat.'

'Sorry?' Anna says.

'Sorry?' Tom wrinkles his brow.

'Did you say something Tom?' Anna asks without looking up.

'No, I don't think so.'

'Could have sworn you said something,' she turns a page over and writes some more notes.

Tom reddens, looks away from Anna.

'You need to go out more,' she says and looks up at Tom. 'Have you been going out at all?'

'It's difficult to get the time,' he eventually responds.

'Well, let me just stop you there,' Anna says. 'If you don't have time to go out now then how are you going to have time for a lady in your life?'

Tom understands that he would have a lot more time on his hands if he didn't have to go out on dead-end dates.

'You need to get out,' Anna stresses her point by chopping the air with her hand. 'It's important that you build a good social life. Have you even been looking for opportunities to go out?'

'Yeah, of course,' Tom nods quickly. 'There's some work thing on soon. I suppose I could go to that.'

'A work outing. Perfect.' Anna makes a note of this in a space in the folder. 'You have plenty going for you Tom. You're independent and you have a job. You're relatively handsome too. Just try not to worry so much about the little things.'

Tom arches an eyebrow.

'You know,' Anna says. 'The little details.'

'There have been some complaints,' Martha says quickly, like it is something that she has been trying to hold in for quite a while. 'From some of the women.'

Anna's eyes widen.

'Look, we realise that everyone is different,' she says while throwing Martha a swift look.

Martha merely taps a page which she has removed from her own folder.

'The furniture,' Martha says.

'People can become set in their ways,' Anna tries to talk over her.

'The cutlery,' Martha continues. 'The location of the table.'

'It's just that relationships are about give and take,' Anna increases the volume.

'Grammar,' Martha says. 'Doors. Hair.'

'Sometimes you have to give a little,' Anna says.

'Hair?' Tom turns to Martha. 'I've never mentioned I had a problem with hair.'

Martha tips her glasses forward and reads from the page.

'"He asked me how many times I washed my hair,"' she says. '"He then informed me that when it comes to head lice, they don't mind if your hair is clean or dirty."'

'You should be more careful about what you say,' Anna clenches her hands together and bends toward him.

'I was only saying that she had nice hair,' Tom says.

'Why didn't you just say that? You have nice hair. That's all you had to say,' Anna says.

'I did say that.'

' "Girls are more likely to be infested by head lice than boys," ' Martha reads. ' "I'm not sure what he meant by this. I don't have head lice." '

'Up to four times more likely,' Tom says.

Martha shakes her head.

'They need to have the same interests as me,' Tom defends himself, pats his chest with an open hand as he speaks. 'It's not about head lice or cutlery. It's about having the same interests as me.'

'Sandra Lyons,' Anna says, her finger scrolling down a page. 'She's forty-one. A little bit older than you but that shouldn't matter. It says here that she likes reading.'

'She likes reading what?' Tom asks.

'I'm guessing books,' Martha says in a dour tone.

'What type of books?' Tom asks. 'What type of authors? Jesus, sure she might only read the *RTÉ* bloody *Guide*.'

'Tom. There's no need for that language,' Anna says. 'And there's nothing wrong with the *RTÉ Guide*,' she mutters afterward.

'I'm sorry. It's just that,' Tom shrugs and exhales. 'I don't know. You say not to worry about the little things but it's all about the little things.'

Anna offers him a photograph.

Tom takes it, his mouth tightens and he shakes his head slightly.

'It's only a headshot.'

'We've been over this,' Martha says. 'A headshot is enough.'

'Besides,' Anna says. 'Body shape shouldn't be that important.'

Tom bows his head and rubs his neck. He doesn't mean body

shape. He is thinking of a couple of his dates. They were nail-biters. The name itself brings up a horrible image of a woman nibbling away at her fingers, pieces of nails thrown outward. And the noise, the clickety-click as her head moves back and forth like the carriage on a typewriter. He shivered when he first caught sight of those kind of nails on a date, nibbled down so far it looked as if they were receding into the fingers. And then that's all he could see for the whole date. This made him think that a headshot isn't enough. There should be a shot of the nails, the toenails too and a shot of the ears, taken with a suitable flash just to be sure that they are good and clean.

'Maybe the form needs more detail,' Tom says. It is something that has been floating around his head for a time now but only really anchors when the words have left his mouth.

Needs more detail.

Of course.

The more detail, the less chance of error.

'Subcategories or something,' he thinks aloud. 'Like imagine if they knew that I liked reading about history or if they realised that they watched the same documentaries as me, I don't know, if they found the same things funny maybe I wouldn't have to go on a million dates to find the right woman. If she knew what I want-ed it would reduce the error factor.'

'And if you knew,' Martha says.

'What?'

'If you knew what you wanted that would help too.'

Tom shakes his head.

'What do you want Tom? You have to tell us. You come in here and you explain what went wrong with your dates and what you think is wrong with the service. You want everything and you want nothing at the same time. Well, I'm sorry Tom, we just can't supply everything and nothing.'

'I want to find someone,' Tom says.

'I know Tom, everybody who comes in here wants to find someone. But what someone do you want? Who is your ideal woman?'

Tom crosses his legs and looks upward, to the grille in the ceiling tiles. He tries to think of what he wants in his ideal woman but there is nothing there. All he sees is the dust which lines each section of the grille. And the third metal bar from the top. It is bent slightly and, in his mind, it has ruined the whole shape of the grille.

Chapter 2

Tom knew the chair was worth saving as soon as he saw it. He found it in a skip around the time he joined the agency, the base balanced on the rusted lip, fabric balding and torn, front legs hanging over the side like a mistreated animal trying to escape its confines. Despite its appearance and without even thoroughly inspecting it Tom had a feeling about that chair. It owned such clean, straight lines, was angled in all the right places, that Tom rescued it from the skip and brought it home.

Later that day, after close inspection, he would consider whether he had acquired some natural skill for measuring objects with the naked eye because the chair was indeed perfect for his bed-sit. And for a couple of weeks afterward, in the time that he spent mending it, the notion that he should hone and improve this natural measuring ability entered his head and he would debate whether he was destined for a career in this kind of area. He imagined himself on a television show, a glittering set and a shiny host.

'Tom Stacey, everybody.'

He saw himself perched on a black leather armchair facing the audience, a number of objects separating them, lined in a row. Tom's challenge was to guess the height and width.

'The antique table Tom.'

'Height 88 centimetres, width 105 centimetres.'

'Pen.'

'14 centimetres in length, 0.8 centimetres in diameter.'

'DVD holder.'

'4.4 feet in height.'

'In metric please Tom.'

'Of course, silly me. Height 134 centimetres, width 30 centimetres.'

'Amazing. What a talented young man. A gift like this can open up doors in so many places.'

The possibilities seemed endless, surveying for road works, design – exterior and interior – architecture. But when Tom tried to rediscover his talent a couple of weeks later he found that his gift was the intermittent kind, the type which afflicts so many people, such as only being able to sing well when husky with the flu and only having a talent for darts when a particular level of drunkenness is reached. Tom couldn't say that his interest in measuring began on finding that chair but it was heightened, his awareness of dimensions and diameters, his consideration of proportions and balance, symmetry, and what comes with this is an awareness of disproportions, misalignments and the knowledge that the world is weighed down with seemingly endless imperfections.

Tom's chair faces the sole window in his bed-sit, a window which Tom believes was probably an afterthought for the architects. It is small and gullet-height, a position which would force a person to bend when standing or stretch when sitting on your average seat. There is an apartment block next to Tom's building, half empty or half full depending on what way you look at things. A lane, about seven feet in width, separates the two buildings and a large window in the opposite building faces Tom's small one.

Tom likes to stare across and think.

There is always a light on in that room opposite his, exposing semi-painted walls and shelves holding the weight of numerous tins and cloths and a scrunched dustsheet. The highest shelf slants at an angle and the cans of paint and varnish stand on the lowest end, long ago drawn into that position by a combination of gravity and lack of friction on the smooth surface. There have been times where he has stared at that shelf for so long that he would begin to feel that it wasn't the shelf that was slanted but everything else. Tom has never seen anyone in that room. Not once. And he has recently been thinking about this and in a way it is beginning to taint the joy of his chair and his window because that room in the opposite building is starting to feel like some kind of shrine to the loneliness which surrounds his life.

Tom's building is a series of identically drab corridors, the atmosphere perpetually damp, the brown carpets laden with a design that can often be found on the cardigans of old men in rest homes or on socks found in shops where old women still buy socks for their husbands. The walls are the colour of latté and nothing has been painted for as long as Tom can remember. Tom only ever sees the owner, Mr Reilly, when he is paying his rent once a month or when the owner is repairing something near the entrance or near his bed-sit.

He is a lump of a man, a dough-like impression to his skin. He wears cords which hang half-way down his arse, dragging his underpants with them. He has a thick Northern accent, nasal and incomprehensible to Tom, and conversation with the man seems more like a series of high-pitched yelps than sentences and Tom finds himself nodding a lot in his presence and trying to end the conversation with long bouts of silence accompanied by polite smiling.

Foreign tongues rattle from behind hollow, wooden doors in the evenings and throughout the day Japanese students leave and return, quietly going about their business. Tom finds the Japanese girls beautiful, the word 'enchanting' rises to mind even though this is the type of word that Tom finds a bit flowery and makes him think of tacky period dramas with lots of big hair and cleavage and farm boys that are played by actors in their mid-thirties. But 'enchanting' does sum up these Japanese girls, they are quiet and graceful, swanlike even, in the way they duck their heads to the side when he meets their gaze.

And they always smile at him. It's nice to have a stranger smile at you, he thinks, it makes you remember that the world isn't all bad.

It is difficult to sleep in his building. The inner walls of his bed-sit are thin. There are frequently bumps in the night. He's not exactly sure what they are. They could be caused by the old man next door, Mr Walters, continuously getting up because of his weak prostate or it could be the movement of Mrs Walters, his wife. From the bathroom on the landing he can hear them some evenings, talking over the constant murmur of the television, random announcements, speech that needs little words, communicating as much through what is unsaid as what is said. Sometimes, usually when he has been drinking, he likes to listen to them, leaning against the cold tiles in the bathroom, the scent of lemon and bleach filling the space, the air outside clicking the vent on the upper wall. Exterior sounds intrude through that vent. There always seems to be a dog barking. And there are always voices in the distance, kids, their hollers and their laughter.

Tonight his neighbours are watching something funny. The man laughs continuously, deep and weighty. Tom imagines it spreading through the walls like heat. She never laughs. Or if she does it is too low for Tom to hear. But he imagines that she usually sits and dreams and offers a little smile when her husband looks in her direction, more of that silent communication.

I'm still with you, love. I'm still on your side.

Tom leaves the bathroom when the cold becomes uncomfortable and he flicks through the stations on his own TV until he finds the programme they are watching. And he forces himself to laugh at the times when the audience laugh. And he imagines they are in the room with him.

But an hour later, when the television is switched off and there is quiet, Tom begins to feel a weight, a weight that he has been feeling a lot recently. It appears in the place where chest and stomach meet, heavy, slightly painful as if he is holding his breath just a fraction longer than he should be. It grows heavier as the evening rolls on and his mind returns to events that happened earlier that day as it often does when he has had a bad one. And he is drawn back into a situation which happened in the canteen in work.

It had been lunch-time. He was eating ham sandwiches, brown bread neatly buttered, cut diagonally so they formed triangular shapes. There were two other people at the table. Claire Doyle, a beefy woman with short hair who has Cup-a-Soups every day for her lunch and who shields the cup with her free arm whilst eating. And Laura O'Driscoll, a woman with straight ginger hair and a face so pale it accentuates any slight blemish or mark on her skin. Her arms are sapling-thin and her form is shapeless except to those who consider a straight line a shape. She works in the packaging department, had a brief affair with one of the forklift drivers and is a friend of someone who Tom had problems with in the past.

Tom knows that she doesn't like him. She isn't one to conceal it either but at lunch there was nobody speaking at the table and sometimes Tom can't help but fill in the silences. He had been talking and carefully opening the tinfoil on his sandwiches, laying it flat so there were no folds in the foil and rotating the sandwiches so that the line separating the triangular sandwiches was perpendicular to his frame on the chair. The topic he was discussing was cheese and in particular a type of cheese in Sardinia which contains living insect larvae.

'They're little white worms from the Cheese Fly,' he explained, bit into his sandwich, chewed and swallowed before continuing. 'The cheese that they eat is in a solid state but when the worms excrete the cheese it takes on a soft form. Then the locals eat this soft cheese. It's important that the worms are still alive when you eat them though.'

'Why are you saying this?' Laura snapped, pushing her sandwich away, a cheese sandwich.

Tom cocked an eyebrow and quietened.

'I'm trying to eat my poxy lunch,' she said, her pale face glowing at the cheeks. 'And you're going on about maggots.'

'I'm just saying,' Tom said.

'You're always just saying stuff. For God's sake. I'm sick of you just saying stuff.'

Her voice was rising all the time and with it attention from the others in the room. It was then that Tom sensed its approach, the weight. It begins with the standing of hairs on his arms and a phantom heaviness on his scalp. It comes on him like the slow building of a thunderstorm and in the cases so far this feeling has always been accompanied by a buzzing which seems somehow both distant and yet only a fingertip away and fair enough, Tom has since mulled it over, there always seems to be an actual object buzzing in the room when the sensation starts but it is more than the actual buzzing. Because the buzzing has never been as loud as it has been the last few weeks. He is sure of this.

Initially Tom tried to ignore it but Laura's whole demeanour was making it worse because she had this face on, this wounded expression, as if Tom had mortally offended her with his talk on flies. Tom understands that it is not a true expression. No, it is more like the demeanour of someone at a funeral who doesn't know the deceased, this effort of portraying a look that they know people are expecting. But it was the attitude of the other workers in the canteen which unsettled him more.

They were angry.

At him.

He was sure of this, even though they couldn't possibly know what had actually occurred at the table.

'I can't even sit here and eat my lunch without you just saying something,' Laura continued.

The buzzing had amplified.

Tom looked around the canteen.

Reflective, rectangular counters.

Dark, imposing, cube-shaped rotary ovens.

Flat wooden trays with short metal grooves.

That fridge.

That great big bloody catering fridge near the window. It was buzzing.

And someone else had noticed it. A canteen worker, a man with a tawny beard, fat-cheeked, long white smock and his hair squashed in a brown hairnet. He gave the fridge a push and the noise stopped for a couple of seconds before starting again.

'Why don't you look at me while I'm talking to you?' Laura demanded.

Tom felt sick. There was embarrassment and anger, building and growing.

And the fear. There was certainly fear and he would ask himself later what exactly he had been afraid of.

The bees?

Was it the bees? The bees that he suddenly believed the fridge was full of, thousands of them, crawling over each other, directionless, confused, just crawling and buzzing and making each other angrier. He followed the movement of the canteen worker as he approached the fridge again. His hand lifted to open the door and Tom felt this sudden lift in his chest.

Don't.

Don't.

The worker's hand was at the handle.

He was pulling it downward

Jesus Christ.

And Laura O'Driscoll's face was red and her mouth was moving so fast that it seemed to shiver because she was on a roll now and whatever was happening in her life, every bad thing that had occurred to her that day or that week, was suddenly the result of Tom and she was going to let him know. Boy, was he going to know.

And Tom looked from her shivering mouth to the fridge again.

He sensed the movement from within, the sound of rapid wings growing louder.

Some of the bees must be lifting, he thought, and he envisaged them forming a shape like in the cartoons, the dotted shape of a hammer in the air.

Three bees deep. Thousands of bees wide.

Bzz

Bzzzz

Bzzzzzz

He held his breath.

And he watched the hand pulling at the handle.

Watched the door opening.

No. No. No.

Heard the fierce noise.

Bzz

So loud it vibrated painfully on the eardrum.

Bzzz

Heard the tone loop higher and higher.

Bzzzz

Saw the fridge rattle on stumpy legs.

Open wider.

Bzzzzzzzzz

And then stop.

Suddenly.

An eerie silence following.

There was no swarm of bees. Not one single creature came from the fridge.

When Tom turned to face Laura again his vision was blurred. The sweat on his back had a stinging heat. He stood up and stumbled toward the door from the canteen. The walk was the unbalanced feeling in his head and the view of entertained faces.

'There really is something wrong with him,' he heard Laura say as he was leaving the canteen. It was followed by a low grunt of agreement from Claire Doyle followed by the noise of soup slurping from a spoon.

Tom prepares for bed and turns out the light. He thinks about how he looked scrambling from the canteen. He considers how people in work view him in general and he thinks about people, about how the damage doesn't always show even when the pain exists and how loneliness can be like a disease, spreading and eating away at you and everything that is close to you. He recalls the words of Martha from the agency, her questions on his ideal woman. And at three in the morning he reaches a decision about something that has been going through his head a lot recently, on something which relates to his past, at a time which he believes was his happiest, that thin sliver of light sandwiched between heavy darkness.

Yes.

He stretches before cupping his hands behind his head.

I will do it.

I will try to find her.

And he leans over the side of the bed and stretches blindly until he finds the pen which he knows is there. And he pats the ground gently with his fingertips until he hears the crackle of paper which is to the left of the pen and he scrawls the words as a reminder for the next day and as an indication that it is a decision and not something that has fallen from his dreams in the night.

He writes blindly.

I will do it.

I will find Sarah McCarthy.

Chapter 3

One of Tom's earliest memories is standing on the outskirts of town, the sky filling with gold and tangerine as the sun dipped and the rumble and groan of machinery as the landscape was shoved and altered to make way for a factory. It took eight months to build and when completed it was a bricked cube structure with hard, lumpy, porridge-coloured walls, wide rectangular windows and an unmarked car park. Initially it was home to a plastics manufacturer but they went bust in the late eighties. Printalux stepped in and took the place over then, a multinational company which initially dealt with commercial printing but has since moved on to the manufacture and repair of domestic and office printers. As a kid, Tom would never have expected that one day he would end up working as a service technician in the factory. Certainly not for fifteen years.

The factory is generally a quiet place to work, aside from the constant buzzing of electrical equipment and the frequent traffic of people to the desk beside his, a desk manned by Dave Roberts. Dave is from a middle-class family, wears hooded tops and baggy jeans, calls himself a revolutionary, an agenda he picked up in college before dropping out in his second year. He spends his breaks in his car smoking joints and eating salt-and-vinegar crisps.

Dave's desk reminds Tom of an old magic trick, the one where someone tries to remove a tablecloth from under a number of items without the items moving. Only Dave's desk is the trick when it goes horribly wrong.

It is Karl Wallace's turn to stop at the desk today. There is something late-nineties about his appearance, the goatee beard and the hair brushed forward. It somehow makes him look more dated and out-of-the-scene than someone who had a sixties, or seventies-era style, possibly even more than someone from the Middle Ages, Tom thinks. Tom isn't sure if the word 'friend' would describe his and Karl's relationship as kids. They did form part of the same group but while Karl was comfortably at the heart of everything, Tom was clinging on to the outer rim.

For the past week Karl has been trying to round up people to head to the Alpha Bar on the quays in honour of Jimmy Byrne's upcoming wedding. Jimmy works in the finance department. As does his wife-to-be, Clarissa, an overweight woman with a deflated-football look to her face. She keeps a photograph of a miniature terrier on her desk and circulates emails relating to animal cruelty from time to time. Jimmy, her husband-to-be, is a lanky-limbed, horse-faced man with taut, almost translucent skin on his face. Everything about him screams laziness, his slow midland drawl, his laborious walk, his extra-long toilet breaks and his marathon-length eating of sandwiches at lunch. They've been seeing each other for the last five years and broke the news of their wedding some weeks before.

Tom is half listening to their conversation while he trawls the internet. The note that was beside his bed when he woke up this morning is now tucked in his pocket.

He types the name 'Sarah McCarthy' into the search engine. The computers are slow in here, infuriating, the hour-glass image flashes. Tom tries to recall what Sarah McCarthy looked like. He repeats her name in his head and he tries to form an image of her. But her face is one which he can't fully grasp. It has a faded quality, diluted in some ways. The hair is almost there though, the colour of teak and long, wavy. He gets a flash of an expression too but it is gone as quickly as it appears.

'Come on Dave. It'll be one last fling for Jimmy,' Karl says.

'No man, I don't think I can make it.'

'We need a group.'

'I don't know,' Dave scratches his collarbone.

'You know what's wrong with you,' Karl says.

'What?'

'You need a midlife crisis.'

'What are ye on about?'

'If you had a midlife crisis you'd be only dying to hit a trendy club like the Alpha.'

'Fuck off.'

The webpage slowly ripples up the screen, stalls momentarily before settling. Tom scans the list of options that appear, mainly social networking links, a couple which Tom knows are dead-ends straight away and one link to a tuba player based in Scotland. Tom clicks on the tuba player link, just in case; a lot can happen in two decades. The social networking site shows photographs. He scans the images, imagines what she would look like today and quickly realises that Sarah is not one of them.

That's not my Sarah.

He runs this statement through his mind again, likes the way it feels, the idea of it.

My Sarah.

He shakes his head and forces a laugh. And he tries a different search engine.

'It can happen anytime,' Karl says. 'A midlife crisis, ye know.'

'I'm only thirty-four.'

'Ye can hit a midlife crisis any time between thirty and fifty. It depends on how long you're going to live.'

'That's a load of crap.'

'The longer you live the later you have a midlife crisis.'

'Are you being serious here? Please tell me you're taking the piss.'

'It's true.'

'So a midlife crisis is based on some kind of clairvoyant skill that your body has.'

'Look, I'm not saying that your body knows when you're going to get hit by a car or anything like that. I'm just saying that your body knows when you are going to die of natural causes. That includes cancer and shit.'

'That means that I'm going to die at sixty-eight.'

'Hey, don't blame me. I didn't come up with the rule. So are you going or what?'

'I don't know.'

Tom begins to hear Anna's voice in his head. You have to get out more, she had said. The way she said this, like he was a slow or stubborn child.

You have to get out more Tom, ignore the little things Tom.

Look both ways before crossing the road Tom.

You have to eat vegetables or your pancreas will rot Tom.

You have to get out more Tom.

'What time does it start?' Tom interrupts the pair.

Dave looks at him quickly and then looks to the ground.

'You thinking of going Tom?' Karl asks.

'I don't know. Maybe.'

Karl bounces on his heels for a moment.

'It'd probably kick off at about eight,' he says.

'You think it'd be all right to go?' Tom asks.

'Yeah, I'm sure it would,' Karl says.

Dave keeps quiet.

Tom hasn't been out with work in a long time. Nor has he been asked. He knows that the accusation has played a large part in this, the accusation from two years ago, from Tara Sheedy, the woman from Administration, a slightly overweight lady but with bumps in all the right places, pretty face, plain clothes, shy manner, the type of woman that Tom at first believed was well suited to him, the inoffensive and nice type of person. The pair seemed to get on okay. Fair enough, they had never sat down and talked in depth about any specific topic but she always smiled when she saw him, those high cheekbones of hers raised even more, enhancing her prettiness. And she laughed when he tried to be funny and replied when he spoke so he figured that there may be something there. He began to look for other signs, tried to read things in her movements, the way she would wave at him, hidden words in her sentences.

Then, Tom watched a wildlife documentary on the tiger beetle, a metallic green insect found in woodland areas. Apparently, after mating, the smaller male beetle rides around on the back of the larger female beetle to dissuade other suitors. There was something inspiring in this, in the way that the beetle didn't have to fight or carry out some flamboyant dance. He didn't have to use force and it mattered little how big he was. All he had to do was get things out into the open and then cling on to the beetle to let her know he was still interested. Tom decided he was going to ask her out. For a meal or a drink, he thought. Well, maybe not a drink. She might think he was just trying to get her drunk. But he was going to do it.

He saw flashes of her the following day. She was in the canteen with a large group, joking and laughing. She was walking with a supervisor across the factory floor. Whenever doubt washed over him he would envisage that little beetle clinging on to the female's back for dear life.

Hey look at me and my Missus. Check me out up here, riding around the place like I'm the king.

And he would get another bout of courage.

He spotted her with a pile of papers after lunch. He knew she was heading to the small photocopier room to the right of the toilets. He followed her, all the while trying to compose himself, going over the best way to approach it.

Tara, I don't normally do things like this . . .

Tara, I think we've been getting on really well . . .

Tara, there's something I want to ask you . . .

Tara, I've been watching you . . .

Tara, I think I love you . . .

His palms were damp, his fingers slipped on the handle as he tried to get into the room. He was aware of heat at his cheeks and sweat at his brow. He eventually managed a clumsy entrance. Tara was on her knees loading a photocopier tray with paper. She turned slightly to see who had walked in. There was little room to manoeuvre so Tom stood directly above her, looking down. His words deserted him and he was momentarily stunned by a blind panic.

She stood up and then he found his voice.

'Tara,' his words were croaky. 'There's something that I want to ask you.'

Her mouth was smiling but her eyes said differently.

Be brave. Be the insect. The insect.

'I was just wondering,' he stammered. 'If you were free this weekend.'

He could see her face dropping before he had even finished the sentence. But he couldn't stop himself now. The words were in full flow, rolling, filling the space about them.

'If you would like to do something with me. It's up to you, ye know, I'm easy. There doesn't have to be drink involved if you don't want.'

She was moving toward the door.

'It's completely up to you.'

She was opening the door.

'If you just want to go to the cinema or out for a meal,' Tom said.

But she was gone. And he was left without a reply and the knowledge that the photocopy room might not have been the best place to ask her out. An image entered his head of that little beetle sliding from the back of the larger one.

Dave stands and announces that he's heading outside for a smoke. Karl shoves one hand in his pocket and saunters over to Tom's desk, picks up a stapler and fidgets with it. He begins the effort of taking back the stapler but stops, withdraws his hand. He looks at the blank space on the desk where the stapler had been sitting.

'You really going to head out with us on Friday?' Karl asks.

'Why not?' Tom shrugs.

'It's not like you.'

'I just need to get out. You know yourself.'

'You want to get a bit shitfaced?'

'I guess.'

'Happy days,' Karl looks to the ground for a moment, nods his head slightly as if debating something. 'The lads are good craic, ye know. They're a little bit messy sometimes. But it's all just for the laugh. You know what they're like, don't ye?'

'Yeah, of course.'

'Good,' Karl says. 'It should be a bit of a laugh.' He places the stapler on the desk and moves off. 'Make sure you bring your drinking head with ye,' he says before disappearing behind a partition.

Tom fixes the stapler back into position and then renews his search for Sarah on the computer.

He discovers a website called Find Them where 'a staff of trained professionals will work tirelessly to find the lost loved ones in your life'. It states in bold writing that they only charge when they find the person. Tom thinks it won't hurt to enter Sarah's details. He fills in an online form. The machine tries to resist by hanging for long spells. It gives Tom time to think. He recalls how he was called into Lionel Gatt's office the day after he asked Tara out. Gatt is the company director, bloated around the edges, a body which has the soft look of an overfed baby but with a saggy face the colour of faded copper. He doesn't talk to the floor staff much but he regularly drinks with the lads from the offices, most of whom are at least a decade younger than him. Gatt imitates their appearance, wears a similar hairstyle, dresses in the same clothes. Tom consistently has this image of the man being dragged toward an older version of himself, scrabbling at anything in hands' reach to try to stay a moment longer with his youth, his nails bending outward and snapping under the force of his resistance.

He folded his arms and explained, in a sombre tone, that a serious complaint had been made against Tom. He went on to say that they were getting all sides of the story before they would deem someone guilty of sexual harassment but Tom could tell by the way he refused to make eye contact with him that he had already made up his mind on the matter.

Most of the women in the factory banded together after the accusation. Tom was the enemy and they weren't shy about displaying their distaste at his presence. Some refused to have any dealings with him at all and he was forced to have a go-between for work-related queries. In the canteen he sat on his own and if he ever happened to find himself beside a group there was always a space between him and the nearest person and talk was rarely directed his way.

Even now, some years later, the stigma of this accusation has never left Tom, even after the whole embarrassing story came out about his misguided quest for a date and despite the fact that Tara herself laughs about the incident. And she does laugh about it because he has heard her joke about the incident, about how she only attracts the 'nutters'. All it took was an embarrassed woman, a few lines on a complaint form, a scene that played out differently for two people and Tom was alienated from the rest of the workforce. He will probably never be accepted back into the group but he understands, in some ways, certain people are easier to exclude than others.

He received a letter some months after the incident, outlining that the company had decided to keep the issue in-house under the condition that:

'Mr Tom Stacey' hereby agrees to only communicate with 'Ms Tara Sheedy' when in the presence of a member of HR with the understanding that the third party is briefed on the incident in question.

It also expanded on this by stating that the complainant insists that she wants 'as little contact as possible' with Mr Tom Stacey and recommended that Tom carry out three sessions with a psychiatrist trained in this area, the cost of which will be deducted from his wages. They were hour-long sessions facilitated by Doctor Bill Duggan. After three sessions the psychiatrist recommended that Tom attend more of the same. The company agreed and Tom found himself attending these sessions for six months.

In the beginning the psychiatrist seemed to think that Tom was suffering from depression.

'Would you say you are depressed?' He asked Tom.

'No, of course not.'

'Okay Tom.'

He would scribble notes in an expensive-looking ledger with a wine cover, notes which seemed more detailed than the succinct answers Tom offered.

Tom couldn't help but think of one of those daytime programmes presented by a medical professional, Doctor Phil or one of those American shows. He began to have the notion that they were filming his sessions and that Doctor Bill or Bill Duggan or Doctor Phil even, whatever he preferred to call himself, would watch afterward and try to pin some tag on him, manic depressive or sexual deviant or any tag that he just so happened to pick from his latest edition of the Collins Dictionary of Crazy-ass Psychotic Disorders. Tom would scan the room, seeking out a blinking red light, or would listen for the whirr of a recording device.

But he had to keep going back.

'You say you'd like to meet the right woman and settle down Tom. Why is that?'

And it was eating into his wages. He was forced to end his subscription to *New Scientist* and he had to survive on potatoes and beans for the majority of the week. This was bad but what was even worse was that he was starting to side with the psychiatrist in believing that a problem existed.

'You say you would like to be a husband and a father Tom. Is that because you have no role now? Tell me Tom, about your role? What is your role?'

'A service technician.'

'No Tom. In society. What is your role?'

'I don't know.'

'As a man, Tom. What is your role as a man?'

'I don't know.' Tom shook his head. He fidgeted with his sleeves and he imagined the camera blinking in the corner. 'I don't know what my role is as a man.' And he looked up at the psychiatrist and returned the question. 'What is my role as a man?'

'Tell me about your compulsions,' the Doc asked one time, legs crossed, the ledger on his lap, a voice which was soft but confident. 'How much do they affect your day-to-day life?'

They are my life, Tom almost said, but thought better of it.

'They're more of a nuisance than anything else,' he lied.

The psychiatrist stared at Tom waiting for him to continue. When he didn't the psychiatrist nodded his head slowly and scribbled something in his ledger which Tom couldn't make out.

'Tell me about your past,' he nodded his head slowly and waited for Tom to speak.

Chapter 4

Tom wasn't aware of the concept of death when his mother and father were involved in the accident. He wasn't aware of anything much except drinking, sleeping and filling nappies, and even then it is difficult to say how aware an eight-week-old baby is of these instinctive actions. But as he moved through adolescence he would sometimes find himself thinking about them, at times imagining what had caused the accident, at other times picturing how differently his life would have turned out if they had never planned that short weekend break to the country, one that Tom's grandmother would have encouraged them to take, one which they probably embraced with the reluctant excitement that new parents so often feel when they are getting a break from the recent additions to their lives.

It was a fire that took them, a hotel on Lampton Avenue, a fire that would also claim the lives of an elderly couple from Sweden and a used-car salesman from Galway. It was years later when Tom found out these details, looking at the online archives of Irish newspapers in a library in the city centre. The news had made the front page of all the national newspapers the day after the accident, the following day it was relegated to page five or six in a couple of the papers, and then it disappeared altogether, the record of their demise fleeting and seemingly all the more point-less from its briefness.

In his younger years in school Tom noticed that he was treat-ed differently by his peers, separated, isolated even. Thinking back, Tom wonders if there was a sense of curiosity at his predicament, the fact that his situation was similar to so many of the fictional stories threaded through the lives of these kids. Didn't all the characters in the stories they read lack parents? From the fairytales of the brothers Grimm to the books by Roald Dahl. Or perhaps, for some children his orphanhood awakened an emotional stew of fear and disgust. Perhaps they believed it could be thrust upon them if they got too close to the boy, like a rare contagious condition that he was somehow in control of. Perhaps his very presence conjured up horrible images for the other children, the bloody and dismembered corpses of their own parents scattered about the work surfaces of their kitchen, crushed beneath a rectangular yellow skip, smeared across the bonnet of a van or the image of mother and father's blue and bloated faces shimmering in the water at the bottom of a lake.

Whatever the reason, the result of all this was that he wasn't very popular during his years in school. Outside school he latched on to a large group of boys on the estate but he would be hard pressed to call any of them friends and his attachment to the group was more physical than emotional.

Tom's grandmother passed away when he was fourteen. Up to that point his grandfather had been driving long-distance haulage for a transport company in East Wall, disappearing for long stretches and on average spending only every second week-end at home. For the rest of the time it was just Tom and his grandmother in the house, her busying herself in the kitchen, hanging out washing, getting him to lift his legs so she could sweep under him as he lounged in front of the television. When he couldn't see her he could hear her, clattering cutlery or bumping around upstairs, thumping the steps with a brush, or the intermittent sound of splashing water as she squeezed out a mop.

She was a grandmother with what Tom would deem to be a typical grandmother appearance, small and round in the way that cuddly beings often are, a preference for dresses and scarves with coloured floral design, rosy cheeked and pleasant smile, an appearance that he would be reminded of whenever he spotted a colourful Russian doll in the years following her passing. Her flushed cheeks enhanced the homely aura of her. Tom and his grandfather never considered that the flushness could be due to the fierce pressure her heart was under. She complained of back pains on the Wednesday. She was dead on the Thursday, the result of a massive coronary. She was buried in a cemetery close to the airport, lowered into the earth with the sound of a Boeing 747 shrieking overhead.

On the day of the funeral the neighbours commented on how mature Tom was in dealing with the loss. In truth he wasn't dealing with the loss. Tom had always looked on his grandmother as if she were his own mother. He never considered life without her around. After her death he felt as if he was drowning in emotions. He felt disorientated and confused. More often than not anger would rise to the surface. And when it did he would allow this anger to flood his other emotions and go looking for distractions to stop him thinking about the loss.

Tom started smoking. He didn't even stop to think about it. He just bought ten cigarettes, some brand that he'd seen in American shows on the telly, and smoked two in a row without feeling ill, enjoying the head buzz it gave him and the feel of it in his hand. He stopped getting haircuts. His hair grew long, not in any style or particular direction. He had already come to terms with the fact that his hair follicles were independent creatures in their own right. They each liked to follow their own course, which resulted in his hair having a blackberry-thicket feel about it.

Tom began to skip school and wear the same clothes for days in a row. His grandfather badgered him about the state of his room, advised him to put the stuff he really wanted in a box and get rid of everything else. Initially Tom thought this was because his grandfather felt some need to take on his grandmother's role after she died. This wouldn't turn out to be the case at all.

Tom's grandfather returned to work for distraction, as early as the Monday following the funeral. Tom didn't see him for six days. His grandfather aged in that week, all that time on the road with memories of his grandmother for company. Quite possibly there were times when he would forget that she was dead and he would probably look forward to seeing her when he got home, only to realise that he would never be seeing her again, not in this life in any case.

When his grandfather was at home he drank heavily. It wasn't as if he was greatly opposed to drinking before her passing but he always had a rule of no drinking the day before he was to return to the road. This rule fell by the wayside. About a month after her death he was due to head for a drop-off in Bantry before heading to Galway for a second load destined for England. He didn't make it as far as Bantry. He took the side off another truck when reversing at the docks. Tom's grandfather never had accidents in the truck. He prided himself on this record. His boss encouraged him to take some time off work. He went one better and quit his job.

'It doesn't really bother me,' he told Tom. 'We'll have a bundle of money before we know it.'

He was referring to an expected cheque in relation to his wife's life insurance policy. That cheque would consume him until it arrived some two months later. He would talk about how much it was going to be, talk about what he could do with it, hover around the hall every morning waiting for it to arrive. During that time it was difficult for Tom to figure out how his grandfather was coping with the loss of his wife. He never gave away much emotion and never showed any signs that he knew what his grandson was going through. Tom couldn't even imagine his grandfather as an emotional man, nor could he imagine him as a young, open-minded man. It seemed to him that people like his grandfather were born old and stuck in their ways from the very first moment they found a 'way' to be stuck in. Tom supposed the fact that the television was switched off was an indication that his grandfather was in some way affected by the loss. Before she died he always had it switched on, the volume loud and intrusive. Evenings in the house became silent, his grandfather sitting at the kitchen table, head down, empty bottles of Guinness lined up in front of him.

The cheque arrived in April of that year. The following day his grandfather informed Tom they would be moving.

'It's a done deal,' he said. 'Spoke to the council and all.'

There was no room for discussion or negotiation. Instead, his grandfather offered a crooked grin and initiated a guessing game. 'Where do you think we're going?' he asked.

And he honestly expected Tom to guess. He wanted Tom to take the whole geography of Ireland, if not the world, and guess where they were uprooting to. Tom rolled off four or five towns, receiving no reaction from him. Then, after realising that he was finished with the guessing game, his grandfather told him that he was correct with all his guesses, offering him a wink when he pressed further.

A week after the cheque arrived he gave Tom an envelope and told him to keep it safe. Although it was sealed, Tom knew the envelope contained money. His grandfather had a system when it came to money. Whenever they would go shopping he would always get his grandmother to hold on to half the money. That way if one of them was robbed they would only lose half of it. It was a system which made sense on a deeply paranoid level. Tom was far from impressed that he was now taking on the role of his deceased grandmother. It would mean that trips with his grandfather would grow in number. The fact that Bicycle Frankenstein was in the front garden was a clear indicator that one of these journeys was imminent.

Tom received Bicycle Frankenstein when he was eight years of age. His grandmother played with the sleeve of her cardigan and blinked her eyes rapidly when she first saw it, possibly hoping that the monstrosity might disappear from view.

'Where did you get that?' she asked.

'I made it.' Tom's grandfather rotated the bike so Tom could get a better look.

It had the curved handlebars of a racer, the grips nothing more than some loose insulation tape, and the brakes skewing dangerously outward. The front wheel and front axle were welded to the crossbar of a thin mountain bike while the back half of the creature was a BMX.

'Does it go?' she asked.

'Of course it fuckin' goes,' his grandfather barked.

It was his grandmother who christened the bike 'Frankenstein'. His grandfather took offence. 'It's not for you. It's for the boy.' He carried it over to Tom. 'Go on. Have a go.'

Tom tried the saddle. The bike sloped uncomfortably toward the back so that the saddle pressed into his groin when he put his weight on the bike. Tom gave him a strained smile, which his grandfather took as a positive signal.

Tom had not seen the bike since long before his grandmother passed away. The fact that it was out again wasn't a good sign.

'You're coming with me,' his grandfather said as he climbed up on his own bike. It was a Raleigh Roadster, a relic of the sixties which had seen better days. The edges of the saddle curled upward, the front mudguard had a long crack up its side. It weighed a ton, too heavy for Tom to move comfortably. His grandfather had not had a car for a couple of years at that stage and his old boss had not allowed the drivers to bring trucks home so his grandfather would cycle this bike across the city to the depot at the docklands. His head would jut over the handlebars and he would pump his legs, slow and deliberate, a constant speed.

Tom followed his grandfather's steady pedalling across the park into Glasnevin with its roads of rippled concrete. His grandfather's bike rattled over these ripples. Frankenstein wasn't too bad. The welding joint at the centre of the bike had loosened over the years and it offered some suspension to the bike, an accidental success in engineering on the part of his grandfather. Still, he was finding it difficult to keep up with the older man. They moved onto the tree-lined route of Griffith Avenue, turned right on to Grace Park Road, down Richmond Road and in the opposite direction to the corrugated roofed football stadium. Tom struggled with the potholes and the bike would whine with each bump or dip. He informed his grandfather of the increased levels of noise from the bike and his grandfather bluntly told him to stop complaining. He had a way of dismissing all forms of disagreements or obstacles as complaints. It was a nice way of avoiding difficult conversations or excusing himself from listening.

The traffic increased as they reached East Wall Road. Each

passing truck pushed Tom to the left slightly so his bicycle was angled and dangerous. There were times that he was full sure he was going to be sucked under a car or flattened by a forty-foot trailer. The creaking in the frame seemed worse in the pockets of silence between passing trucks, the rear of the bike seemed to take a bit longer to follow the front. It was at a junction on the East Wall road when the inevitable happened. The front of the bike disconnected with the back. For a moment the handlebars veered to the right while the saddle end continued on forward. Tom had the good sense to let go of the handlebars but his one-wheeled jaunt lasted a few metres before he crashed to the ground, cutting his elbow and knee.

His grandfather stopped pedalling and faced Tom.

'You've wrecked that bike,' he said. He then turned back and cycled onward.

Tom went the rest of the way on foot. It was a relief when his grandfather veered towards the entrance of a yard at the top of the road.

The depot had a dark gateway about fifty yards to the right of a pub. The wall surrounding the yard was made of the type of bricks that would later remind Tom of wartime in Britain, those orange, tan and teak colours that give character and history to an area regardless of how poor it is. Poverty seems less depressing in places like that to Tom, more sentimental in a sense.

Inside, there was rubble in the corners of the yard. It smelled of rubber and burning and diesel. Welding irons buzzed and sparks danced, engines let out sudden barks before issuing a relaxed continuous rumble. A truck sat at the front, the cab bent forward as if it had somehow been cracked open.

'That's how they get at the engine,' his grandfather explained when he saw Tom staring at it.

They walked to an office at the rear, a few plastic chairs and a table with a woodchip top. While they waited his grandfather warned Tom not to mention his grandmother. Tom hadn't planned on saying anything about his grandmother. He hadn't planned on saying anything about anything.

Eventually, a wide man entered the office, Mr Promley. His hair was blonde, short and dense so it resembled fur. His voice was wheezy, the type which almost disappears by the time the person reaches the last word in a sentence. He smiled constantly but the creases running across his forehead told a contradicting story about the man.

'Sorry to hear about your wife,' he said and Tom's grandfather looked sharply in his grandson's direction as if Tom had somehow instigated this comment.

'I'm looking for a box truck,' his grandfather said. 'A cheap one.'

'You're not starting your own business now, are ye?' Promley laughed. It ended too suddenly to be genuine and his smile was looking more like a grimace the longer Tom looked at him. His grandfather told his ex-boss that the truck was to live in.

Promley laughed.

Tom laughed.

His grandfather didn't.

'Me and the boy,' he said. 'It's going to be our home.'

Promley led them out to the yard. Old truck parts lay in rough heaps, the bones and organs of long-deceased vehicles, lengthy exhausts, lone seats free from their cabs. A trail of small rubble pieces led to a Ford Box-lorry. It wasn't a bad-looking thing, a bit rough around the edges. Promley offered it for seven hundred. His grandfather made a face that he so often made for Tom, the bemused rise of the mouth and the dipping of his eyebrows.

'I wouldn't pay that much for that heap of shite,' he said. 'But

I might be interested in the old Bedford.'

He walked over to a lorry that was partially hidden behind a trailer. There was something tortoise-like about it, the green colour of the front cab, the low headlights like eyes and the large brown box structure that hugged behind like a large shell. It was a Bedford TK, six-cylinder petrol engine, a model which was popular in the sixties. Not only was it not designed for comfort, it was also not designed for humans to live in. It was a horse-box lorry, long wooden eroded planks held in place with a lined metal structure. It was missing its crest but it still had two wide wing mirrors extended on long bars from the cab and indicators extended in front of the driver and passenger doors on both sides.

They agreed a price of three hundred, with the added stipulation that Tom's grandfather could work on the truck in the yard until he got it running. They shook hands, the other man twitching at the mouth in the effort of hiding his good fortune. When Promley walked off, Tom's grandfather touched the front of the cab gently like it was an old acquaintance. He then opened the bonnet at the front with the relaxed and sure attitude of someone who knew exactly what they were going to find inside.

Chapter 5

Tom hears voices when he reaches the stairwell in his building, the familiar voices of his neighbours.

'Jesus.' It is the old man, Mr Walters. 'We're only going for three weeks.'

'I need everything,' his wife replies.

Tom continues upstairs and meets the man on the landing. He moves aside to allow him to pass with a large suitcase, navy with tan edging. Tom nods and smiles but the old man doesn't see him. Or if he does he chooses to ignore him. Mr Walters stops at the top of the stairs and holds a palm against his forehead, flat, directs his eyes toward the ceiling.

'Come on, we'll miss the train,' he says.

'I'm coming.' Mrs Walters is at the door to their bed-sit. Tom thinks of an unmade bed when he sees her. She is hidden amid layers of material, ruffled and creased, folds of different colours, the jaded flop of a massive sunhat on her head, scarf over cardigan over blouse, coat draped across her arm, the tail of it disturbing the dust on the carpet. A square, bloated suitcase trails her movement.

'You have the tickets?' she asks.

'Of course I do. Come on.'

She pauses before closing the door, narrows her eyes as she reads what is on a piece of paper in her hand.

'Come on.' His impatience has turned to anger.

'I want to be sure that we have everything,' she says but follows in any case, swinging the door closed behind her as she moves. 'We'll be back on the Wednesday, won't we?'

'Yes. Yes. Yes.'

'Okay,' she offers Tom a strained smile and a roll of the eyes before rushing down the stairs.

Tom listens to their clatter as they round the stairs onto the floor below. When he turns, he notices that the door to their bed-sit has not closed properly.

It is open slightly.

Tom doesn't call after them to warn them.

He doesn't close the door either.

It is a couple of hours later when Tom returns to his neighbours' bed-sit. The door is still ajar. He pushes and it opens with a whine. There is a rug to the right, a slanted hump in the centre, skewing out at the edge. It is this edge that has stopped the door from closing properly. Tom stands in the one spot and surveys his surroundings. The wallpaper is radioactive yellow. There is a fat, flumpy sofa in the centre, bombarded with pillows, a throw and a couple of doyleys on the armrests, an area so cluttered that it takes him a moment to decipher one object from another. The armchair beside is a mismatch of the sofa, straight-backed with long, bone-like armrests. All the seated furniture is aimed toward the hulk of a television in front of the kitchen area.

This bed-sit is bigger than his, the kitchen area tucked away toward the rear, a door-less frame separating it from the seated area. That counts as two rooms, he thinks.

Two whole rooms.

The floor is wooden, raised to the left of the kitchen area entrance, and the bed sits on top. Tom briefly wonders if they are paying the same rent as he is.

He slowly walks around the space, initially shy about touching off anything. He stops beside an interesting vase, pale with ochre-coloured Chinese figures in different poses, fishing, digging, holding a small bird cage. There is a chip in the rim, a crack near the base. A coffee table sits beside the settee, a stack of envelopes on top, the paper returned to them in a slanted manner so the corners stick out. This is something that Mr Walters would do, Tom thinks, the old man impatiently shoving the letters back in, complaining about the price of gas or electricity. It was probably his impatience that caused the damage to the vase too, moving it from one area to another, Mrs Walters directing him where to place it and telling him to mind his back and take his time.

Every couple has the stubborn one. Every couple has the one that will push and the one that will bow, the one that will demand and the one that will reason. Isn't that always the case? He supposes it is only true for those relationships that last. He wonders if Sarah is still as headstrong as she used to be. He doesn't mind if she is. There are times when pushiness is as essential as reason.

Tom moves to the kitchen area, a gas cooker with four black hobs, a metal sink and a small, humming fridge. The counter is slate grey with chalky arcs of residue from a half-hearted clean. The area smells of lemon. It wouldn't be an overly exciting kitchen, to those normally excited by kitchens, Tom thinks. But it does have something which Tom envies, something that makes his apartment pale in comparison.

A window. A large window.

Wooden frame with flaky paint, dirty with old spider webs in the upper corner.

It is much bigger than his minuscule window and it looks out on to the front of the building, to a partial section of the street and an apartment block which faces the building. Looking down he can see the black knobbled roofs of the lower sections, mounds of shiny black tar at the edges, battered walls meeting new extensions, square cage-like extractor fans, drops of shade and long thin corridors that fall away to open space.

It is a window made for dreamers.

Tom rests his elbows on the counter. Somewhere out there Sarah McCarthy is going about her business. And she may be married or divorced, with kids or without, in a house or flat. But that doesn't matter. What matters is the fact that she is out there or that someone like her is out there, someone for him, someone that will potter through this life with his needs on her mind, someone who will laugh at his jokes, someone who will share his happiness and his fears.

And listen to his stories.

And take his hand.

And what was that noise?

Tom closes his eyes.

There it is again, a creak on the landing outside. It is followed by a tapping.

'Hello?' a voice calls, dampened by the front door.

Tom ducks to the side of the door-less frame and leans against the wall.

There is the whine of the bed-sit door opening and the soft sound of footsteps.

'Gabby,' the voice is clear, inside the bed-sit now. 'Hello?'

He hears her movement in the groan of the floorboards on the right-hand side of the bed-sit.

Tom presses his back against the wall and wills himself smaller. He hears his own breathing, the slight whistling in his nostrils. He opens his mouth and drags in a long, steady breath.

He has to do something.

Think.

Think.

He slowly ducks down and opens the cupboard under the sink. Inside is the glaring greens and yellows of bleach bottles, a packet of surface wipes, j-cloths, some spare rubber gloves behind a dirty white pipe. He remains still this way, listens for her movement.

All is quiet.

Perhaps they are both waiting on the other to move, stuck in a pose, still as two figures in a photograph.

Move.

Move.

Tom turns to the side slightly, spots a number of spanners on the upper shelf, a vice-grips, screwdrivers, Philips and flathead.

He grabs the vice-grips, brings it up to the pipe and keeps this pose while listening for her movement.

But the floorboards don't creak any more and the only sound is a scuffling noise, faint and quick.

Tom holds this pose until his arm begins to ache. He can't hold it for much longer. He quickly wipes his finger along the grime of the pipe and smears it across his forehead. He draws his frame away from the cupboard and stands, coughs a warning before leaving his hiding place behind the frame.

He recognises the woman near the bed. He has seen her bundle about the building, her pastel blouses billowing behind her, her bright necklaces resting across her massive bosom. She is

Maureen Hill, a tenant from downstairs. He has never spoken to her but he assumes she is a widow because she hangs her head as she walks, like someone who has lost someone and is afraid to look skyward in case they discover that there is nobody up there smiling down at them.

Tom holds the vice-grips at his side.

Her eyes move from his face to the tool, widen, her mouth contorting sideways.

'I was just looking,' she says and holds her left hand in front of her. There is a gold chain wrapped around her palm, a couple of rings loose on her fingers. 'They're so lovely,' she says. Her tone is the dotted-line type, the type that causes faltering and stammering between words.

Tom looks from the jewellery to her ankles. They are fat and trunk-like. Once they catch his attention he can't release them.

'I'm doing a bit of work for the Walters,' he mumbles.

'I'm sorry,' she says. 'I saw the door open and I was just checking that everything was okay.' She brushes the rings from her fingers into an opened jewellery box and swiftly unwinds the necklace from her hand. 'I was worried that someone might break in.'

'Yeah,' Tom says, still staring at her ankles.

'I was passing, you know. Just walking by,' she moves away from Tom. 'I just saw the door open.'

Tom suddenly looks up and raises the vice-grips to shoulder-height.

'There's a leak under the sink. And I've to do a bit of work while I'm keeping an eye on the place. They're away.'

'They are?' She inches toward the door, all the while maintaining her sight on Tom.

'Yeah, they've gone to England.'

'England?'

'Yeah.'

'Well, it's good to know that someone is looking after the place.'

'Grimsby,' Tom says. 'They've gone to Grimsby.'

'Lovely,' she says. 'I'm glad the place is safe. You can't be too careful.' She offers a chuckle. It is low and fake.

She turns when she is on the landing. Tom gets one last glimpse of those ankles before she waddles from view.

His head feels full and weighty as if he has been hanging upside down. He exhales, kicks the rug flat and closes the door behind him. The space changes, becomes smaller, more confined.

He is alone with his lie.

He rests the vice-grips on the coffee table, sits down and patiently waits for the pressure to drain from his head. Tom picks the vice-grips up again. His grandfather had one just like it. He didn't use it solely as a grip. He would hammer things with it, remove nails, smash tiles and break wood. Tom spins the bolt so the grip tightens. He puts his finger inside the mouth of the tool and applies pressure slowly to the handle so the mouth tightens and loosens at the tip of his finger. He presses and releases the lever for a time.

Close. Open.

Pressure. Release.

Continuously, so he hardly realises he is doing it. Thoughts wash back and forth.

And the pressure in his head reduces like a slowing locomotive.

And he becomes aware of a photograph to his right. Mr and Mrs Walters, both smiling that awkward smile that comes with the awareness of a camera being in close proximity. Tom places the photograph on the table, face down so the eyes are no longer looking at him. He suddenly becomes aware of other photos in the room and a vague memory enters his head, a girl and her mother in a café or fast-food place, he isn't one hundred percent sure where. They are talking about glass eyes, the young girl unable to get her head around the fact that it is impossible to see with a glass eye. She had a book about pirates on her lap, the drawings in the book deliberately lacking detail and the dots for eyes askew. The girl would point to each character they came to and ask if the eye was a glass one.

'No, just the pirate,' her mother would patiently reply each time.

About halfway into the book they came across a spider with a multitude of eyes, thirty or forty.

'Are any of those glass eyes?' the girl had asked.

'No, only the pirate has a glass one,' her mother replied.

'So the spider can see with all those eyes?'

'I guess so.'

'Why has he got so many eyes?'

'He has a lot to see.'

'If they fell off could the spider still use them to see?'

'No, that's impossible.'

Impossible, yes, but it stayed with Tom, this idea that the spider could still see with the eyes he was missing. And there have been times when Tom has pictured the ground littered with tiny eyeballs just like the spider, eyes which are watching his every move.

There is a cold crawling sensation along his spine.

He stands and begins to face every photo on a flat surface into a downward position. When he has finished this he starts on the photos which hang on the walls, turning the wooden frames so the photographs face the wall. He feels better when he can't see any eyes watching him.

He doesn't lock the door on his way out. He puts it on the latch and wedges a folded page in the end to prevent it from opening without force. There is little evidence of his presence in the room. Apart from the photograph frames which lie on the flat surfaces and the fact that the garish wallpaper is broken up by small, wooden rectangles on strings.

Tom thinks about his neighbours' bed-sit, about the muddle of the room and the large window. This terrible feeling of wastefulness comes over him. He tries to distract himself. And at times he does, enough to eat his dinner, enough to clean the counter in his kitchen, enough time to change into his blue and white stripy pyjamas, the ones which help him keep warm in the drafty bedsit at night and the ones which he knows will have to go as soon as he meets the right woman.

At around half ten he begins to hear the bees. At eleven he has gone to the bathroom on the landing three times. By twelve he is doing laps of the kitchen. At six minutes past twelve he is outside his neighbours' bed-sit. He stalls for as long as he can, studying the number on the door. It is slightly crooked. There are bubbles in the paint on the door. There is a fuse-box above it.

Bzzzz

Black squares in a dusty mould, a counter behind a dim glass shield, the end number rolling slowly on to the next.

Bzzzz

He pushes the door open and enters.

What a mess.

He immediately removes the cushions from the sofa and arranges them into a rough pyramid shape. He puts them in the corner of the room to the right of the door, ensuring that they are pushed in as far as possible. The sofa is in the wrong spot. It is slap-bang in the centre of the room. This doesn't make any sense to Tom, the fact that if you are sitting on the sofa there is a television blocking a clear view of the window, the fact that you would have your back to the door.

Everyone knows that a sofa goes against a wall.

Tom has his own sofa against a load-bearing wall but that isn't essential. Any wall will do. He moves it so that it forms an L-shape with the bed, pushes the television and stand so they are at the opposite side of the bed. He does the same with the armchair and the table, any other piece of furniture that is in the central area. When finished he rotates to look at all the furniture framing the empty space. He exhales slowly, a sigh of relief. There is even a free space at the wall to the right of the kitchen area. He moves across and places his palms flat on this wall. It feels cool against his skin. He stands this way for a time, neither pushing nor being pushed, just feeling the plainness of the wall.

After a time he moves to the window. With a window like this you can think clearly, he muses. You can map out a few things. You can really analyse the little details.

Don't worry about the details, Anna from the agency had said. But it's all about the little details.

He blinks and sees an image in his head, a white rectangle, A4 in size.

He knows what it is. It's an agency form. His form.

The words are covered the way someone would censor a document, with rectangle blocks of black ink. He'd love to be able to peel back those blocks to see the word which is hidden, but those words don't exist yet. He sees the shape of the form though, the structure of the headings and the space available for subcategories and square borders, the space available for drawings and diagrams, maybe even photographs.

He could include details about himself, the little details, about what he would like in an ideal woman. And his match doesn't even have to tick all the boxes.

Not all.

Just enough to increase compatibility factor, which could equal relationship, which could equal . . .

What?

He's not sure.

Everything?

But first he will have to make some lists, prioritise, create a plan.

He sits for a time and thinks about the key compatibility characteristics needed in his ideal woman. Soon, he is drafting up a chart. He feels that it isn't important which section the characteristic goes into because he has already come to the conclusion that no single component should take priority over another. In that way he won't be unfairly swayed toward beauty or personality. The headings will merely be a series of areas to think about so as to find the ideal-case scenario.

He tapes the chart to the wall. In keeping with his indiscriminate approach Tom takes a pen in his right hand, closes his eyes, spins his hand in circles before randomly landing it on the page.

'Sense of humour,' he says to himself and moves away from the chart.

Sense of humour.

He smiles, arches his back and places his hands at the base of his spine.

He inhales deeply.

He likes this place, really likes it.

And it will be nice to look after it for the neighbours.

Sure, isn't that what good neighbours do?

Chapter 6

The only thing new about the Alpha Bar is the name. At one time it was called Brandy's Nightclub and before that it was Magnums. It is situated on the ground floor of the Manhattan Hotel and it looks like it was designed from an oral description of what a typical Irish pub should look like, from a person who had never actually been in a typical Irish pub. Things are a little bit off kilter, the snugs are too small, the bar is too long, the pictures on the wall are scenes of Ireland but they are depressing ones, lonesome people standing in fields, sheep in the rain, a battered cottage seemingly cowering in a storm. There are wide wooden shelves set high near the rafters with trinkets and vintage bicycles and small mechanisms that look like they belong to farm machinery.

The tables are square and chunky and uncomfortable to sit around but at the moment there is barely enough room to stand and Tom has to continuously lift his pint above shoulder-height to stop other patrons knocking against it. There is a dancefloor in the centre. The music is loud. The women don't look old enough to be referred to as women to Tom. He's not sure when the kids had taken over the pubs. It was done quietly, a silent coup.

The night is small-talk and plenty of alcohol. The lads drink much quicker than Tom. There is a round of shots which Tom refuses to take part in. The lads take on a rubbery quality the more they consume, lolling on the ledge next to them and lolling on each other, spilling drink on the floor, their necks bowing forward as if they are wilting flowers.

Tom lines up the glasses on the ledge, tallest to the back, smallest to the front.

'That's some watch you have there,' Karl grips Tom's arm and shows the rest of the group.

They move closer to see.

'Where would you get a watch like that?' he asks.

'Jaysus, looks ancient,' Jimmy says, drawing out the words slowly. 'Here, what time is it in 1973?'

Tom laughs with the group, even though he doesn't want to laugh.

'Here, give us it for a second,' Karl says. 'I'll show you a trick.'

'You're all right.' Tom takes a sip of his beer to distract.

'Come on, it'll only take a minute.'

'Jesus, give him a shot of your watch, would ye,' Dave waves his hands and shouts. The sudden movement causes him to stumble to the left.

'All right,' Tom says. 'Just for a minute. And mind you don't get beer on it.'

He reluctantly removes the watch and gives it to Karl who ushers the group closer.

Karl places the watch on the ledge so everyone can see.

'Check out the second hand,' Karl says. 'It's working grand, isn't it?'

They all agree it is.

'Watch this.'

Karl places his hand over the watch for a moment. When he removes it, the second hand has stopped rotating.

'Jesus Christ,' Dave says.

'How did you do that?' Jimmy smiles.

'Magic,' Karl says.

'Have you broken my watch?' Tom finds his voice.

'Wait,' Karl blocks Tom from grabbing the watch. He then gently taps the watch with his finger and the second hand begins to move again.

'No way,' Dave slaps his thigh. 'No fuckin' way.'

'Give me my watch back,' Tom says.

'Hang on.' Jimmy holds his hand out for the watch. 'My uncle showed me how you can use a watch as a compass, ye know, if you ever get lost.'

'You live on a housing estate,' Dave says. 'What would you need a compass for if you live on a housing estate?'

'You'd need a compass to find your way around a pair of knickers,' Jimmy answers. He holds his hand out again but Karl is distracted.

'I'll be back in a second,' Karl moves away from the group. He stops to talk to a woman who wears a coat buttoned up to her neck. Her hair is blonde, an old-fashioned style, shoulder-length with a fringe. She has a small chin and large eyes. She is pretty.

Karl shows her the watch and she laughs.

He's probably doing his trick again, Tom thinks.

What if it goes wrong and the watch breaks? What'll he do then? He needs that watch.

Ticka-ticka-ticka

The woman soon disappears through a door to the left of the bar and Tom gets that lifting feeling in his chest that comes with hope. It lasts until Karl exits through the same door.

The toilets are in that direction, he thinks.

That's where Karl is going. He'll be back any minute.

Tom waits. He thinks of his watch.

Minutes pass.

There is no sign of Karl returning.

Ticka-ticka-ticka

Tom stands and pushes through a crowd on the dancefloor. The air feels hot and compressed. Drum and bass vibrates through the soles of his shoes. It instantly dampens when the door beside the bar closes behind him. He finds himself in a corridor, the Ladies and Gents toilets in the centre and another door at the far end.

Tom enters the Gents.

There is a man swaying at the urinals and a self-admirer in front of the mirror.

No Karl.

Tom exits and investigates the door at the far end of the corridor. It leads to a set of stairs which lead to a number of hotel rooms. There is no sign of the woman or Karl. He hurries back to the nightclub in case Karl has somehow returned without him seeing.

The two lads are still next to the ledge. Dave is leering at the dancefloor. Jimmy is texting on his phone, most probably to his soon-to-be wife.

Having a great time. Give my love 2 the dog. Jxxx

Tom goes to the bar and queues for a drink. After a few minutes of being ignored he roams the floor.

Ticka-ticka-ticka

He follows a corridor which sits to the left of the main entrance. The carpet is yellow diamonds on a wine background. There is artwork along the wall, colourful streaks on a dark canvas. It resembles oil splashed on a roadway. The corridor leads to a door which is the mirror of the one he has just walked through.

Tom likes the uniformity in modern hotels. He likes the strong lines and shapes, the way one area is the same as the next.

His walk leads him to a small bar with a couple of snug areas and a few tables in the centre. The place is dark wood and calm lighting. It is quiet here. A couple sit in the corner, whispering, the woman with a concerned face, her hands cupped together as she stresses a point. There is a man at one end of the bar. He sips coffee from a white cup, his newspaper spread out on the counter. There is a bartender facing away from him. She is writing in a ledger and, on hearing him approach, turns.

Tom slowly takes a seat at her end of the bar. The beer-mats sit in even stacks of two in front of the taps. The bottles of cordial are tucked away under an arch on the left side of the bar. Everything is nicely placed, fine rows and columns.

Except for a stack of menus behind the bar.

Two menus on top are askew. Tom leans forward so as to fix them.

'Ah, ah, ah,' the bartender slaps him on the hand.

'Hey,' Tom withdraws his hand quickly.

There is something cat-like about her, the shape of her head, her plump cheeks and wide eyes which curl upward slightly at the outer edge. Her dark hair is clipped tightly on her head. A badge on her top tells him that her name is Fiona.

'I was only trying to fix the menus.' Tom moves for them again.

She raises her hand and he stops mid-air.

'It'll only take a second,' Tom says.

'See this point here,' she directs his attention to the edge of the bar with the swift guide of her right hand. 'And everything behind this point.'

Tom offers a grunt of understanding.

'This whole area is mine. You can have any part of that area out there.' She rotates her two hands outward in unison like a flight attendant. 'You can touch anything. Go ahead. Tip the back of the chair. Sit at any of the tables. Hug the poxy pillar for all I care. But don't touch anything past this point.'

Tom frowns and slumps his shoulders.

Fiona begins to hum, takes a cloth from beside the sink and wipes the area under the taps.

'Do you want a drink?' she asks as she does this.

'Give us a pint.'

'Are you a hotel resident?'

'Will I still get a pint if I say no?' Tom asks.

She shakes her head.

'Well then yes,' Tom says. 'I am a resident.'

'Room number?'

'Sixty-three,' Tom picks a random one.

She moves to the electronic till and types in his room number.

'Well Mr Zhang Wei,' she turns. 'I think this is your first time visiting the bar.'

'It is,' Tom says. 'Don't bother charging the drink to my room though. I'd rather pay in cash if that's okay.'

Her left eyebrow drops slightly but she smiles.

'It is Mr Wei.'

She pours him a pint and takes the money. Tom throws the change in a large tip-jar on the counter. She thanks him and returns to cleaning the counter.

Tom sips his pint.

Ticka-ticka-ticka

He contemplates having another search for Karl.

Ticka-ticka-ticka

Surely he's back with the lads now.

Ticka-ticka-ticka

He has to get that watch back.

'Ten past ten,' Fiona says.

'What?' Tom blinks.

'You keep looking at your wrist like you're checking the time.'

'Sorry, I hadn't noticed,' Tom says.

Fiona smiles and nods and moves to the end of the bar.

Tom folds his arms tightly in an effort to control his actions. He sits straight in the chair. Soon, he begins to imagine the watch on his arm. He can almost feel the band hugging his wrist, can almost feel the coolness of the metal plate on his skin.

Ticka-ticka-ticka

He sees an image of it in the corner of his eye. It is quick, the barest of flashes skimming across the surface of his thoughts. He knows the longer he is without the watch the more concrete the image will become and the more he will feel the urge to act in order to dispel it from his head.

He tries to ignore it.

Ticka-ticka-ticka

He clenches his fist and grinds his teeth together. There is this horrible sensation in his chest, a kind of crawling.

And it will not leave him until he acts.

Ticka-ticka-ticka

There is a cooler at the back of the bar, loaded neatly with various beers.

It buzzes gently.

Bzzzzz

Tom unfolds his arms and takes a large mouthful of his pint.

The buzzing is increasing.

He taps the glass with his little finger, a steady, constant beat.

'Have you ever been stung?' Bill Duggan, the psychiatrist, had asked once.

Tom recalls how he had been fishing for any memories which may have involved buzzing and considering if they are in some way associated with his anxiety or compulsive behaviour. At the time he wondered what term the psychiatrist had written in his ledger to describe Tom's condition. Tom would label it as a trap. Because it is a trap, Tom thinks, a hole or vast cavern in the earth whereby a single thought or notion can echo around in his head like a call in a cavern until he feels as if he is going mad.

'Maybe when you were a baby?' Bill Duggan had prompted.

'No.'

'Were you afraid of bees as a child?'

'No.'

'Have you any memories to do with wasps even?'

'Not really.'

Tom remembers only one, a fairly insignificant memory of a wasp nest in the shed of his grandmother's back garden when he was a kid. Tom remembers their constant arrival and departure, the way they squeezed through a small hole in the grouting between the bricks, back and forth constantly as if they were being controlled by some outside force. And thinking about it now, Tom understands that this wasn't so far off the mark. They were controlled by something, some basic primeval thing that is etched into the make-up of all wasps. And perhaps this is what he should link his problems to, not to a single event but to some instinctive glitch in his make-up, some survival mechanism that won't turn off, that is urging him to protect or to seek or even to flee, which relates to a danger that doesn't actually exist. Because how can you protect if you don't know what you are protecting from or how can you seek if you don't know what it is you are looking for? How can you flee if the thing which you are escaping is yourself?

Tom looks at his wrist.

The buzzing stops. He decides to replace the momentary quiet with something else.

His sight moves to Fiona and he speaks.

'Do you think you're funny?' He leans on the counter.

'What's that supposed to mean?' She walks to his side of the bar, folding the cloth as she moves.

'It means what it means,' Tom shrugs. 'Do you think you have a good sense of humour?'

'I have my moments like everyone else,' she says.

'Try to make me laugh,' Tom folds his arms and sits back.

'Feck off,' she gives an exaggerated look of exasperation.

'Go on, I'm trying something out. An experiment.'

'You a scientist?'

'No.'

'I didn't think so.'

'What's that supposed to mean?'

'I can't say. My boss won't let me be rude to the customers.'

Tom stares at her. She bows her head to hide her reddening cheeks.

'I was trying to make you laugh,' she says quietly.

'Oh yeah. It didn't really work.'

Tom looks across the bar to the skewed menus. He reaches over to fix them.

'If you try that again I'm going to have to ask you to leave.'

'Sorry. I wasn't thinking.'

'You'd better start thinking.'

'Sorry,' Tom mumbles. He takes a sip of beer. 'What do you think is the best way of finding out if someone has a good sense of humour?'

'Try to make them laugh I guess.'

'And if you aren't face to face?'

'I don't know,' she shakes her head slowly. 'I suppose, judging by the people that come in and out of this place, I guess that most people have a good sense of humour. They just find different things funny. Ye know, some people might like slapstick. Others might have a dry sense of humour. Everybody is different.'

'What about you, what sense of humour do you have?'

'I'd probably have a quirky sense of humour,' she plays with the nail on her thumb.

'And you seem pretty normal,' Tom says.

'Thanks a bunch.'

'Yeah,' Tom takes his notebook from his pocket.

He opens it and writes the words 'common sense of humour'.

'It's not about finding out who has the best sense of humour,' he says. 'It's about who laughs at the same things as you.' Tom stands. 'Thanks.'

'You're welcome,' Fiona looks confused.

'You missed a bit,' Tom says and nods to the far end of the bar.

'Where?' Fiona takes the cloth from the counter again.

'Over there,' he points.

Fiona turns and Tom quickly reaches across the bar and fixes the stack of menus before hurrying toward the corridor which leads to the nightclub.

Chapter 7

Tom's hangover is a parched, sandy mouth and a steady throb-
bing in his crown, a pain which intensifies as he shuffles to his
neighbours' bed-sit. He sits on an armchair and rings Karl on his
mobile phone. His call gets directed to the message service.

'Karl,' Tom leaves a message. 'Give me a ring when you get a
chance. It's about the watch. About my watch, about the watch
that you borrowed last night. You might have already tried to get
in touch about it. I did have my phone on but I know that sometimes the connection isn't great, especially if you were trying to
ring me from the nightclub. Sometimes it's just the sheer volume
of people in the place that can cause a problem with the signal.
Or it could be a mast on the roof. Or it might even be where
you're ringing from in the building. Anyways, I just want a word
about the watch. My watch. If you could let me know how I can
collect it from you that would be great. I'd rather have it sorted
out before Monday if we can. Otherwise I'll get it from you when
I see you in work. But again, if we can sort it out before Monday
it would be better. All right? Okay. Bye then.'

Tom hangs up and stands. He stares at his phone for a
moment, half-expecting Karl to ring straight away. The phone
remains mute and the screen stays dull and grey, almost resentful-

looking, Tom thinks as he mopes around the bed-sit.

Ticka-ticka-ticka

He considers ringing again, just in case there is a problem with the answering service, but decides he will give Karl a little time to respond. He sets a reminder on his phone for an hour later.

Reminder: Watch, Karl

He moves to his chart, closes his eyes and randomly selects a heading. When he opens them again he finds that his finger has landed on 'Features'.

Tom thinks about this while he returns to his own bed-sit. He supposes features could cover body shape and facial features. This might take some research, he thinks.

Tom has an old pair of binoculars. He picked them up years ago, at a swap-day organised at work by Clarissa from Accounts. Tom brought an old radio along and a set of place-mats. He swapped the place-mats for a picture of Elvis that now covers a crack in the wall to the left of the door to his bed-sit, and traded the radio for the binoculars. They have been sitting in a drawer ever since. Tom only removed them once when drunk and spent a few minutes gazing through the reverse side, imagining he was in a larger room. The novelty of that lasted until he almost fell against the sink.

Tom fetches the binoculars and makes his way to the roof.

He has been up here before, a couple of years back, when his television reception had gone on the blink. Mr Reilly, the land-lord, happened to be on the premises at the time and he led Tom to the roof and explained, in his customary high-pitched yelping, the best way to fix the aerial. It mattered little that Tom could barely understand a word he was saying because he soon learned that fixing the aerial consisted of hammering the metal prongs at random points while cursing at the top of the voice. He attempted this method a few months later when the reception went on the blink again, and was delighted to find that he had two additional television stations on his set when he returned to his bed-sit.

The building is five storeys high and the roof is a series of level areas of different heights broken up by sections of sloping tiles. A frail wooden stairwell sways to a narrow door which opens up on to one of the level sections. There is a lip of concrete at the front of this section. A deckchair lolls beside a disused, red-bricked chimney stack, a colourful piece of shredded fabric curling around the wooden frame. Tom figures that this is where Mr Reilly likes to come to smoke. There are plenty of cigarette butts crushed into the concrete to reinforce this theory.

Tom tests the strength of the chair by pressing both hands into the fabric before he eventually sits down. It is a nice spot, apart from the frequent fluttering of pigeons with the bite of cold on his face and the stomach-warbling scent of the local takeaway which hangs in the air. The noise of the street reaches him in drifts, contorting with the distance, the blaring of engines, the monotonous thump of dance music filtered through obstacles, the squeal of tyres, the whoosh of extractor fans. It is the outside world but from a different angle than normal, the angle of hidden solitude, a position that he feels a lot more comfortable with.

From the roof he has a clear view of the apartment block on the other side of the street. He can see the paved footpath below from both sides and about half a kilometre worth of passing traffic. He scans the area with the binoculars, quickly discovering that they are more difficult to master than he had expected. It is tricky to get the timing right when following a target. He overshoots on occasion and loses his target when others cross their path. But he perseveres and eventually he begins to get the hang of it.

Tom aims for a figure approaching in the distance on the left-hand side of the street. He wiggles the focus wheel at the top of the binoculars until the image clarifies. It is a man, bald, wearing tight tracksuit bottoms and an undersized T-shirt. His large gut oozes over the elastic band of the bottoms and he grips a lead, the other end of which is attached to a tiny King Charles pup. Tom aims for the man's face. There is a hazy element to the view, a lack of distinction between different facial features. Tom plays with the wheel but the image worsens. Tom realises that they are not as good quality as he originally thought.

He tries another figure, a woman pushing a buggy, limp blonde hair and a puffy yellow coat. He has the same problem as before. It's as if he is looking at a hazy projected image instead of a form. There is a man standing across the street. The man is picking his nose. Tom aims for him, steadies his arms. The longer Tom stays in the one position the more clearly he can make out his target. The key is stillness.

If only everybody would stop moving around so much.

He lays the binoculars on his lap and rubs his eyes.

Then again, he isn't really looking for a definite, is he?

His ideal woman is not going to come strolling down the street just because he happens to have a set of binoculars. That's like expecting to see a UFO just because you've allowed yourself to believe in them. No, if anything this field-trip is merely an exercise in creativity, something to stir the mind, a warm-up for the task ahead. In fact, the blurriness of the features is a good thing. He read somewhere that people don't see the detail in faces, on a conscious level at least, and that memory fills in any missing gaps. There must be thousands of faces stored in his head. In reality he already knows the face of his ideal match. He just has to remember it.

Besides, the face that he is most attracted to may not be the perfect face, scientifically or traditionally. It just has to be the face most appealing to him. Because there are flaws in even the plainest of things, always a notch in the seemingly flat board, always a blemish on the porcelain urn, always a taint in the clearest of diamonds. So, no, it doesn't have to be perfect. He merely has to be aware of all the possible options for each characteristic before he makes a final decision on his number-one face.

So a hazy scan will have to do.

Down to the people who hurry about their business.

Down to the partners who hold each other's hands, to the boys that bounce off each other and joke around, the girls balanced on high shoes, the old men with sticks, the dogs that piss against the lampposts and the crows that land on electrical wires to watch the world bustling below their feet.

Down to the woman who stops in front of the entrance of the building, who is taking a phone from a red handbag and pressing the buttons.

She is familiar to Tom.

He quickly rotates the focussing wheel on the binoculars. A blurred impression of her face expands and contracts in the lenses before the image improves.

Tom's phone rings.

He fumbles with his pocket while trying to keep his sight on the figure. He loses the image but finds his phone.

There is a woman on the line. Karl's wife. Angela.

Karl's wife!

That's who is standing at the front of the building.

'I want a word with you,' she says.

'Hang on, I'll be right down,' Tom says.

She looks up quickly and scans the windows at the front of the building before returning her phone to the bag.

Tom moves downstairs. He meets the trundling Maureen Hill

on the way. She acknowledges him without smiling and Tom doesn't hang around to chat. He jogs down two more flights and exits onto the street.

'Where is he?' she asks as soon as she sees Tom.

'What?' Tom says. His forehead wrinkles.

'Where the fuck is he? He didn't come home last night. And I know you were with him.'

'What?'

'I know you were with him. Karl told me you were going to be there. He said,' she deepens her voice to mimic her husband. '"Tom is going, that bloke that used to live on my road." And I said, "That odd bloke that works in the factory?" And he said yes. So I know for a fact you were there.'

She folds her arms and indicates, with a nod of her head, that it is his turn to speak.

'Yeah,' Tom says. 'I was out.'

'Then what are you lying for?'

Tom runs his hands down his face. He can't think straight.

'What?' he asks.

'Where is he? Is he up in your place?'

'No, of course not.'

'Come on,' she moves toward the door. 'We're going to check.'

'He's not up there.'

Her eyes partially close with suspicion.

'All right,' Tom doesn't want to argue with her. He opens the front door and leads her upstairs.

'He's gone out with the lads from work before and he's always come home,' she says. 'He goes out with you once and he's out all night. What does that say?'

'I don't know,' Tom mumbles over his shoulder as they move upward.

'It tells me something is going on,' she says.

Maureen Hill is still hanging around the stairs. She raises her eyebrows on seeing Angela and gives her the once-over. Tom pretends he doesn't notice and quickly rounds the banister rail onto the next flight.

'Is this the only door to your place?' Angela asks when they are outside Tom's.

He nods and unlocks the door. Angela bolts to the next flight of stairs and scans upward and around like a threatened meerkat before entering the bed-sit.

She assaults the room, kicks the door which hides the boiler, pulls the bedclothes onto the floor, shoves the set of drawers so they knock against the wall. She crouches and checks under the bed.

'What have you done with him?' she asks.

'I haven't done anything with him.'

'He's not answering his phone or anything. Jesus,' she snatches her phone from her handbag and stares at the screen. 'Where the fuck is he gone? Where the fuck is my husband?'

'I don't know. I thought he went home last night.'

'You must know. Someone must know. What time did you leave the pub?'

'I left at half twelve but I don't know about Karl. I didn't see him leaving.'

'So he was still there when you left?'

'I don't know.'

'Are you trying to cover for him or something?'

'No.'

'You're doing a terrible job of it, ye know.'

'I'm not trying to cover for him. I don't know whether he left because I didn't see him leave.'

'He just disappeared?'

'Kind of. With my watch.'

'What?'

'He has my watch.'

'My husband is gone and you're worried about your watch.'

'Well, if you find the watch there's a good chance you'll find your husband.'

She grips her hair tightly and presses her teeth into her bottom lip so the skin fades to white.

'Jesus Christ, where is he? What happened?'

'The last I saw of him was when he was at the bar waiting to be served. He might have gone to the Gents then.'

'After he got served?'

'He didn't get served.'

'Was he too drunk to get served?'

'No, nothing like that. The place was busy. He was waiting for a bit at the bar but then he went to the Gents. Or I think he went to the Gents. He went through the door that leads to the Gents but when I checked the toilets about ten minutes later there was no sign of him.'

'Davey told me he didn't see him leave either.'

'You spoke to Davey?'

'Yeah, he gave me your number and your address. I have that other fella's address too.'

'Jimmy?'

'Yeah, so don't think you can hide him there.'

'We're not hiding him anywhere,' Tom says. 'I don't know where Davey got my home address from. People from work shouldn't have access to your home address.'

She widens her eyes in disbelief and paces the room.

'Last night,' she says. 'Did any of you even think it was strange that my husband just disappeared?'

She stops beside Tom's chair, the one which faces the tiny window.

'Everybody was pretty drunk,' Tom says.

'Yeah, I'm getting that feeling all right. Jesus, you lot really are useless.'

She bends down and looks through the window, frowns, turns to him again and to the binoculars that hang around his neck.

'What's with the binoculars?' she asks. 'No wait,' she holds her hands up. 'I don't want to know.' She looks at the phone again. 'I'll head over to Jimmy. I bet he's hiding there.'

She hurries towards the door.

'Probably,' Tom follows her, removing his notebook and pen from his pocket as he does.

'He's a fuckin' eejit,' she says. 'Wait till I get him.'

'He is,' Tom agrees.

'He'll wish he really had vanished.'

'Look,' Tom says. 'When he turns up will you give him this?'

Tom scribbles a short message on a page in the notebook, rips it out and folds it in half.

She takes it from him and unfolds it.

'Karl,' she reads. 'Ring me about the watch as soon as you can.'

She looks from the notebook page to Tom and back to the page. She shakes her head.

'I need it back as soon as I can,' Tom explains.

'Why did you give him your watch in the first place?'

'He was showing us a trick.'

She nods her head knowingly and steps outside the bed-sit.

'It's a magnet,' she turns as Tom is closing the door. 'That's how he stops the watch. He uses a magnet on his keys. Christ, he's so predictable. He probably showed the trick to half the people in Bradley's last night.'

'In the Alpha Bar,' Tom corrects.

'What?'

'The Alpha Bar. The place in the Manhattan Hotel.'

'I know where the fuckin' Alpha Bar is,' she says, her cheeks turning red. There is a vein in the centre of her forehead. Tom can almost see it pulse.

'That bastard.'

She storms from the landing and stomps down the steps.

Tom closes the door. His phone begins to vibrate. He removes it from his pocket.

Watch, Karl

The reminder flashes on the phone.

Watch, Karl

Tom walks to the library in an effort to shake off his hangover. Two young staff members work there most Saturdays, a slight girl who wears hippy-type summer dresses all year round, has an unusually short fringe and goes by the name of 'Ell'. Tom guesses it is a shortened version of 'Ellen' or 'Ellie' but really it could be short for any number of names. The other staff member is Nigel, a stocky man who wears his mop of ginger hair to the side and tends to lean toward the hairy-jumper look. Tom thinks of him whenever RTÉ's *Nationwide* is focussing on farms in Ireland, which it so often does.

They are an interesting pair, seeming to get excited about the simple things in life, the fact that they might have had the same cereal for breakfast or that they share a particular brand of tooth-paste.

'Do you know what I hate?' he heard Ell say once. 'I hate the way that when you are having a nice dream, ye know,' she likes to fold her arms and arch her back when she has something worthwhile to say. 'And the alarm clock wakes ye.'

Nigel nodded his head like one of those bobble-headed dogs kept in the rear window of cars.

'And then you can't remember what you were dreaming about,' she continued. 'And then you spend the whole rest of the day trying to remember the dream. I hate that.'

'I hate that too,' Nigel shook his head. 'Jesus, yeah I hate that all right.'

Tom approaches the counter and asks Nigel if the library stocks any books relating to body shape.

He then straightens the books on the counter so the edges are lined up while Nigel checks the PC. After a minute the library assistant points him in the direction of healthy eating and diets.

Tom browses the shelves, picks four interesting books, one by illustrations alone, two by contents and one merely because he likes the image on the front, a hamburger with facial features chasing a man.

When lunches go bad!

He begins to read but it isn't long before he comes across a problem. There is a common description in the books whereby three of the four body types are related to fruit shapes, banana, apple and pear. He finds it difficult to visualise these. He finds it much easier to replace the images of fruit with numbers. The banana shape becomes the number one, the top-heavy apple shape becomes a nine and the bottom-heavy pear shape becomes a six. While the hourglass body shape becomes a number eight.

The shapes are now easier to visualise but soon the four numbers begin to scroll through his head and he begins to think of handwriting, how most people write letters and numbers differently and how one person's number six will be wider than another person's, how the curve of a number may be shorter or a base may be longer. And he begins to panic and starts to believe that the whole exercise of picking an ideal body shape is as pointless and random as a kid picking his favourite number.

Em, hi, I'm Tom and my favourite number is six, my favourite colour is blue and I like running from one place to another and jumping over stuff, and if that stuff moves then I like it even better and if there is water near the stuff that I'm jumping over then that is really great. Or if there is muck near, that is cool. But not worms, I don't like worms. They have no eyes.

And the sheer weight of the number of possible varieties within the four body-shape categories makes him feel as if there is a weight on his chest and he has to force himself to inhale deeply a number of times in an effort to calm down.

Eventually he composes himself.

He returns to the book.

He flicks through the pages, stopping when he spots a significant detail. He reads how a major model association in Britain recommends that their models should have a ratio of around 34-24-34 and he thinks how strange it is to have a standard for humans, especially as, unlike a lot of the creatures on this planet, human beings seem to be so utterly different to each other.

34-24-34

Bust-waist-hips.

34-24-34

In order to visualise these dimensions he draws a rough sketch of a figure with scaled-down proportions. It doesn't help him much but a thought gradually emerges from his sub-conscience. It is one of those wobbly ones at first, the type that could just as easily lose its shape and collapse under itself, drain off to somewhere out of sight. But Tom gives it a moment. And then it starts to solidify, gradually becoming something he might be able to pick up and run with.

If only I had a body to work on.

Not a real body, of course, a model of some kind that he could play around with.

It would make the whole process easier.

There are options. Not a great deal of options, true, but there are definitely options out there.

Chapter 8

The truck was parked at the end of the street near a trodden and dejected green. The neighbours would stand in clumps, folded arms and dark faces, complaining about the leaking oil and the space it was taking up. Some were disgusted with the mere existence of such a vehicle. Tom's grandfather would watch the truck from the front room, each evening a long silent vigil. If Tom tried to talk to him he would grunt at the boy and wave him off. On occasion his grandfather would rush to the door, his shirt open to reveal the greying hair on his chest and bark at children who he viewed as a threat to the truck. Then he'd hurry back into the front room to his old position at the window, all the while muttering under his breath about the uselessness of parents and the unruliness of kids in modern times.

During the daytime he worked on the truck, mainly repairing the boards in the box on the rear. He was more like his old self when working, scooting around the floor, cursing at his tools and at the boards if they didn't fit nicely, at the nails that would bend when hit at the wrong angle. He was more aware of Tom's existence at these times and he would give out about the state of Tom's room, telling him to get a box to store his things in. Sometimes he would comment on one of Tom's many developing ticks, like Tom's need to continually grind his jaw from left to right or his compulsion to frequently scrunch his eyes together in a forced blink.

'You're doing that thing with your eyes again,' he would say. 'Stop doing that thing with your eyes. I don't like it.'

His grandfather added a sleeping compartment for himself in the rear directly above the truck's cab and a bunk for Tom beside. He also constructed a wooden counter on the left-hand side, fitted a stove next to it, the chimney of which funnelled up through a hole in the roof section. He had purchased a second-hand generator from a scrap yard to provide electricity for light and appliances. This generator was loud enough to rattle teeth and to cause temporary tinnitus; loud enough to let the people in a mile radius know when they were making a cup of tea. Candles quickly became the preferred choice for light in the box.

Tom would ask his grandfather where they were heading to and he continually received the same answer.

'We're hitting the road,' he'd say. 'Seeing the world.'

There was adventure in this statement, a landscape of possibilities, the chance to dream. Tom would lie on his bed, hands tucked behind his head, and imagine that he was going to be the one to drive the truck. He imagined stranded girls hitching on grassy verges and tattooed, leather-wearing musicians heaving their gear into the back.

Rock and roll, brother. Rock and roll.

The end of the school year neared and the days grew longer and one evening Tom returned from the library to find his grandfather in the back garden, his face flickering from orange glow to shadow with the movement of fire. There was a bottle in his hand and a low mound of items beside his feet, pieces of broken furniture, music tapes and books. Panes of glass jutted from the ash at the outer edge of the fire, flames licking the sides, glass that once covered photographs of Tom and his grandfather, of his parents and his grandmother.

'It's time we cleared the place out,' his grandfather said.

'Is that all our stuff?' Tom asked.

His grandfather didn't reply.

Tom slinked back into the house and upstairs, only to find that his bed was no longer there.

Two weeks after the fire in the back garden, the first week in June, and his grandfather told him they were ready to go. Tom helped load the horsebox with the last of their supplies and climbed into the cab. The broad window offered expansive views. There was a magnet of St Michael on the dash, a Yankee flag behind the seats and stickers on the door advertising Bandag tyres, a cartoonish image of a blonde woman provocatively sitting on a pile of tyres, wearing a pair of tight jeans, her opened waistcoat only concealing a fraction of her breasts. Tom would glance at her when he thought his grandfather wasn't looking.

The engine started first time. It vibrated through Tom's body. His grandfather allowed it to rumble for a good five minutes, frequently pressing his foot on the clutch, allowing air to leave the system. Eventually he eased his left foot slowly off the clutch and with equal pressure and speed pressed his right foot down on the accelerator.

They were in motion.

Let the adventure begin.

They moved off the street, the engine seeming to inhale in the pause as his grandfather changed gear. The suspension would bounce wildly as the truck reared over bumps on the road surface. There was the sound of something sliding and knocking off the sides of the box as they took corners. Tom hoped it wasn't his bunk.

Tom's grandfather's face changed when he drove, his eyes intense, the skin at his mouth tight with his concentration. There was something bird-like in his expression, a hunting type of bird, one with an acute awareness of its environment. There was also fluidity to his movement, the way he manoeuvred the gears and positioned his arms, a gracefulness, as if he were dancing with the wheel. He was sure and confident, experienced, no pause for thinking, no stuttering, it was one fluid movement into the next as they took the corner behind the shopping centre on the main street and chugged past a dilapidated Esso garage, took the first exit at the large roundabout at the town centre and drove northward.

The engine heaved.

The cab heated.

Tom daydreamed of what was in store.

Down the dual carriageway.

Past the scrap yard.

Left. Left. Right.

Then his grandfather clicked the indicator to pull over. A few yards later and they were stopped in the car park of the Fortress Pub.

'Sure we'll hitch here for a bit,' his grandfather said.

'We've only just started,' Tom said.

'I need a pint. And sure,' he used the tone that he often used when he was in a joking humour, 'isn't one place exactly like another when you live in a truck.'

But he wasn't joking.

The truck would be parked in that car park for the next two weeks.

The Fortress Pub was the kind of place that someone might open if they had a whole chunk of money to waste. It was built on a dangerous road at the back of the town, too awkward to attract walking customers, and situated on a road too infrequently used to catch passing trade. It was constructed from concrete cinderblocks, the ones on the roof section spaced so the build resembled a castle in the way that a child's drawing might resemble a castle.

Most of the trade came from the housing estates to the west of the town, young men dressed in bomber jackets, who would arrive in the back of vans or four-door bangers, piled in so tight that they seemed to explode from the vehicle when a door was opened. They would pop pills and drink gallons of cider, dance the night away or beat the crap out of each other in the car park. Tom would sit in the rear of the truck at night and listen to their antics, praying that they wouldn't go too near the truck. Each thump and Tom would picture someone receiving a kick to the head, each squeal and he would imagine someone screaming for help. The world was a more frightening place when he was judging it by hearing alone. But they never came near the truck. They had quickly got wind of his grandfather's travel plans. The likes of young working-class men usually have respect for the old. And the eccentric.

The interior of the pub was typical of the time, long cushioned benches with dark, furry coverings. The carpet was tough and the bare walls painted a soulless green colour, not much to look at but it did have toilets and running water which meant they could keep themselves clean, Tom at least. His grandfather didn't seem too bothered with washing. His grandfather spent most of his time at the bar on his own looking at a small television in the upper corner of the room, regardless of what was showing or regardless of whether the sound was on or off. Tom would sometimes wonder whether he was actually looking at that television and wonder if he would ever be the same again.

Tom didn't hang around in the Bedford during the day. He

usually walked the half-hour trip back to his old estate, trying to keep a nominal amount of normality in his life. He would cut through fields with rotten and discoloured weeds and shrubs, through wasted factory ground piled with rubble and old rusted iron just to maintain the weak link with the lads. Perhaps it was that place, the Fortress Pub, or perhaps it was because it was so early in their move or the fact that the lads didn't seem bothered that he was no longer living on the estate, but it was the first time that Tom became aware of his insignificance to the group and his insignificance to the world that he had once felt part of. Of all the places they would stop on the journey Tom hated that place the most. There was something hopeless about those two weeks that can often catch Tom off-guard and make it seem as if all his teenage years were like that place, isolated and depressed. Those weeks, as short as they were, can sometimes infect and corrupt all other memories of that time.

In the mornings, before the bar opened, his grandfather would listen to an old transistor radio. It was covered in oil, the aerial snapped and the front casing cracked to reveal a single speaker inside. He kept the sound at a low level so the voice of the presenter or the newsreader would be continuously lost to the slightest external noise. He would huff angrily when this happened and Tom would wonder why he didn't just increase the volume on the radio.

One of the mornings a chirpy presenter's voice was replaced by a haunting tune. Tom's grandfather had been rolling a cigarette and he stopped suddenly, the tobacco in a small heap in the centre of the cigarette paper and his fingers gripping each end.

'That's her song,' he said and he slowly leaned toward the radio.

'Who?' Tom asked without thinking.

His grandfather frowned, shook his head. And Tom felt

embarrassed. After a moment Tom stood, shoved his hands into his pockets and made his way over to the radio. The voice was wavering, the notes high for a man. It made Tom think of an American Cadillac for some reason, ice-cream sundaes and drive-in movies. Perhaps the song had been used in some film about the fifties in America that he had seen. Or perhaps it was merely a song that sounded like it should be in one of those films. He wasn't sure.

'I never heard Nan sing,' Tom said.

'No,' his grandfather shook his head. 'She never sang.' He redirected his attention to his hands and began to evenly spread the tobacco along the cigarette paper. 'She had a shite singing voice. Really shite. But she liked to listen to the song.'

He shaped the tobacco into a neat line and skilfully tucked the opposite edge of the paper backward before swiftly rolling the end closest to him in a forward direction. He licked the gummed edge and gave it one final neat roll. 'She said that we danced to it one time,' he continued. 'I can't remember. But if she said it then it must be true. You take after her that way, don't ye?'

Tom widened his eyes questioningly.

'You're good at remembering stuff, aren't ye?' his grandfather asked.

'I don't know,' Tom shrugged.

'Don't be shy about letting people know what you're good at. Jaysus, it's easy enough for them to see the bad.'

His grandfather lit the cigarette and they remained quiet until the song finished. Tom thought of how his grandmother would always have the radio on when she was ironing, a mound of clothes beside her and a cup of tea on the counter. He saw her in his head, smiling, lost to her own thoughts, and he imagined the scent of the steam and the fabric heating as she swept the iron from right to left across the board.

Over the next couple of days Tom would regularly consider the song on the radio. He began to feel he should take note of it in some way.

'What song?' his grandfather asked when Tom brought it up again.

'The one you told me about the other day,' Tom said.

'I can't remember the name,' the old man muttered.

His grandfather stared out the window for a time. Tom wasn't sure if he was trying to recall the song or if he was thinking about something else. When he didn't respond after a couple of minutes Tom went and sat on his bunk.

'I'm heading across for a couple,' his grandfather eventually nodded his head in the direction of the pub. He stood and stretched his arms before opening the door. He paused before exiting.

'You're all right, aren't ye?' he asked without looking in Tom's direction.

Tom paused before answering. The question had caught him unawares. If it had of been evening and if his grandfather was settled maybe he would have given a different answer. But the door was open and his grandfather had one foot out and Tom felt there was only one answer to give.

'Yeah,' he said, tensing, a part of him wanting his grandfather to push for a different answer.

But he didn't.

'Good,' he said and climbed from the rear.

Tom had an early night that evening, partially waking to the sound of his grandfather's clumsy and unsteady return. When he woke in the morning there was a piece of paper on the table, a mug weighing it down. On the paper his grandfather had written the words 'Only the Lonely' and the name of the singer, 'Roy Orbison'.

Their stay in the Fortress car park ended the following night with his grandfather flopped over the steering wheel of the truck, the engine running. He was muttering to himself, repeating something about an orchard that he robbed as a kid. He would often revisit his youth when drunk, recount stories from those days, colouring the tales with wistful enthusiasm and talking as if life after his childhood was just a weak shadow. He had two pals as a kid, Byrner and Goosey, and they usually weaved their way through each story. His grandfather supplied little detail on their appearance and always referred to them in a collective sense in that '*they*' were a gas laugh and '*they*' were great at scaling up trees and you should have seen '*them*' do a little bit of this or you should have been around when '*they*' did a little bit of that. Tom would draw his own mental images of the pair, imagining Byrner as a round character with a small cap and a grey uniform a couple of sizes too small and Goosey as a tall skinny lad with a snotty nose and the sleeves of his jumper so long they almost trailed the ground. Tom isn't sure if he stole this image directly from a comic he had been reading when he first heard his grandfather's stories or if the image is one of his own creations.

Judging by his grandfather's stories life seemed to work on the general principle that poverty equated to happiness. The less you owned the better the time you were having.

Shoes! What the hell do you need shoes for?

We were so poor that we could barely afford to breathe.

The stories would vary in setting, the Tolka river, hitching their trousers up and catching slippery pinkeens with a bucket, Cabra, stone fights with other lads, chasing the cars on O'Connell Street, sliding on the ice in winter on Marlborough Street.

Depending on his humour the stories would sometimes veer onto his later life, dances at the North Strand and films in the picture house in Fairview. But when he was really drunk the story was always the orchard, a place that he had robbed with Byrner and Goosey when they were about twelve. It was as if that scene with the lads was his default setting and any time his mind was overpowered by the drink he would seek safety in that orchard.

There was always this feeling of falseness for Tom when his grandfather reached a deep state of drunkenness, the impression that he was acting out the part of another man because he was always so different to his normal self. He even looked different, his eyes taking on this wild look, like a creature that is being chased or cornered. When Tom saw this expression on his face he knew there was little reasoning with him and that it would be best to agree with everything he said and hope that tiredness would overtake the drunkenness. Anger might only be a misconstrued sentence away in this state so when his grandfather tried to fit the key in the ignition of the truck Tom just watched him. And when he succeeded on his third attempt Tom remained silent. When his grandfather turned the key and started the engine Tom waited it out, praying he was only kidding around.

'I have to go home,' his grandfather spoke through clenched teeth. He could barely lift his head from the wheel.

'We *are* home,' Tom replied softly.

His grandfather just shook his head.

It wasn't the first time Tom had been in a vehicle with him drunk. It mostly happened in his younger days when his grandfather owned the Cortina. It wasn't an abnormal occurrence so Tom didn't think much of it. Later in life he would consider how he never believed that anything bad was going to happen. There might be the odd grab of the seat if a foot is too heavy to the floor or there might be a sudden intake of breath if the sign passed is a little bit closer to the vehicle than usual, but mostly there is a confidence in the fact that accidents always happen to other people.

His grandfather had never tried to drive in a state this bad.

The truck stuttered forward like a reluctant dog being pulled on a lead, small bounces along the earth, whining at the mistreatment of its owner. He reversed the truck and somehow managed to aim the front of the vehicle in the direction of the road. It was as much out of instinct as it was out of awareness because most of the time he was looking at Tom while he did it and for the times he wasn't his eyes were at the same level as the steering wheel. His upper body rotated with the gear-stick as he moved it into first and they slowly made their way toward the car-park exit. Tom was immediately aware that their course was slightly off-kilter and that they were heading straight for a pillar to the right of the exit. Their sluggish pace gave plenty of time to change course and even today Tom remembers looking from the pillar to his grandfather on a number of occasions in the time it took them to get to the pillar, waiting for him to stop joking around and rectify the direction.

'The pillar,' Tom said a couple of metres in front of the wall. His grandfather's movements were slower than the vehicle and he only managed to change direction slightly before they connected with the wall. It was possibly the slowest car crash that has ever occurred, Tom thought, after the truck jolted to a halt and the engine stopped suddenly.

'Oops,' his grandfather said. The expression on his face would have been comical if Tom had not been terrified. His grandfather then lay back on the chair and was asleep in seconds.

The next morning they checked the truck over. There was a dent at the front and some scratches from the collapsed wall. It was minor aesthetic damages though and the engine started first time. They left before the owner arrived to see the state of the wall.

Tom was glad to see the back of that place. In some ways he wished they had ploughed through the rest of the building before they left. But it was easier to have this notion of bravery in the sobering light of day. The first leg of their journey had come to an end, like all things that come to an end, Tom would muse some years later. They don't come to an end because you are enjoying them or they have a nice conclusion, they come to an end because it is their time to die and because they have run their course. This is why so many memories have the shadow of disappointment hanging over them. Even the best memories lead up to the bad. And even the darkest memories can take on a deeper tone.

Chapter 9

After the library Tom visited shop after shop in the city centre, sniffed around the mannequins on display, scrutinised the details to see if any would suit his needs. They all bore similarities, frame-wise, in that they had an insect-like slenderness and were ghostly pallid. Tom found some with heads and some without, some with hands removed and others which were merely upper torsos, a jacket or shirt draped over them and a pair of trousers tied to the centre to give some idea of an outfit. He made excuses for not choosing each one, blaming height or flimsiness or lack of appendages and limbs. Eventually he decided to give his cousin Pete a call.

Pete is a relation on his father's side, a side of the family that Tom has seen little of in the last two decades, and if he is being honest, little in the years leading up to that point. But there was a period in Tom's youth when his grandmother felt it was important that Tom keep in touch with his father's side of the family. So she began to invite some of his relations up to the house for dinner, the odd weekend, mostly on Sundays. Tom's Uncle Ted was the only one to take up the offer, and even then it was probably the notion of a free meal which enticed him to the house rather than as a support for family ties.

Pete and his parents would arrive in the afternoon. And, just as the doorbell rang, Tom's grandfather would say that he was going for a lie down and trample upstairs. But he wouldn't sleep. He would sit on his bed and read true-crime magazines, chain smoke Players and only come back down when their muffled goodbyes reached him from the hall and the front door closed behind them as they left.

Ted was his father's eldest brother and he looked like his father in some ways, in the photos at least. He had the same blocky frame and the same reddish-brown hair. There were similarities in the face too, the meaty nose and thick lips. Their eyes were different though. Ted's had a much sterner quality to them.

Ted worked intermittently, holding down a job for a few months before returning to lengthy periods of drinking and daytime TV. His wife, Maggie, was a secretary in a primary school. Tom always remembers her as a head-shaker, her perm bouncing on her head as she did this, arms folded so she was gripping both elbows, her eyes aimed at the heavens. She was one of those people who could unearth the bad in any event and had a skill for manoeuvring conversation onto the negative things in life. Some of her stories have never left Tom, like the story of a neighbour's child who lost two of her fingers through the slamming of a car door or the story of how an aunt of hers had been dead in her flat for three days before they found her.

'Her cat had started to eat her, ye know.' She turned her body away from Tom and Pete when she said this, as if the change in direction would prevent them from hearing.

'She was unrecognisable when they found her. It makes you think, doesn't it?'

About what, Tom wasn't sure at the time, but now, he does wonder what drives a person to focus so much attention on the miserable aspects of life. Perhaps it is the same thing that compels people to watch reality programs about hospitals and cancer and tragedy. Maybe these people feel a sense of relief in the fact that the event is not happening to them, or perhaps the discussion of terrible events is a way of displaying their empathy, the ritual of misery a way of portraying their love for mankind.

Pete was a whiner of a child. When Tom visualises him as a young boy he mainly sees him with a red, angry face. He was stubborn too, a child who only wanted to do something when someone wanted him to do the opposite. He was skinny and freckled, with dark, straight hair that his mother cut herself. There was a piece of hair at the base of Pete's nape that he wouldn't let his mother cut, his 'tail'. He wore it outside his jumper as often as possible and liked to show how long it was by curling it around his neck so it reached the other side. Tom admired that tail and would ask his grandmother if he could grow one too. She made the excuse that it would only get caught in his tie for school, a tie which was merely a piece of fabric on an elastic band. His grandfather wasn't so polite.

'Why would you want the back of your head to look like a rodent's arse?' he'd ask. 'Leave the tails to the mice and the rats.'

Pete didn't eat as a kid, proper food in any case. On their visit to Tom's grandmother the boy would fold his arms at the table and refuse to budge until the ice cream and jelly appeared. His mother would make comments about starving children in Africa and carefully transfer his dinner to a bowl which she had purposely brought for this reason. She would claim that Pete was going to eat the dinner when they got home but Tom knew better. Pete had told him once that his mother throws the dinner in the bin as soon as they get home.

'I wouldn't eat that crap,' he'd say when they were out of

earshot of the adults. 'I'd rather eat dog-shit.'

The visits ended after a few months and with it Tom's link to that side of the family. There has been the odd email over the years, usually with news of a death or a marriage in the family, where they have filled each other in on brief details of their lives. And Tom has seen Pete a couple of times since they were kids. The last time was at the funeral of Pete's father when they were teenagers. Pete didn't cry on the day. Or carry the coffin. He spent most of the time after the funeral moping around his parents' house.

Tom sat quietly in the kitchen, near the door, listening to the relatives try to outdo each other with stories about how successful their lives were. He watched the kids playing in the back garden. Tom doesn't usually pay much attention to kids. They are a bit loud for his liking, overly unhygienic and unpredictable at the best of times. On the day of the funeral the kids were charging around the garden, either with complete aimlessness or in a game too sophisticated for him to comprehend. Their game took them to the furthest part of the garden and to a small area of flowers in the corner, tulips, those flowers that for some reason make Tom think of snooty ladies when he sees them. Pete suddenly came storming from the house with that old boiled look on his face. He ran those children out of the area like an angry bull.

When they had escaped inside Pete moved over to the tulips. The way he collected the petals which had fallen from the stems of some of the flowers, the way he gently straightened the stem of a damaged tulip and watched it bend forward again when he released it, the way he patted the earth around the flowers, Tom knew that his cousin's father had planted those flowers and he knew that his cousin wasn't as heartless as he liked to make out.

Tom meets Pete at a taxi rank beside the waxwork museum in

the city centre, the museum where his cousin has worked security for the past ten years. When Tom rang Pete earlier and explained that he needed a body, Pete didn't even enquire as to what he needed it for. He just asked how much Tom was willing to pay. Tom said seventy and when his cousin agreed to seventy straightaway Tom wished he had only said fifty.

'You only want the one?' Pete asks. 'Because you can have more if ye like.'

Tom says that one should be enough and Pete shrugs his shoulders as if he couldn't have cared less either way. They move past the rank, through the doors of the museum into the lobby. Another security guard sits at reception to the left of the door. He is eating a banana. Without speaking he acknowledges their presence by pointing the half-eaten banana in their direction.

'That's Gerry Carney,' Pete says as they are clumping down steep steps into the basement. 'It's his shift tonight. I'm not even supposed to be here. Gerry's all right though. Split up from his missus about a year ago. I warned him that she was a slapper. He wasn't having it.' Pete unlocks a door which leads to a corridor. He flicks a switch and a bulb weakly illuminates the dark space. 'They have three kids. Three fuckin' kids man. What a mess.'

There are two doors at the end of the corridor. Pete unlocks and opens the one nearest to them. A dark shape immediately falls toward him. Pete catches it.

'Fuckin' Terry Wogan.' Pete drags the body from the room. 'His leg is all busted up.'

He grunts as he balances it against the wall of the corridor. 'Here, I'll get the others.' He ducks through the door, into a small room containing other dark shapes, and drags a second waxwork body from inside.

'How many are in there?' Tom asks.

'Five or six. Hang on, have a look for yourself.' He pulls on a string and a bulb lights up with a continuous fizzing sound. The waxwork models are crammed inside, leaning on each other. Tom helps to take them from the small space and they line them up against the wall in the corridor.

'They don't have enough room upstairs for any of these fellas.' Pete has his hands on his hips. 'So these will just sit here until one of the display ones gets damaged. Or if someone dies I suppose.'

'What do you mean?'

'If one of these fellas die then they'll put the waxwork back out on the floor. Ye can't beat death for boosting your career.'

Tom scans the models. There are five in total. Terry Wogan with the busted leg and Bob Geldof are closest to him.

'Is that Daniel O'Donnell?' Tom motions to a neat figure at the end.

'Yeah.'

Tom nods slowly.

'The jumper?' Pete asks.

'Yeah,' Tom agrees. He walks up the line of models.

'Who's that supposed to be?' He points to a man wearing rags, long tangled hair, black circles around the eyes. His skin is a rain-cloud-grey colour with scattered red blemishes.

'That's just some man from the Middle Ages exhibit. He has TB or something. There's a whole history-of-Ireland section.' Pete taps the model on the face. 'He's an ugly bastard, isn't he?'

'Um,' Tom agrees, examining him from the side.

'They were thinking of moving him to that Viking exhibition over by Christchurch but supposedly some director got into an argument with another director and one thing led to another so they just shoved him in a closet instead. You know the way these things work. It's all politics.'

'Yeah,' Tom says even though he's not sure what his cousin is talking about.

The selection of waxwork models isn't ideal. They are all men for one, all a bit dated and the worse for wear.

'Who's that supposed to be?' Tom asks about the final figure in the line-up.

'That's William Shatner.'

'William Shatner.' Tom moves closer. 'Doesn't look anything like him.'

'I don't know. If you look at him from a certain angle and close your eyes a bit. It's from the eighties, around the time he made T.J. Hooker.'

'That would explain the police outfit. Was he ever really that thin though?'

'I guess so.'

'Or tall? I always thought William Shatner was short. This figure is, what,' Tom stands straight, places a hand on top of his own head and moves his hand towards the figure until it reaches a point above the figure's head. 'Must be about five-nine or five-ten. Tall enough.'

'What am I?' Pete says. 'Some kind of William Shatner expert? They probably just made it up from a picture of the man. Jesus, for all I know somebody was just chancing their arm and William Shatner doesn't even know this waxwork exists.'

'Waxwork piracy,' Tom says as he investigates William Shatner's hands. They have a feminine quality to them. 'Interesting,' he says.

'Well, who do you want?' Pete asks. 'Pick one.'

Tom is undecided. Really there are only three figures which would come close to what he wants: Bob Geldof, William Shatner or the man from the history-of-Ireland exhibit who has TB. The

TB model is more feminine around the face but his arms are quite butch. Shatner, surprisingly, seems to have the most feminine frame. But Geldof is tall and thin. He could do a lot with Geldof.

Who to pick?

Tom taps his foot quickly, stares at each model, and this terrible image enters his head, the three rigid figures tied to tall metal stools with rope, a colourful TV setting behind them and a partition beside.

Hi there, I'm Tom from Dublin.

(applause)

I like to look at the structure of school jotters, enjoying the straightness of lines, the equal gaps between each one. What do you do for fun and how would it involve me? This question goes to number three, Bob Geldof.

Well Tom, when I'm not saving the world from famine there is nothing that I enjoy more than reassembling old Atari game consoles. So if you pick me tonight perhaps I can bitmap your sprite and maybe we can create our own graphics interface together.

(laughter)

The rock star, the TB victim or the actor? They each have their advantages and disadvantages. Eventually it is the connection with *Star Trek* that sways his decision.

'William Shatner,' he says.

'Good choice,' Pete agrees.

They return the other figures to the small room and Pete carries the model upstairs, where he wraps it in a grey, frayed and bobbled blanket before taking the money from Tom.

'If anyone asks, you didn't get this here,' he warns Tom.

'Sure,' Tom says and exits through the door of the sole wax museum in Ireland.

Tom takes the bus home.

He stands Shatner in the space normally reserved for buggies and sits next to him. There is an old man at the top of the bus, bundled in jumpers, a scraggy hat on his head. He smells of Parmesan cheese and offers a loose, rumbling cough frequently. A boy sits with his mother at the back of the bus. He gradually makes his way forward as the journey lengthens, closer to Tom and closer to the blanket-covered model. He has red hair and a scowl, is probably about eight or nine, but Tom can't be sure. His eyebrows are low and he continuously looks from the model to Tom as if he is trying to decide which of the pair he is most disgusted at.

'Is that a dead body in there?' he eventually asks and points to the blanket with his thumb.

'Corpses can't stand,' Tom says and turns towards the window slightly.

The boy exhales loudly. 'What is it then?' he asks.

'What's it to you?' Tom keeps his voice low enough so it doesn't reach the boy's mother in the back row.

'Nothing,' he exhales loudly again, moves seats, taking the one in front of Tom.

The bus moves through Drumcondra, stopping at the teachers' college. Two women get off. Tom studies their shape. One of the women is small and curvy, a number 6 maybe, Tom thinks. Her curves give her a smooth, slinky movement. The woman beside her is thin with a long slender neck, a number 1. There is something elegant about her movement, athletic too. It is too difficult to pick a preference. The complexities involved in sorting through the variety of bodies make him feel tired.

What do you want?

What does he want?

What does anybody want?

The boy has turned in his seat and he is staring at Tom.

'What's wrong with you?' he asks.

'There's nothing wrong with me.'

'You were doing this,' the boy blinks continuously for a few seconds.

'No I wasn't.'

'I saw you,' he says. 'What's that?' he asks quickly, nodding to the blanket.

'William Shatner,' Tom mumbles.

'What's a Shatner?'

'William Shatner. It's a person.'

'A real person?' The boy grips the blanket and moves to lift it.

'Here, leave that.'

'Give us a look.'

'No.'

'Who's William Shatner?' The boy sits down again.

'He's an actor.'

'What was he in?'

'Loads of things. *Star Trek*, he played Captain Kirk.'

'Let me see him.'

'If you see him will you piss off and leave me alone?'

'Yeah.'

Tom briefly removes the blanket from the top end of the model.

'That's William Shatner,' the boy says. 'The state of him.'

'There, I showed you. Now leave me alone.'

The boy tuts and moves to the back of the bus.

Tom's thoughts drift with the movement of the vehicle. Up and down and forward to his plan for the waxwork model and backward to the sexual-harassment incident in work and to

Doctor Bill Duggan, the psychiatrist.

'Your compulsions Tom, tell me about them,' he had asked.

Tom explained about the bees.

But the bees hadn't been as bad at that stage, not nearly as bad as they are now.

'It's like the bee is in the air near me,' Tom said. 'Its wings are buzzing and this buzzing is accompanied by whatever idea is stuck in my head, ye know like,' Tom drags his fingers down his neck. 'Like maybe the idea to squeeze my fists tightly three times or something.'

'Why would you want to do that Tom?'

'I don't know. Ideas just come into my head like that. Like if I turn off the television I might get the compulsion to squeeze my fists tight and then every time I turn the television off after that I'd feel the urge to squeeze my fists together.'

Doctor Bill wrote something in his ledger.

'I'd try to ignore it and then the buzzing would get louder and would sound kind of angry. And the longer I leave it the louder it gets and then there is so much buzzing that I'd just squeeze my hands tightly so that everything would return to normal.'

'And it's always bees?'

'No. It's been other things. The bee thing seems to be more common though.'

'Do the bees make you feel anxious?'

'It's hard to say.'

'Why?'

'Well, I'm not sure if I feel anxious before the bees arrive or after.'

'So you might feel anxious turning off the television?'

'No. That was just an example.'

'Can you give me a real-life example of when the bees have arrived?'

Tom thinks for a moment.

'Not right now.'

'Can you remember the first time you ever had a compulsion?'

'Not really.'

'Before the bees, in what way did your compulsions manifest?'

'I don't know. I guess I just felt that I had to do them, like the thing with the bottle-top.'

'The systematic turning before removing the cap.'

'I just felt like I had to do it.'

'What do you think will happen if you don't do it?'

'I don't know.'

'Think about it Tom,' he had closed the ledger. 'And try to think about how far you would go in the effort of keeping everything in order.'

Tom nodded.

And he thought about it.

And he couldn't come up with an answer.

Chapter 10

Tom checks Karl's office on six separate occasions on Monday morning. By eleven he realises that Karl is not going to clock in. The calls he makes to Karl's phone after eleven are all directed to the message service.

Ticka-ticka-ticka

On the way home from work Tom stops at a camera shop, a place that smells of plastic and leather, with excessive lighting on the ceiling, the walls busy with cameras on small Perspex ledges. The only camera he had ever owned before was a Polaroid Sun 600, black and silver with a built-in electronic flash. He was ten years of age.

It has been a long time since he has seen one like the Sun 600 but he did come across some Polaroid snaps in work a few months before, taken at a staff night out. Up to that point Tom had believed Polaroid cameras to be extinct, proof of their existence only found in the bare bones of older models following explorations of neglected attic spaces or excavations of junk rooms. But here was evidence of their existence, small photographs tacked to a notice board, uncannily similar in size and colour contrast to the photographs taken from his childhood. The style made Tom think that this type of camera doesn't actually capture a scene. Instead it merely transposes the characters onto a retro background. Unfortunately, he knows a Polaroid camera won't be suitable for the job he is planning to carry out.

Tom has some issues with cameras, the main ones being the risk of photograph underdevelopment and the fragility of film and the pause between the pressing of the shutter button and the moment when the camera reacts. It may only be one or two seconds but a lot can happen within this moment of time, a level smile can become crooked, a movement of the eyes, dropping of the head, dropping of the shoulders. The randomness is a cause of anxiety for Tom and this is why he asks the shop assistant for a fast camera as soon as he enters the shop.

'How fast do you want it?' The shop assistant is a tall, thin man with dark hair and circular designer glasses.

Tom isn't sure how to answer that.

How fast is a camera?

How fast is a washing machine, a television set, a shiny chrome-plated four-setting toaster?

'I'm not sure,' Tom says. 'The faster the better I guess.'

'I suppose it really depends on your price range. What is your price range?'

'Thirty euro,' Tom says.

The shop assistant grunts, rummages in a box near his feet before placing a small silver digital camera onto the counter.

'Is it fast?' Tom asks.

'It's the Usain Bolt of the thirty-euro cameras,' the shop assistant says without smiling.

There is a charity shop near his building that sells cushions; horrible gaudy things that cause a phantom itchiness on the skin of

Tom's arms and legs when he is in close proximity. He hurriedly searches through a pile, scooping up the cushions which contain spongy foam and throwing the fluffy feathery type back in. There is a rack of women's clothes near the door, dresses and blouses, a pile of trousers in a waist-high metal cage. Tom selects a dress, light material, daffodil yellow with red dots. He pays for everything at the till.

Tom then buys a couple of rolls of black insulation tape from a store that sells an unsettling variety of clothes pegs and plastic drainers, and follows this up by purchasing the cheapest Stanley knife possible in the hardware store next door.

He picks up a six-pack of beer and returns to his neighbours' bed-sit and to the wax model.

Tom holds the dress up to the model. It is long enough to reach the ankles and there is ample room to add some lumps and bumps to the model in the places where women commonly have lumps and bumps. Tom rests the dress on the chair, fetches his measuring tape and discovers that William Shatner is exactly five-nine. Tom is six-two. He is comfortable standing next to the model, even taking into account the loss of height due to the slant of the model when Tom leans it against the wall. Tom is happy to go with five-nine as a height for his match. It will simplify future measurements to do with the model. He carefully writes '5ft 9in' in the Height section on his chart.

The decision causes a small flutter of excitement in his stomach.

Tom opens a beer. He cooks some rice, studying the model while the water bubbles away. The body should be easy enough to alter, he thinks, but he isn't sure how to sort out the face. Perhaps some modelling clay will work for the nose and ears, papier mâché even. It might be possible to alter the face into a new shape, file the nose or thin the cheeks. The colour of the model's skin has dulled from age. The eyes are very detailed though. In the light of day the model has a surreal quality to it. The painted skin, the hardness, the lack of movement, it makes Tom think of a character in a skilled portrait painting, one which has somehow escaped the background and climbed from the frame.

The figure alters as the light leaves the day. The dimness adds a realistic quality to the model. It becomes more human but with an empty quality, as if it is just the hollow shell of a human. This makes him think of taxidermy, whereby somehow removing the core of the animal makes it seem even more dead than if it was splayed open on a roadside, pink guts protruding through wiry, dark fur.

More dead, Tom thinks and laughs.

Dead is dead.

Tom tidies his rice into a mound in the centre of his plate. He eats, starting at the edge and working inwards. When finished he cleans his plate before fetching the dress and insulation tape. He removes the packing from the cheap Stanley knife and tests it. The retractable blade moves with a stuttering movement when forced, and the plastic casing has sharp defects in it. It is usable, but only just.

'Sorry about this, Shatner,' Tom begins to unbutton the police jacket. 'But needs must and all that.'

He removes the clothes from the model to reveal a body with little detail to it. He puts the dress over Shatner's head and gets one arm into the sleeve easily enough. The lack of flexibility makes the second arm more difficult. It is only when he stretches the fabric as far as he can that he manages to get it to fit and even then he hears the crackle of the fabric tearing slightly before he is successful. He rests the model against the wall.

'Not bad, Shatner,' he scrutinises it from the side. 'Not a bad fit at all.'

He opens the cushions and removes the foam from each one. He cuts and rolls pieces of foam into circular shapes large enough to sit in his palms and uses the insulation tape to hold them into shape. He then pulls the dress up and over the model's head and tapes the two foam balls to the chest. He drops the dress to see how they look on the frame.

He adds and shapes, checking frequently to see how the dress sits against the model. It is all about proportion, about how the width complements the height. When he is relatively happy with the chest area he moves on to the waist, using the foam to widen it. He then moves on to the hips. It is more time-consuming than he had expected because if he feels the proportions don't sit well he must decide where to remove the foam from. This alters the whole shape and then he has to begin the process again.

Eventually he is happy with the dimensions. He pulls the dress at the back so it hugs the frame and he ties a knot in the material to keep the size. He takes to the armchair and nods slowly, examining his creation. Ignore the head and it doesn't look too bad, he thinks.

The hips are big compared with the bust. A mistake or on purpose, he isn't truly sure, but he is happy with it. He can always make alterations if he feels the bust is too big or too small or if he feels the waist could do with another inch or two.

He drinks a beer to celebrate his progress.

When finished, Tom notices a telephone directory under the small table next to the door. It is an old one, 2008, the thick end has blackened from dust and the cover is shredded at the edges, crinkled.

It rests on a Yellow Pages directory, a pile of magazines underneath, newspapers, a number of copies of *Ireland's Own*, *The Big Issue*, *The Local News* from early last year. There are half a dozen free ad papers too. He carries the telephone directory over to the armchair with the bone-like armrests and begins to look for the name 'McCarthy'. The beer has affected his judgement and he opens it on 'E', then skips to 'H' before landing on 'L'. He moves in a forward direction bit by bit until he gets to 'M'.

There are a lot of numbers with the name 'McCarthy' in the book. He skims down the columns and eventually finds a small bunch with the name 'Sarah'. There are none in her hometown of Rossboyne, a couple in Meath and Kildare, three in Dublin.

It's worth a shot, Tom thinks. What have I got to lose?

Tom's first call reaches an answer machine. The recorded voice is female, a heavy Dublin accent. It is certainly not his Sarah. He tries another and his call is answered after a wait. It is a woman again, her voice groggy, as if she has been disturbed from sleep.

'Speaking,' she grumbles when he asks for Sarah.

Tom suddenly realises that he doesn't know where to go from here. This is partly because he had never really expected to reach this point. It is just a series of small actions that have somehow led him to be talking to a stranger on the phone.

'Hello, are you still there?' the woman asks.

'Yes, sorry. I'm looking for Sarah.'

'Yes,' her tone is angry. 'I'm Sarah.'

'I was just wondering,' he stumbles on. 'Did you know a Tom Stacey when you were younger?'

'Who is this?'

'It's Tom Stacey.'

'Are you asking me if I know a different Tom Stacey or if I know you?'

'Me, I'm Tom Stacey, do you know me?'

'Do you realise what time it is?'

'Yes. I mean, no. Hang on,' Tom looks to the spot where his watch usually is.

'I'll tell you what time it is,' she says. 'It's ten past twelve. That's what time it is.'

'That late?'

'Yes, that late,' she rasps. 'So why don't you and Tom Stacey just fuck off.'

The line goes dead. Tom's face burns with embarrassment.

He puts the telephone directory away and returns to his own bed-sit.

Chapter 11

Tom takes his camera for an outing after work on Tuesday. It is draped from his neck by a shoelace as he walks the main street of the town. There are plenty of women worth photographing but every time he approaches one an image flashes into his head, a photographer rapid-clicking in front of a semi-naked young girl. For some reason the photographer has a cockney accent and has shoulder-length blonde hair, blow-dried and brushed backward on his crown.

Lovely babe. Jus' lovely.

He needs to sit down.

He sits down.

He takes a deep breath.

He forces himself to think of the expedition in scientific terms, in that he needs the input of these photographs in order to get a reliable output and that the more varying the inputs the better the chance he will have of finding his perfect match.

You can do this.

He thinks of Charles Darwin.

What if he had just hidden in a lava cave when he reached the Galapagos Islands?

What if he had not had the courage to explore?

Do it for Darwin.

Do it for science.

Do it for the evolution of Tom Stacey.

The blood pumps in his temples. His nerves jump and tingle. His eyesight becomes tunnel-like.

Adrenaline, he thinks. He needs this adrenaline.

I am a photographer.

I am a scientific photographer.

He stands and walks over to the nearest woman to him. She is a grey-haired lady in a pale raincoat. She clutches two bags of shopping and is trundling towards the butchers.

'Can I take your photograph?' Tom blurts out when he is next to her.

'No,' she replies quickly, her bags swinging forward with the suddenness of her halt.

'Okay,' Tom says, aware that his voice is too loud.

He turns and walks away, his cheeks a burning heat. That wasn't so bad, he thinks.

Tom holds on to this thought and the adrenaline. He uses it, makes his way down the main street and asks another woman if she would like her photograph taken. He receives the same answer, always the same answer, but the more he asks the less uncomfortable it feels.

Pretty soon he is asking every woman he meets.

Tom quickly realises that people don't have the time to stop. Or smile, nod or acknowledge you in any way if you are trying to get their attention on a street. Of course there is the camera to add as another disincentive. He has always been aware of the fact that some women don't like to have their photographs taken but he never knew the extent of their resistance. Near violence in some cases.

Tuesday could be another part of the problem, he thinks. To Tom, Tuesday is the kind of day that likes to hide amid the other days, the type of day that could fall out of the week with very little reaction. Nothing usually happens on Tuesdays, and for this reason people are conditioned to expect little from the day, which means they don't make much of an effort, certainly not in the sense of choosing what to wear for the day. As soon as he mentions the word 'photograph' to some of the women their initial reaction is to check their outfit, followed by a flat refusal. And on the occasions where Tom has pointed out that it doesn't matter what they are wearing, the angry reaction seems to intensify.

Bloody Tuesdays!

So the first part of his task involves a lot of negative responses, rapid twisting and turning amid the traffic of people, a variety of mumbled curses aimed his way, and the half-hearted raising of his arm in an effort to gain more attention. He only finds one willing participant, a forty-something blonde woman with an excessive amount of make-up and a T-shirt that says 'Come and have a go if you think you're hard enough' on the front. She places her right hand on her hip and sticks out her behind when he moves to take her photograph.

Tom concentrates on the face area.

'Your eyes really stand out,' he says and clicks. 'Did you know that some cats have blue eyes too?'

'Yeah?'

'Yes, unfortunately it's caused by a neurological disorder.'

'Oh.'

'There's also a lemur with blue eyes. It's called the Black Lemur,' he steps closer and takes another shot. 'They are prone to weight issues though, ye know, especially in captivity.' He brings the camera to his side. 'Yes, obesity is a big problem for the Black Lemur.'

Her behind retreats, her arms fold and she walks off with a cold look on her face.

Tom needs a different tack. He contemplates how photographers take pictures of fearful animals in the wild all the time, considers how they take up positions where the animal will not see them.

If the animal doesn't come to them, they go to the animal.

Bus stops.

Of course, why didn't he think of this before? There are always women at bus stops. And he'll be gone before they even know he was there.

Tom goes on the hunt.

He strikes it lucky straight away. Two women are standing in a queue, one staring at the ground, the other looking at approaching traffic and tapping her foot impatiently. He conceals the camera within his coat and pretends to read the timetable on the rotating section of the bus stop. Before long he is not pretending any more and he notices that the 327A departs from the city centre every fifteen, minutes apart from a twenty-minute gap between 4.15 and 4.35, and this seems like such a strange alteration that he can't help but think that the whole timetable is ruined by it. The roaring of a car horn breaks his concentration. He looks away from the timetable to find that the women are still there.

He lifts the camera, focuses and clicks.

He ducks behind the timetable and is gone.

Tom believes they are probably wondering if they had even seen him at all.

The Shadow.

He moves in silence.

Smooth and sleek.

One minute he's there, the next he is gone.

The Shadow!

A woman in a café. She is nibbling on a scone while flicking through a magazine. He readies the camera at his side before moving in front of her. She looks up at his presence. He clicks and is gone.

The Shadow.

Like a flicker in the water.

Or the blink of an eye.

Was he here or is he there?

The Shadow!

A woman waiting at the traffic lights. Click.

Two women standing in front of a parking meter. Click.

Exiting a clothes shop. Click.

Topping up a phone. Click.

Reading a book. Click.

Searching in a handbag. Click.

The Shadow!

Is he real or in your imagination?

As stealthy as a cat.

As fast as a thought.

Can you see him or can you not?

The Shad—

'What the hell do you think you're doing?'

The policeman is tall and broad at the shoulders, mid-twenties, with a face that looks like it has been removed at some point, ruffled up a bit before being carelessly thrown back on again. There is a gorilla in Dublin Zoo, a fat-headed beast of solid muscle with a back like a worn rug, perpetually watchful and perpetually scowling. His name is Harry. And Tom sees this gorilla when he looks at the policeman. Garda Harry, he thinks, and lowers his camera.

'Nothing,' Tom says. 'Just taking a few pictures.'

'Of what?'

'People.'

'I've been watching you for the last five minutes and it seems to me that the only people you're taking pictures of are women.'

Tom nods.

'Why?'

'It's kind of a long story.'

'Well you better start telling it because I've had a complaint that there's some pervert taking pictures of women at bus stops.'

'No,' Tom says. 'It's nothing like that. Jesus, no.' Tom rubs his hands together, briefly wonders if this is something that a pervert might do and stops immediately. 'I'm not a pervert.'

'I'll decide that,' Garda Harry says. 'Go on.'

'The pictures are for research purposes.'

Garda Harry raises a single eyebrow.

'I'm trying to gather photographs for,' Tom stops.

There is an electricity box adjacent to a nearby wall. It buzzes gently.

'For what?' Garda Harry asks.

'For the,' Tom scratches his head. 'To represent a kind of ideal female face.'

'What?'

Bzzzzzzz

'What?' Tom shakes his head.

Bzzzzzzzzz

'Who's the research for?' Garda Harry questions.

'It's for a dating agency.'

'And you work for this dating agency?'

'No, I'm just a member.'

Bzzzzzzz

'So it's not for a dating agency?'

'It is. It's just, I've told them that I'm doing it. I didn't go into too much detail but . . .' Tom trails off. 'You know.'

'No, I don't know,' the policeman shakes his head. 'I don't like the sound of this at all.' He begins to bite his lip.

Tom recognises this as a sign of someone coming to a decision. He sees himself in prison, a stripy outfit and a ball and chain locked to his ankle. He can't go to jail. There are no windows in jail. The buzzing intensifies.

'It's the truth,' he says loudly. 'It's like pandas, ye know.' Tom speaks quickly, filling the space, not sure if it is the link between gorillas and wildlife which causes him to think of pandas. But once he starts talking he finds it difficult to stop, despite the darkening of Garda Harry's face, and the fact that a number of people are standing beside him, watching, unmoving, heads bowed and mouths open. 'People think they're fussy at choosing a mate but it's not true,' Tom blabbers. 'You see, the female panda is only in her reproductive cycle for about five days. Now, I'm not saying that women have the same reproductive cycle as a panda or anything like that, but what I'm saying is that it's mad that a male can find a female in the wild in that space of time, while she's still fertile, ye know. But it happens. And it happens because for those few days he knows exactly what he wants and the female panda knows exactly what she wants and so it happens. And that's what I'm doing. But in a slightly different way.'

'What are you talking about?'

'I'm just trying this out for the agency, that's all. I'm not a pervert.'

The policeman stares at him. Tom is afraid of those eyes. They are hard and unblinking and he gets the feeling that they see a lot more than what is right in front of them.

'Give me your name and address,' Garda Harry takes a small

black notebook from the inside pocket of his coat, flicks through the pages, finds a blank one and writes down the address that Tom gives him.

'This is the deal,' Harry says. 'I'll give you two seconds to get out of here but don't think you're off the hook or anything. I'll be watching out for you and if I see you taking any more pictures or hanging—'

'I'm not a—' Tom tries to interrupt.

Harry holds his hand up.

'Or hanging around any women,' he continues, 'I'll arrest you. And if I hear of any complaints about creepy perverts around here I'll be calling straight to this house,' he taps the notebook.

'Bed-sit,' Tom corrects.

'Fuck off,' Harry says.

Tom doesn't hang around.

Tom spots the eyes as he passes the apartment block opposite his bed-sit. They belong to a woman exiting the building, a knobbly type of woman, so thin that the contours of her bones are clearly defined under her white blouse. She has brown hair, dyed so it has a coarse and stringy appearance. Her other features are overshadowed, outplayed even by those eyes. They are large and round, a glossy white and the irises the fairest of blue, so fair that they are almost grey.

They are beautiful.

He has to have a picture.

What about the policeman?

The eyes are worth the risk.

Her walk reminds him of a foal some hours after it has been born. It seems to lack full control, her bony limbs flung outward as if compensating for her limited balance. She is quick though and Tom has to push himself to keep up. She stops at a second-hand clothes shop. Her breath fogs the glass. Tom is almost upon her but she moves again. Down a side street, cobblestones the colour of jaded flower pots, framed with moss and slender blades of grass. Her step looks even more precarious on these, clown-like.

Tom hears circus music.

Pa-Rump Rump Rum-rump.

Par-ra-rump Rump Rum-rump.

Roll up, roll up.

The elasticated, elongated, dingly-dangly dancing lady.

Pa-Rump Rump Rum-rump

Par-ra-rump Rump Rum-rump.

A higgledy-piggledy performance of preposterous proportions.

Under the archway in the eternal shadow of corroded brick-work, a hurried rush two steps ahead, by the small record store which offers music to the minority, anti-popular protesters and haters of chart, past the second-hand bookshop that seems to have an unhealthy obsession with military memorabilia. She stops again in front of a café. There are metal chairs with hollow legs, the type so light that they slide too easily and tilt when someone moves to stand. A border separates the café from the pedestrians, waist high, made of canvas with the café's logo print-ed on it, a series of thin posts with fat bases keeping it in place.

She checks her watch.

Tom walks up to her and she looks at him.

He looks at her eyes.

She bites her lip and fidgets with the sleeve of her blouse.

'Can I take your photo?' Tom asks.

She looks at the small camera.

'No thanks.'

'It'll only take a second.'

'I'd prefer if you didn't.'

'Maybe I could just take a photo of your eyes?'

'No,' she slowly moves to the side away from him.

'One eye?' Tom asks.

A man comes from their left, dark hair brushed to the side, pointed nose and chunky Desperate Dan-type chin, a blue V-neck jumper, the shirt underneath buttoned to the top.

'What's going on here?' he asks. 'Is this fella hassling you?'

'It's all right, John,' she tugs on his arm and starts to walk. 'Let's go.'

'Are you hassling her?' he asks Tom.

'No,' Tom says and raises the camera half-heartedly.

'Come on John,' she says.

The man's teeth are clenched and his mouth is tight. He keeps his sight on Tom as she pulls him away. Tom should be afraid. He knows this. And true, his heart does pump madly in his chest. But those eyes, he thinks, those eyes are perfect.

Chapter 12

Wednesday, Karl is not in work again but there is a message on Tom's phone from him, an angry message. He insists that he doesn't have Tom's watch and warns him to stop leaving voice messages.

Tom rings Karl to clarify things but his call is unanswered.

He considers where the watch might be if Karl doesn't have it.

Ticka-ticka-ticka

In the nightclub maybe?

Tom retrieves the number for the Alpha Bar from the telephone directory in the staff area and rings.

'Hello, Manhattan Hotel,' a woman answers. 'How can I help you?'

'I'm looking for a watch,' Tom says. 'I mean, I was in your hotel last Friday night. Not the hotel part. I was in the nightclub.'

'Yes.'

'And I lost a watch. I was wondering if anybody has found it.'

'The Manhattan Hotel can't be held responsible for lost or damaged property, sir,' she says.

'I don't care about any of that. I just want the watch back. Maybe it was handed in or something?'

'It could have been,' she says.

'Could you check please?' Tom asks.

'Of course, hold on a second and I'll get one of the porters to check.'

'Thanks.'

There is a short crackle on the line and then music begins to play. The volume drifts up and down, disappears at times. Tom wonders how this is even possible. He pictures a woman bracing herself against a wild, whipping breeze, a telephone in her hand held up in front of an outdoor orchestra.

'Hello, sir,' the woman returns.

'Yeah.'

'The porter is checking for your watch. While you're waiting I'd just like to let you know that there are special business discounts on our conference rooms for the rest of the month.' She speaks in a tone usually used by a child who is reading something mind-numbingly boring in class. 'There is also twenty-five percent off bed and board. Wi-fi is available in all rooms and our restaurant, Bongos, has a fine à la carte menu.'

'Yes,' Tom mutters. 'Very good.'

'And if you are planning a weekend break with the family you might be interested in our special aquarium deal. Half-price aquarium passes for you, your wife and two children when you stay two nights at the Manhattan.'

'I don't have any kids,' Tom says.

'Of course, the same applies for you and a partner. Half-price passes.'

'I don't have a partner. I have nobody.'

'Well we have a,' she coughs. 'There's a,' she clears her throat and a lengthy silence follows.

Tom taps his index finger against the top of the phone for a moment.

'That's what's after getting me into this bloody mess in the first place,' he says. 'I don't even like going to nightclubs. But you know when someone says something to you and you just do it without really considering what could go wrong? It was like that, the power of suggestion, that's what it was.'

'Okay sir.' There is the sound of shuffling paper on the line. 'Oh here comes the porter now,' she sounds relieved. 'Hold on a second.'

The breezy music returns. Tom taps his finger quickly until she speaks again.

'There are no watches in the Lost and Found at the moment.'

'None?'

'Yes, none.'

'Can I leave my number? You can ring me if it turns up.'

'You can ring again tomorrow but if it hasn't turned up by now there is a good chance that it won't turn up at all. Can I help you with anything else, sir?'

'No, I'm okay.'

'Goodbye and thank you for choosing Manhattan Hotels.'

Tom hears a buzzing. Even after the line has gone dead.

He decides to go to the library after work.

Tom thinks of loyalty on the way to the library and how he could use it in his form. When he does this he thinks of a dog. The two are entwined, canines and loyalty, and this gives him the idea that there are specific levels of loyalty relating to different animals. Every so often he slows his walking pace, removes his notebook and writes down the name of an animal under one of two headings, loyal or disloyal. Just before he enters the library he writes the word 'elephant' and the image of the animal's trunk brings his mind around to the task in hand and to a question which he directs at the librarian on duty.

'Noses?' Ell asks from behind the counter.

'The human nose in particular,' Tom says.

'I don't know. I can't imagine there are too many books about noses. I suppose you could check the biology section.'

'I'm not really interested in how they work.'

'I'm sorry, I don't understand. What else would you need to know about noses?'

'I'm not sure,' Tom shoves his hands in his pockets. 'I was hoping that I might see something interesting.'

Ell moves over to the computer and types in what Tom can only assume to be the word 'nose'.

'Here, Nigel, do you know any good books about noses?' she asks her colleague, who is rustling through some papers on the opposite end of the counter.

'What's the computer say?' Nigel strolls over to her.

'There are two books with "nose" in the title but they're both fiction.'

'*The Nose of Bradley Hughes,*' Nigel taps his pen against his bottom teeth. 'Never heard of it. What does he want to know about noses?'

'Not sure,' she shakes her head.

Nigel sidles over to Tom.

'What do you want to know about noses?' he asks.

'I guess I want to know what makes a good nose.'

'One that works,' Nigel nods slowly.

'Aesthetically, I mean.'

Nigel hums an upward, curious sound.

'Back in Roman times,' Tom says, 'the nose was used as an indicator of character. One that stood out, usually a good long one, meant that the person was thought to be powerful or intelligent.'

'Yeah?' Ell joins him in front of Tom. 'What would my nose say about me?'

She arches her head forward.

'It's not very big,' Nigel says.

She smiles.

'So you wouldn't be considered strong or intelligent,' Tom says.

'Oh.'

'Average, I guess.'

'Average,' she repeats quietly before folding her arms.

'Your best bet is to check the online journals on one of the PCs,' Nigel says. 'I think we have a subscription to some of the cosmetic ones. You might find something there.'

Tom thanks them and moves to the computer area adjacent to the back of the counter. The machines in here are quicker than the computers in work. Tom checks his email first. There is nothing of any interest. He logs on to the Find Them website, only to see that the status under Sarah McCarthy says *In progress*. He stares at the status for a time, hoping that it will change to *Found* while he is looking. He thinks about how amazing it would be if Sarah had her hand resting on a mouse too, *Tom Stacey* in dark-green font on a computer screen in front of her, *In progress* next to his name.

It isn't the first time he has tried to find Sarah. Over the years he has been overwhelmed with memories of her, so vivid that it seems as if he has always had her in his life and that the lost years were only lost minutes. It is easy to think that he is young again at these times, easy to think that he has a grip on his life, easy to think it is not merely sliding away from him. But they have been short-lived searches, rarely moving beyond the point of wishful intentions. Tom reluctantly closes down the website and begins a search of the online cosmetic journals.

Tom reads articles on facial expressions and cosmetics, on the history of phrenology and on symmetry. He comes across a study on toddlers which found that children prefer to look at symmetrical faces longer than at asymmetrical faces. This makes Tom consider ugliness and its place in mankind. He looks at his reflection in the glass panel that separates computer sections, at the crooked apex of his nose, at the eyelid that has a tendency to droop when he concentrates. If the world is weighted towards the beautiful then why does ugliness even exist?

Tom comes across numerous articles relating to noses. He begins to make a list of his findings in his notebook.

Blind people cannot detect odours better than sighted people.

He reads articles comparing people's differing perceptions of odour.

A Dutch wine-maker once insured his nose for 8 million dollars.

He reads how people each have their own distinguishing odour identity and the effect this has on the opposite sex.

Humans can detect over 10,000 smells.

Eventually he hits the jackpot, in aesthetic nose terms at least. He reads how a survey carried out in the *Journal of Craniofacial Surgery* identified that there are fourteen human nose shapes. The article not only lists the types but there are pictures as well. Tom studies each one, the upturned nose, the straight nose, aquiline, snub and Nubian. He lists them all and then eliminates his least favourite one by one. Eventually he is left with the thin pointed nose. He gathers a number of images of this type of nose from the web and prints them out on the library printer, in colour, at a cost of twenty-five cents per page.

This research is going to break the bank, he thinks as he leaves the library.

There is a newsagents on the main street, O'Reilly's, a shop swamped with cheap toys and racks of magazines. The place is a nightmare for Tom, aisles that seem too small, nets draped from the ceiling bulging with coloured balls, electronic toys rattling and whizzing in displays and a system of queuing where a person is served by being in the right place at the right time. Towards the back there are shelves cluttered with toothpaste with foreign script on the boxes and dodgy bubble bath in human-shaped bottles, items similar to popular brands sold in supermarkets but with packaging the wrong shade or size, the boxes opened or damaged so they look like they literally fell off the back of a lorry.

Tom stands next to the rack of magazines. There are children's ones at the bottom with free gifts taped to the front, luminous whistles and plastic ducks, bright cartoon animals on the covers, the right height for sticky little fingers to grab. The shelf above is for music and cars and the two shelves above those are the women's magazines, about twenty varieties. Tom chooses three by the cover alone, two of which are glossy and one that looks like a magazine which might come free with a Sunday tabloid. He pays for them and brings them back to his neighbours' bed-sit.

Tom trawls through the magazines, his Stanley knife in hand, carefully cutting out any characteristic that seems interesting. The non-glossy magazine contains mostly small pictures, the kind of ones taken from a distance with little detail and where the target doesn't seem particularly aware that they are even a target. There are captions under the photographs commenting on hair and weight, references to gym use, plastic surgery and cellulite. Some pictures contain a close-up of different parts of the target, showing a rip in a pair of tights, runny mascara, a spot.

'A spot, Shatner. A fuckin' spot. Christ sake.'

The only useful thing he finds is an advert for hair dye and he makes a note of this in his notebook.

Hair colour. O'Reillys.

He flicks through the other magazines. There are some nice shots of pretty women with trendy haircuts. Eccentric seems to be in. And punk. There are a lot of punk haircuts, shaved sides, tall, messy, strong dyed hair, more like bright brushstrokes than hairstyles. Most of the women are skinny and some have boyish haircuts. Tom is drawn to the long and straight type of hair. He finds that a fringe frames the face and he likes this. It is neat and purposeful and it makes him think of squares, a very appealing shape in his mind. Most of the other cuts seem a bit unbalanced, some downright weird.

The majority of the models have soft faces, beautiful to glance at but not very memorable. That's the thing about faces, Tom thinks. Some haunt you long after you've seen them. Others just melt away. The same can be said for hair.

'Take blonde, Shatner,' Tom says. 'In a group of dark-haired women it certainly stands out. But if there is more than one blonde in a group they cancel each other out. I'm just not a blonde type of man.'

He couldn't really explain what type of man usually goes for blondes. He just knows that it isn't him. Red is beautiful but it comes in too many shades. And, after examining a group of photos of the same model in one of the glossy magazines, he realises that red has a tendency to change a lot depending on the light. This inconsistency is a complication that he doesn't need in his life.

Dark brown hair seems to be his type.

He writes a list of pros and cons just to be sure.

PROS	CONS
It is common	*It is common*
Subtle	*May mask dirt*
Contrasts nicely with the face	*It is harder to see in the dark*
Will highlight a dandruff problem easily	

'Dark brown it is,' he says and fetches the Yellow Pages. He flicks through until he finds sellers of wigs, and rings a couple, enquires about the cheapest wig. It turns out to be too expensive for him. He moves to where the telephone directory is kept and to the magazines and free ad papers underneath. Tom sorts the ad papers by date and checks the latest edition for wigs. He methodically works his way down every column so he doesn't miss a thing. When he finishes the latest edition without success he tries the previous edition. When he has finished this he works on the one before. He's not sure how long he does this for. At one point he looks at his wrist but his watch is still missing.

Ticka-ticka-ticka

He returns his focus to the paper.

The week before.

Three weeks before.

A month ago.

There are no headings for wigs but he checks the edition from cover to cover.

Six weeks ago.

Bingo.

Under the heading 'miscellaneous'.

Bag of Wigs from stage productions. 10 euro.
Contact Frank Mundy.

Tom writes the name and number in his notebook and rings on his neighbour's phone. The call is answered by a man.

'Hello,' Tom says. 'I'm looking for Frank Mundy.'

'Bastards,' the man hisses.

'Sorry?'

'You mean Grundy.'

'No,' Tom says. 'Frank Mundy.'

'My name is Grundy.'

'I must have the wrong number. Sorry about that.'

'No you don't,' the man corrects. 'You're looking for me.'

'You're Frank Mundy?'

'No, I'm Frank Grundy. You're calling about the ad, aren't you? Christ, I put that in weeks ago. There's a typo in the paper ye see. The bastards. It should read "Grundy" with a "G" and an "R", not with an "M". You got that?'

'Yeah.'

'You should write it down maybe.'

'I will,' Tom amends the name on his notebook.

'I wouldn't mind. I could have sworn that I said "Grundy" on the phone to those people. I certainly didn't lose any letters. I'm able to spell me own name. They probably put these mistakes in on purpose so ye have to get on to them again.' He coughs, a loose, rattling cough that lasts for a good fifteen seconds. 'Statistics,' he says when finished. 'It's probably something to do with statistics. They get paid more if they get more phone calls or something, so ye have some young upstart putting the names in wrong. Some fella from Kilbarrack or something, some fella who drives a Polo or something with a muffler on it, ye have him putting the names in wrong on purpose. Isn't that always the case?'

Tom hesitantly agrees.

'But there was this fat woman in the post office behind me when I was making the phone call,' he pauses. 'Sorry, you're not fat are you?'

'No.'

'Thank God for that. That could have been a bit embarrassing. What was I saying? Yes, the fat woman. There was this fat woman standing behind me and she kept tutting. I don't know why. I was just making a phone call. And I couldn't talk properly then. It's a bit like peeing in a public urinal, if you'd pardon my comparison. But that's exactly what it's like. But you're getting off the point a bit here, mister. What can Frank Grundy do for you?'

'I'm ringing up about the wigs. I just need one really. It's for a project, kind of like scientific research. Do you still have them?'

'Scientific research?' Mr Grundy asks, drawing out the word 'scientific' as if he is giving it a lot of consideration.

'Yes.'

'You're not going to use the wigs for experiments are ye?'

'It's kind of an experiment.'

'It won't involve mice or anything. I don't want these wigs being used to harm mice.'

Tom has this sudden image of little mice running around a cage with tiny wigs on.

'No, it's more at the research end of things. I'm just going to stick one on a model.'

'Of course you are. Sure why else would you be wanting the wigs? Don't be minding me. Well, I'll tell you what I told the last three people that rang. I don't know how many wigs are in the bag or what state they're in. All I know is that the bag is a bit melted because it was too close to the water heater in the attic and that they smell a bit. After that, well Jaysus, sure it's up to you.'

'That sounds good to me,' Tom says. 'And you're looking for a tenner?'

'A tenner indeed.'

'And there's definitely more than one wig in the bag?'

'I can count past one if that's what you're thinking. I have the certificate to prove it. Well I don't really have a certificate. I don't think they give out certificates for things like that. But if Frank Grundy says something is the truth then it is the truth. Ask me anything and I'll give you an honest answer.'

'I believe you Mr Grundy.'

'Let me prove it. Ask away. Anything you want.'

'I can't really think of something to ask.'

'Please mister. I won't rest easy till you ask.'

'I don't know,' Tom thinks for a moment. 'Do you have any kids?'

'I don't have any kids mister. We did have a Gobshite though.'

'What?'

'Gobshite, that was the name of me dog. He's the closest thing to a child I've ever had. I know what's going on in that head of yours. You're thinking to yourself, what's this daft old mentaller doing giving his dog a name like "Gobshite". Well, you'd be right in thinking that. I am a bit of a mentaller. But only when I don't take me tablets. That being said, it's a long time since I forgot me tablets. I have a note to remind me. I stick it to me glasses before I go to bed. That way I see it as soon as I put on me glasses. And if you're thinking to yourself, what if the old mentaller forgets to put on his glasses? Well, I'll tell you mister. If that happened then Frank Grundy wouldn't be able to see a damned thing. Now, what did I ring you for again?'

'I rang about the wigs.'

'Jaysus, of course ye did. Sure half the buttons are missing from this phone. I wouldn't even be able to ring ye if I wanted to. Yes, you were asking about the dog. Gobshite really was a Gobshite. I'll tell ye what I told everyone else. There was something seriously wrong with that mutt. I mean in the head compartment. Ye hear about these things with humans, ye know, someone thinking that they're Napoleon Bonaparte or Cleopatra or some other fecker who just happened to be on the television the evening before. Ye hear about it with humans all right but I'd never heard of it with animals until I met Gobshite. The dumb bastard thought he was a bird.'

'Look, Mr Grundy,' Tom interrupts. 'If I could just get your address I'll drop over and get the wigs.'

'The dog would drag everything in the garden into the corner,' Grundy ignores him. 'Exactly like a nest. Then he'd sit right down on his fat behind and start howling. I'd swear the thing was trying to sing. Of course the vet didn't agree with me. She says it's impossible for a dog to think it's a bird. She said that their brains aren't wired up the same as humans. She said that if she was being honest, dogs don't even know that they're dogs. They don't analyse themselves like us. They just do things by instinct. I says to her, sure could he not instinctively do things like a bird? She couldn't answer that one. But it wasn't even just the nest and the singing. Gobshite had a tendency to jump off the wall. And I'm telling you this for a fact, he'd be trying to wiggle those hairy legs of his on the way down. Answer me that Mrs Big-shot vet, I said. Answer me bloody that.'

'Can I get your address Mr Grundy?'

'Of course,' he rattles off another cough and then gives Tom the address. 'The afternoon suits me,' he says.

'Grand,' Tom mutters, knowing that he will have to ask for a half-day in work.

'Just a word of warning. Don't use the bell. I hooked it up to the mains a few months ago and it did something with the bell tone.'

'Grand Mr Grundy.'

'Just use the knocker.'

'Okay.'

'Give it a good bang now.'

'See ye.'

'A good bang.'

'Bye,' Tom hangs up the phone.

Chapter 13

Tom's grandfather often said that he wanted to live beside the sea. That's why they ended up in Howth, parked next to the pier, fellow trucks beside, bare trailers and a blue Volkswagen van with tartan curtains drawn across a window on the side, the words 'WASH ME YA LAZY BOLLOX' smudged into the grime on the rear. It was the latter part of June and yet it rained constantly the first night they arrived. That, combined with the fact that his grandfather had decided to give up the drink following the Fortress Bar incident, resulted in a whole new dimension of claustrophobia in the horsebox. Tom could almost feel his grandfather's reserve as a pressure in the air. Between long bouts of silence he would suddenly clear his throat and shuffle from one end of the horsebox to the other. After a couple of hours of this Tom braved the weather just so he wouldn't have to look at his grandfather any longer.

His clothes were soaked by the time he reached the shops which hugged the Harbour Road. A phone booth outside a chip shop offered some relief from the rain. The interior smelled of plastic and wet dog, graffiti was etched into the door. Tom dropped a coin into the slot and rang one of the lads from the estate. The call was answered by the mother of the boy, who informed him that she hardly sees her son any more and advised Tom that the only way he'd reach him was if he was living in the knickers of her son's new girlfriend. Tom wished he knew what to say to this and wished he had the nerve to draw out the conversation. He wanted to ask her what was happening on the estate and he wanted her to tell him about her day, to complain about her husband, to give out about the neighbours or the kids or the economy. He wanted her to talk. Just talk. And he would listen, for the rest of the night if he could. Just listen. But the line went dead and he was left with the sound of the rain pelting against the roof of the booth. Eventually he opened the door to the cold.

There was an arch, head-height, in a wall next to a bus stop. Tom stood inside the arch and clumsily removed a cigarette from his pack of ten. His clothes were itchy with damp and the top of his head was so cold it pained. Tom sat on his hunkers, curled into a ball and lit a cigarette. His wet fingers made the tip soggy and pretty soon he could no longer get a drag on it. A bus came and went and Tom wondered how long it would take to get a bus into the city centre and then a bus to home before he remembered that his home was parked on a load of old fish guts beside the pier. He dried his hands on the inside of his jacket and smoked cigarette after cigarette, pulling so hard it hurt his chest. When he eventually stood, his joints were painfully tight and the clothes he wore felt like a burden. His grandfather was asleep on a chair when he arrived back at the horsebox, a bucket next to his feet. Tom would fall asleep to the steady sound of water dripping from the roof into that bucket.

The next day was a dry one. And with sobriety his grandfather's interest in the truck was renewed. He spent a whole day cleaning and waxing the cab so the paint shone like the skin of an apple. Tom offered to help but his grandfather was used to working alone. In his own way his grandfather was always alone, even when he was with other people.

Howth quickly grew on Tom. He would sit at the top of the embankment beside the pier and stare at the water, the breeze as soothing and luring as a drug. The rats would come out as it darkened, scurrying about the boulders on smash-and-grab food missions. The rigging on the boats in the harbour clinked and echoed constantly. There was magic in that sound. It was calming, as a mobile is calming to a child. His grandfather seemed calm too.

Tom didn't know whether it was the sea air or the absence of drink but there were signs that his grandfather was returning to his old self. After a week in Howth he even decided they should visit the graveyard where Tom's grandmother was buried.

'You ever been on a boat?' he asked as they drove along cramped, bumpy roads.

'No,' Tom said.

It took so long for his grandfather to reply that he wasn't sure he had heard him over the noise of the engine.

'We should rent one out, ye know, when the weather picks up a bit. Maybe we could try a bit of fishing.'

'Can you fish?' Tom asked.

'I don't know. I've never tried.'

The springs on the chairs creaked and the truck groaned as the surface of the road became more uneven.

'It can't be that hard,' his grandfather said. 'All you're doing is feeding the fish really. Isn't that right?'

'I suppose,' Tom said.

'What?'

'I said I suppose,' Tom shouted.

'Sure that's all they do, those fish.' His grandfather controlled the vehicle with small movements of the steering wheel. 'They eat and eat. Christ, they don't know when to stop eating. Don't ye hear about goldfish that eat so much that they burst or something? If ye hide the hook well enough I'd say ye could catch hundreds of fish.'

'Yeah,' Tom agreed.

'We'd better make sure we get a big boat then.' His grandfather looked to him and smiled.

Tom wasn't expecting it and by the time he returned a smile his grandfather had his eyes on the road again.

The graveyard was a place of savage brambles and chalky pathways. An ancient chapel sat at the entrance, grey and humble, built at a time when buildings were designed to complement their surroundings. There was a frail-looking hotel adjacent to the graveyard, fractured front painted a stale pink colour with a wooden sign affixed to the side wall. The Bedford was parked in the car park next to the hotel beside a beat-up old hatchback and a fat oil cylinder.

The freshness of his grandmother's plot stood out against the other weed-ridden and collapsed ones beside. Tom felt okay with this. He couldn't explain it at the time but he felt some comfort in the idea that death was not a new phenomenon. He blocked out the brightness that shone through the branches overhead with his hand and he listened to the movement of that place. When he closed his eyes he felt freedom.

He soon heard a voice coming from the distance, an accent noticeable for its neutrality.

'Hey there. Who owns this truck?' The voice was angry in a reserved way, the way a parent might be if their child is misbehaving in public. It was coming from the hotel direction and when Tom looked up he saw a man exiting the car park and walking in their direction. He wore a white shirt, so clean it seemed to radiate light, contrasting with a pair of dull slacks on stumpy legs. Tom's grandfather muttered in the way that he usually muttered, and moved from the grave towards the hotel. Tom hung back, hoping that the distance would save him from getting involved.

The man was a chinless, fat individual, his small legs looking out of proportion to the balloon shape of his top half. His hair was thin and greasy so it seemed to be pasted to his head.

'Does this thing belong to you?' he asked Tom's grandfather, nodding his head in the direction of the truck.

His grandfather answered with a grunt.

'I want it out of here,' he said. 'Now.'

'I'll move it,' his grandfather muttered.

Taking the acceptance as proof he was in the right, the man began to badger Tom's grandfather about the difficulties in running a hotel, about how he didn't need people making it more difficult by parking ugly lorries in his car park. Tom's grandfather quietly walked past the man to the driver's side. He took one last look at the graveyard before heaving himself into the cab. Tom climbed into the passenger side and they left that place in silence.

As soon as he parked the truck in Howth his grandfather went to the pub to pick up from where he had left off in the Fortress Bar.

Some days later Joe O'Donnell appeared on the scene, a small, squat man with a tangle of dark hair which he liked to sweep from one side of his head to the other in an effort to hide the balding middle. He claimed he was in Howth to fish but he would never have any fishing gear with him and he would avoid talking about fishing when asked. But Howth attracted the likes of Joe O'Donnell, the sea called the drunks and the bums. They would arrive in the morning with a bag of beer cans or a bottle wrapped in brown paper, full of notions of freedom and adventure. The sea offers the illusion that it is easy to escape your life, that happiness lies just beyond the horizon. Perhaps this is partly the reason why so many people have jumped on a boat to England only to find themselves alone and homeless in a city so big they feel even more insignificant. Tom could spot them a mile off, walking from one end of the pier to the next in filthy coats, blooming with the many layers of cardigans and jumpers underneath, possibly believing that they looked no more inconspicuous than the other tourists that visited the place.

Joe stank. It was this undercurrent of drink and sweat, old rotting newspaper and soil. It made Tom think of smell as being a living, breathing creature, one that slumbered on O'Donnell and was disturbed into action every time he moved. And he was creepy. He reminded Tom of an unwanted magician at a kid's party, the type with a dead flower hanging out of a lapel, the big coat with the many pockets. Tom could imagine children crying at his approach and parents shooing their offspring away from him. Tom imagined he could make things disappear without anyone noticing. He could certainly make things appear. He magicked a bottle of whiskey onto the table and drank the whiskey from a ceramic mug along with Tom's grandfather.

For days they got drunk together in one of the local pubs and then announced their approach with an off-key rendition of 'Spancil Hill', trying to sing over each other the way drunks do. Tom would watch them, his grandfather's frame angled backward as though he was walking up a hill even though the pathway was level. Frequently he would totter sideways until he met a wall or lamp-post for support. Tom would help his grandfather into the back of the lorry but he was afraid to touch O'Donnell so he let him awkwardly climb in by himself.

They would play cards, poker, with a deck that didn't start out as a single deck of cards. Tom's grandfather had compensated for missing cards from one deck with cards from another so some of the cards had a red pattern on the reverse side while others had a blue one. Two Jokers remained in the pack but the number two and a crude spade-shape had been drawn on one Joker in black pen while a six and a diamond had been drawn on another in red pen. One evening O'Donnell began to talk about upping the stakes. Tom became suspicious. The fact that his grandfather had been winning every hand up to that point was another cause for suspicion.

Tom's grandmother had been the card player in their house. She learned how to play from her father, who worked night security in a large biscuit factory on the south side of the city. They would play cards to make the shift go quicker. Unfortunately he had the gambling gene, that curse that compels a man to risk everything he has on a game of cards. He was one of the breed who believe in luck and see life as one big game of chance. And it excuses their actions, this belief, because in a way it doesn't matter how hard you work at something or how long you think about your options because if lady luck is not on your side you will never achieve anything, in their minds at least. There were times when he lost his whole weekly wage on one game of cards. Tom guesses that seeing the devastating consequences of gambling was why his grandmother only allowed herself to play cards on one day a year, Christmas Eve.

The table would be covered with a green tablecloth, coppers were retrieved from the money jar under the sink, cards were removed from on top of the cabinet and the lamp was moved from the front room to the kitchen. They would play cards up to eleven at the latest or up to the point when his grandmother won all the money, whichever came first, usually the latter. His grandmother would share all her expertise with Tom, knowledge that was passed on from her Dad about shuffling and dealing, flushes and blues and straights and full houses. Her knowledge was impressive and as she flicked cards in front of each player with confident ease and skilfully shuffled the cards so they were a blur, joked about her winnings. It was easy for Tom to imagine her a different person, not a grandmother or mother or wife but an individual with hopes and dreams that didn't revolve around the family environment.

Some of his grandmother's knowledge served him well. Tom was soon aware of what O'Donnell was up to. He began by talking excessively, mostly when it was his deal, go off on a rant about the police or the government, shuffling the cards clumsily so that a clump of them would fall onto the table, face-side up. He would then slowly collect them and put them at the end of the deck. Tom knew he was putting all the best cards at the bottom of the deck and then dealing them to himself. Tom considered getting his grandfather aside and alerting him but he was probably too drunk to listen and even if he did, God knows what it would have led to. Tom just watched and hoped O'Donnell would make an obvious mistake.

His grandfather's luck must have been in or his drunkenness was clouding his bad card-playing because he was winning at least every second hand, one of which had a nice big pot.

'I told you,' he'd say. 'You can't win a winner.'

He always fancied himself as a card player and a gap of a year between games at Christmas seemed to reinforce this belief and push all the lost games out of his head from the previous Christmas. Because that's what would happen. He would lose game after game to Tom's grandmother, drink too much whiskey and sulk until he went to bed. Then, the following year, he'd be at the table again, rolling his sleeves up for the first game and repeating the words, 'You can't win a winner'.

This was the first time his words made any sense.

Tom could see that O'Donnell was getting pissed off with the way the night was turning out and he was constantly proposing that they play a different game, like Acey-Deucy or Three-card Stud, a quick way to win a big hand and a lot easier to cheat on. Tom's grandfather refused. He still had enough sense to stick to a game he was winning at.

'Do ye know of those fellas in Las Vegas that remember all the cards?' O'Donnell gripped the mug by the handle, held it out for a refill.

'Yeah,' Tom's grandfather blinked a number of times before sloshing whiskey into the mug.

'That's some living, isn't it?'

'I guess so.'

'Some fuckin' living,' O'Donnell took a mouthful of the whiskey and squeezed his eyes tightly before placing the mug on the table. 'That's some fuckin' living isn't it?'

'Yeah,' Tom's grandfather picked up his cards. His head dipped and his eyes partially closed. He suddenly bolted upright and took a deep breath. 'Christ. How long have we been playing? What time is it?'

'They earn a good living out of it,' O'Donnell didn't hear him. 'A damned good living. It's something that I've always wanted to do, ye know.'

'What is?'

'Remembering the cards in the casinos.'

'You any good at remembering?'

'Yeah. Too good. Forgetting, that's my problem.'

'Can you open or what?' Tom's grandfather nodded towards O'Donnell's cards.

'Especially the bad,' O'Donnell picked up the cards. 'If you can't forget the bad then you carry it around with ye.'

'I can't open,' his grandfather said.

'Ye wear it like a jumper,' O'Donnell shook his head.

'Like a bleedin' polo neck, is it?' Tom's grandfather snapped.

'Fuck off,' O'Donnell threw his cards down. 'You wouldn't understand.'

'Can ye open or what?' Tom's grandfather raised his voice.

'That's a damn good living in Vegas though,' O'Donnell swayed on the chair before steadying himself by gripping the table. 'A damned good living.'

'Christ sake,' Tom's grandfather stood. 'I'm going out for a slash.'

He tottered outside to urinate at the rear of the horsebox.

Tom would usually move to his grandfather's bunk when he was alone with the man, as far away from him as possible. This night, the night of the cheating, Tom was brave. He stayed where he was to make sure that O'Donnell wasn't going to steal any of his grandfather's money.

In the candlelight the man's eyes were murky puddles.

'You ever gut a fish?' he asked and removed a knife from his pocket, a straight, sharp blade about four inches in length. It didn't look like the type of knife a fisherman would use. It was scalpel-like.

'You have to jab the knife right into the fish's stomach,' he said, jutting his hand outward. 'Then you run your hand along its belly so that all the guts and shit comes out. You've to be careful. They're slippery little fucks, they are.' He smiled. 'I'd say you're a slippery one. I'd say you get up to a lot of mischief when your old man isn't here.'

He stood up then and took an unstable step toward the young boy. Tom tensed and readied himself to run but there was the creak of his grandfather returning. O'Donnell quickly hid the knife under his coat and fumbled for a time, trying to get it back into his pocket. He took a step backward and fell against the side of the box before letting out a soft cry. When he brought his hand from under the coat there was blood. It was a murky black in the poor light.

'My hand,' O'Donnell slurred. 'There's something wrong with my hand.'

Tom's grandfather staggered over to the table and picked up O'Donnell's cards.

'What's wrong with your hand? It looks like a good enough hand to me.'

O'Donnell just stared at him, too drunk and shocked to comprehend what he meant. Then he stumbled through the opened door and ran in the direction of the pier.

They would never see him again.

The next day Tom's grandfather was working near the bumper of the truck, scraping paint from the section that was damaged at the Fortress Pub. He still had the wide-eyed deranged look of someone who wasn't wholly clear of the drink. Tom swept around the rear wheels, adding to a pile of dirt which he had previously swept from inside the horsebox, bottles, cigarette butts, bloodied playing cards. There was a dried trail of blood leading from the horsebox, a whole lot of blood, Tom thought as he swept along the side of the vehicle. He came across what at first he assumed to be a stumpy, gnarled piece of wood. On closer inspection he discovered it was the top of a finger, pale and dirty, the nail long and stained yellow. Strangely, at that immediate time, Tom wasn't shocked by the find. He quickly swept it up and put it in a bag with the rest of the rubbish. Later, when they left Howth and began to move around Dublin, whenever he was going through a hard time he would dream about that finger, picture it in the mouth of a gull as it fluttered above a cluttered dump. Tom would wake up in a sweat and ensure that he still had all his digits by touching the tip of each finger against his thumb.

One-two-three-four.

Still there.

One-two-three-four.

Chapter 14

There is a cotton-wool appearance to Mr Grundy's hair and beard. He wears hefty black spectacles that make his eyes look large and cartoonish and his mouth is dark gaps between scarce crooked teeth so that when he smiles his face takes on a drunken pirate kind of expression. He likes to talk and to Tom he sounds like the kind of man who has not spoken to anyone in years, the kind of man who fears he may never speak to anyone ever again.

Tom recognises this trait. He sometimes sees it in himself.

'The wigs were my wife's,' Mr Grundy says. 'She used to do the amateur dramatics.' He pulls a large refuse sack from the hall. It is stretched in places with uneven bulges and a melted section in the centre. 'But don't you be thinking that Ted Grundy was just sitting around waiting for her to get home. No way. I had plenty to keep me busy. Jesus, I'm not saying that I was a wild man or anything. But I knew how to have a good time. Understand?'

He stares at Tom until Tom nods his head.

'What are you using them for again?' he asks. 'Mice, wasn't it?'

'No, it's for a model.'

'Of a woman?'

'Yeah,' Tom says. 'It's for some project to do with a dating agency.'

Mr Grundy smiles his pirate smile.

'Dating agency,' he laughs. 'Jaysus sure what would you need a dating agency for? Fetch me a tie. Someone fetch me a tie,' he shouts behind him. 'Old Ted Grundy needs to show this man a thing or two about getting the women. Dating agency,' he shakes his head as he opens the bag.

The wigs are bunched together.

They smell of wet carpet.

'I met the queer one in a cracker factory,' he nods to a photograph on the mantelpiece. 'Crackers about each other, that's what I'd say all the time, ye know, when anyone would ask how we were getting on. Acting silly and all that. She'd call me mad. Ted Grundy, you're a mad man,' he laughs, ties a knot in the bag. He lifts and drops the bag a couple of times as if he's testing the weight.

'She could play any part,' he says. 'That's why she had so many wigs. She was very talented.'

'Yeah?'

'I'd say she could have gone professional if she wanted.' Mr Grundy carries the bag to the front door. 'She was involved with it right up to the end mind you. Not a lot of them can say that. Sure they can't?'

He keeps his hand on the bag for a moment, stares at the ground. When he looks back to Tom he is smiling.

'Good luck with the dating agency,' Mr Grundy says. 'They're gas, aren't they, dating agencies? Ye wouldn't see me getting mixed up with all that at this age. No, I think when you're on your own this long ye kind of get used to it. It just becomes a habit. Sure Ted Grundy Junior has retired a long time ago, if you get my meaning,' he winks. 'A brother of hers was into all that dating and shite. He's lived in America most of his life. They all seem to be into that stuff over there. It's different here though. Or it used to be different, I guess. Jaysus, sure we weren't as picky as people are now. We'd just go with the first thing that came along. Well, second thing if you counted Willie Dowd's sister. But nobody ever counted her. I suppose it just came down to luck. Those that were unlucky, sure, they just got on with it, head down and all that. Some of us, the very few of us, well, we struck gold really. Didn't we?'

Tom gives Mr Grundy the ten-euro note at the door and the old man carefully folds it three times so it is the size of a stamp before putting it in the pocket of his cardigan.

'Don't be shy about calling in if you're ever in the area,' Mr Grundy says as Tom closes the front gate behind him.

Tom smiles and nods before moving down the street.

There is a row of shops a couple of streets from Mr Grundy's house. Barbed wire twirls up the side walls and across the gutters. There is a glass-sheltered bus stop with a view of a dental surgery with drooping blinds.

Tom waits for a bus there.

He feels the vibrations of the engine through the ground before the coolness of its shadow.

He takes it to the city centre and gets off near the Manhattan Hotel. A revolving door sweeps him inside and he feels the push of cool air behind him until he reaches a modest counter in the lobby. There is a second, lower level behind the counter, two grey cushioned chairs behind, a tourist stand on the far side with rows of leaflets and a dumpy sculpture on the side closest to the door, a metal tree with tiny, detailed leaves.

'It's you,' the receptionist says as he approaches.

It is the bartender from Friday night, Fiona.

'What are you doing here?' Tom asks.

'I don't know how to break the news. I work here.'

'But you work in the bar.'

'I work wherever the hell they put me.'

'What's that you're reading?' Tom nods to an opened book in front of her on the lower desk.

'What?' She looks around nervously. 'Nothing. I'm not reading anything.'

'Looks like a book to me.'

She closes the book. There is an image of a small, furry creature scaling up a rock on the cover. The title is in bold letters, *The Bolivian Chinchilla Rat and Other Endangered Rodents*.

'Do you read a lot of books like that?'

'No,' she shakes her head. 'I mean, yes.' She lifts an A4 diary and shoves the book underneath. 'Sometimes I do.'

'Can I have a look?'

'No,' Fiona quickly cocks her head to the side in an effort to see behind Tom. 'What do you want?'

'I'm looking for my watch.'

'And?'

'I was hoping that someone handed it in.'

'Nobody has handed it in.'

'How do you know? You haven't checked.'

'Let me see. I've been on the desk since you rang an hour ago and nobody had handed it in then. And wait,' she scrolls her finger down the A4 diary on the desk. 'It says here that you've rung at least seven times before this. And there was no sign of it then either.'

'Has anyone mentioned anything about it?'

'I think it might have made the ten o'clock news last night.'

'What about the blonde woman? Has anyone seen the blonde woman that I mentioned?'

'You didn't say anything to me about a blonde woman.'

'I was talking to some man. I told him about a blonde woman with an old-fashioned haircut? She might have it.'

'What makes you think that?'

'Not sure. I saw her looking at it.'

She nods her head slowly.

'Will you be able to ring me if it turns up?' Tom writes his name and phone number on a page in his notebook and rips it out carefully.

'What's the big deal with the watch? Is it expensive? Sentimental?'

'Yeah, I suppose.'

'You suppose,' she laughs. 'That's such a man thing to say.'

'What?' He hands her the page.

'If it's sentimental just say it is. There's nothing wrong with keeping things because they remind you of somebody.'

'I got it off my granda. He's dead,' Tom suddenly leans on the counter. 'You have great arms ye know.'

'You think?' She scans her arms.

'They really stand out,' Tom says.

'Compared to the rest of me you mean,' she laughs.

'Yeah,' Tom nods. 'Here, let me have a look.'

'Go away.'

'Come on. Hold them out,' Tom says.

She tuts loudly before raising her left arm. Tom gently takes her by the wrist and slowly rotates her arm.

She reddens as he does this.

'I wish I had arms like yours.'

'You'd look funny with these arms,' she says.

'No, they're not for me.'

She moves to say something but decides against.

Tom carefully brings her arm down to the lower level of the counter before releasing it.

'So you'll let me know if the watch turns up?' Tom asks.

'I might,' she sighs. 'So is that all?'

'Yeah.' He shoves his hands into his pockets. 'Actually, no, wait. Kindness, what do you think about kindness?'

'I don't know,' she shrugs. 'It's a good thing.'

'I know that. What I want to know is how could you tell if someone is a kind person?'

'I don't think kindness is just about gifts and money,' she bows her head for a moment. 'I'm not sure. I'd say you'd cop on fairly soon if someone is kind or not.'

'That doesn't really help me,' Tom says.

'Fair enough.'

'I gave you that piece of paper with my number, didn't I?'

'Yeah.'

'And it has my name on it?'

'Yes,' she exaggerates the roll of her eyes.

Tom walks away but stops and turns.

'It has the right number on it, doesn't it?' He begins to walk back to the desk. 'I might check.'

'It's the right number,' she says. 'I have a record of it in the reception diary in any case. Right beside your name, Tom Stacey.'

'Yeah, of course,' he turns back toward the door, hesitates only once more before exiting.

This is no use, he thinks. I need to talk to Karl, find out when he last saw the watch.

He decides to pay him a visit.

From the moment Tom enters Karl's house he can't help but compare the Angela of today with the Angela of his youth. Back then she seemed so sure of herself, so in control. Now she is almost kite-like in her actions. She drifts towards the sink in the kitchen before rapidly changing direction. She talks as if it is an effort to do so and her character is diluted in a way, a mere hint of the person she once was.

'I warned him,' she takes the seat next to Tom in the kitchen. 'I warned him. No one can say that I didn't warn him.' There is no anger in her words, just resignation. She runs her palms down her cheeks, stretching the skin so red arcs show under her eyes. 'Karl never listens,' she says. 'No, he has to do everything his own way.'

Tom nods. He wishes he hadn't called in. He tries to avoid looking directly at her, tries not to get drawn into her situation.

Angela's dressing gown has slipped to the side at her waist, revealing the stubbly skin of her crossed legs. Tom glances at them and feels embarrassed. He looks away, towards a collection of drawings that are tacked to the side of a cupboard: owls, ladybirds, some kind of egg-shaped creature surrounded by coloured circles. One of the sheets contains a child's name in various different colours, Freddie, written at least thirty times. Tom guesses they're going to have trouble with that child.

'Yesterday was grand, ye know,' she says. 'Like I was ready for it this time, like I was used to it by now and I could cope. Then this morning I saw this packet of biscuits on the counter and for some reason this really messed me up. Jesus Christ, it's only a packet of custard creams, I kept saying to myself. But it was more than that. He had bought them last Wednesday, before any of this happened. Does that make any sense to you? Do you understand? They were more than just a packet of custard creams.'

Tom nods again, his eyes move to her bare legs. She catches his glance and fixes her dressing gown roughly. But when it opens again she leaves it.

'I threw him out,' she says. 'I did it. Jesus.' She closes her eyes.

Her hair is limp, more yellow than blonde, clumped together in parts. 'I don't know how he's going to cope on his own. The man can barely dress himself. But I had to do something. I can't live like this.'

Tom looks at the ground. He's not exactly sure what has happened between them and he doesn't have the courage to ask.

'I can't even bear to think of how we're going to arrange things with the kids,' she says.

She bows her head and Tom remembers how Angela used to sing in the choir when they were just kids, eleven or twelve. She was Angela McGuire back then, striking, angelic in some ways. Mrs Trevor, the woman who organised the choir, knew it. She put her in the most prominent position in the group, central, in front of the candles so the flames made her blonde hair glow. Tom remembers the hard benches pressing against his knees, the cold draft that crept in through a gap in the church doors, its chilly embrace. He remembers the voices of the young girls, and how Angela would stare at the ground when she sang, her hands tight at her sides, the concentration causing her to frown.

Tom liked to watch her during Mass. He enjoyed looking at her without her being aware that he was looking at her. And when she was singing he could do this because those eyes of hers just focussed on the floor and he could gaze for as long as the song lasted.

He watches her now, her hands clenching the dressing gown to her chest. She looks smaller than she did as a child, more vulnerable. He tries to see some of the girl that illuminated and enchanted so many boys in his youth. He only sees her sadness.

'I remember you in the choir,' Tom says.

She blinks a couple of times. Her eyebrows dip.

'Do you still sing?' he asks.

She looks at him for a time, looking without looking in a way. Soon, she begins to cry. It is silent and her tears are large. They weave down her cheeks. She leans forward, into him. He awkwardly puts his arm around her shoulder. He feels her weight against his chest. She shivers and Tom thinks of how it feels as if she is made of warmth and solidness while he is made of nothing but anxiety and air.

They stay that way for a minute but it seems longer to Tom.

She sits up when she is finished crying and fixes the dressing gown at her legs.

'I've thought about singing, ye know,' she says softly. 'But singing is for the young.'

'I don't believe that,' Tom says.

Her tears glisten when she smiles.

'I don't think I knew you back then, did I?' she asks. 'Karl mentioned that you were from his street but I don't remember ever knowing you.'

'I was away for a bit,' he says.

'And you came back?'

'I don't think I ever wanted to leave.'

She smiles again.

'You're not married Tom, sure you're not?'

He shakes his head.

'A bit of advice,' she places her hand on Tom's knee. 'Keep it that way.'

On the way home Tom considers how important it is for people to have a hobby or an interest. He thinks of Angela, wonders what she replaced her singing with and who she gave it up for. Was it for work or the kids? Did she give it up for Karl?

When Tom was younger he was afraid of his true interests. At the time he wasn't aware of this fear. He just knew that on some level he wanted to be defined by things that other people thought cool or acceptable. Because aren't we defined by our interests, he thinks, in the eyes of others at least. Think train-spotting and a type of character jumps into the head. Wrestling, the same happens, guitar player, ice-skater or hunter. Perhaps this kind of association could be used in his form, he thinks.

Especially in relation to hobbies.

Because respect for a partner's hobby goes a long way in a relationship. It doesn't have to move to participation but acceptance and understanding is essential.

Tom begins work on a hobby section when he gets home.

The form is really starting to take shape, he thinks.

Chapter 15

Tom is in his neighbours' bed-sit watching wigs tumble in the washing machine. There are six in total and a hat which was buried at the bottom of the bag. He is feeling guilty. Most of his workday was spent searching for Sarah McCarthy on the PC. Nobody seemed to notice, and if they did notice they didn't seem to care. He found some tips on the internet in relation to people looking for lost loved ones. But Tom's information is limited and he has no contact with any of her friends or relatives from that time.

After lunch Tom began to think that head office was monitoring his internet usage in some way. He then started to imagine all the managers sitting around a table.

What are we to do about Tom Stacey's behaviour?

He dodged the PC for the rest of the day, tried to make up for the lost time and awaited the imminent call from the offices.

It never came.

Tom taps his left hand twice on the top of the washing machine. Almost immediately, he apes this tap with his right hand.

There is a box of dark-brown hair dye on the counter which he has purchased from the damaged-goods section of Riley's Newsagents. The packaging is battered and opened at the end. The instructions are missing.

Tom can only think of one person who might be able to help him. He rings up the Manhattan Hotel and asks for Fiona. After some mild persuasion she agrees to help.

'What colour are you thinking of dying your hair?' she asks.

'It's not my hair,' Tom says.

'Okay,' she pauses before continuing. 'Two questions Tom. Number one, who does the hair belong to? And two, do they know you are dying their hair?'

'No,' Tom laughs. 'It's not real hair. It's a wig.'

'Thank God for that.'

'So, do you know how to do it?' Tom asks.

Fiona slowly explains the basic steps involved in dying hair.

Tom thanks her and hangs up.

He listens to the rolling of the washing-machine drum and thinks about how the wigs will smell of detergent when they are finished. There is something deeply comforting about this smell for him, like the smell of freshly baked bread or the scent of a rainy day. He feels it is a pity that all hair isn't so nice-smelling. He recalls the hair of one of his dates from the agency, a hyperactive woman who praised the mediocre restaurant they were in as if it was a five-star establishment and gasped every time the waiter came to the table. She seemed clean to Tom. There was no evident sign of a lack of hygiene in any case. But somehow her hair smelled of compost. It was baffling. It still is baffling, he thinks. Some rational reason for the stench might have made it easier for him to deal with.

The wash cycle finishes and Tom rummages through the wigs until he finds the best one to suit his model. He places it in the sink and pours the dye on top. He massages the dye into the hair, places it on an old newspaper and notes the time.

After ten minutes he rinses out the excess dye and dries it using a hair-dryer.

Not bad.

Not bad at all.

The sink is pretty messy though. He places the wig on some sheets of newspaper on the table, retrieves a scrubbing cloth from under the sink and works at removing the dye. Might as well clean the whole area around the sink, he thinks, and scrubs behind the taps and the drainer. He throws the stained newspaper in the bin and grabs the empty box from the hair dye. He opens both ends, squashes the box for recycling and crumples the clear packaging which had previously held the dye. An object falls to the floor. It is similar in colour to the semi-transparent packaging which it had been stuck to.

Tom picks it up for a better view.

It is a set of gloves.

Oh.

Tom looks at his hands. They are a reddish brown.

'Shit,' he says.

Tom turns on the tap and places his hands under the running water for about five minutes, scrubbing them with soap. It has little effect.

Shit.

He tries the scrubbing cloth normally used for cleaning pots. It doesn't work either. He rings the hotel reception for help. A man answers and tells him that Fiona has finished her shift for the day. Tom asks about his watch and is told that there is already a note in the diary regarding the missing watch. Tom thanks him and hangs up. He stares at the stains on his hands.

Hair dye washes off. It's no big deal.

'It's no big deal Shatner. It's just a bit of hair dye.'

He repeats this in an effort to convince himself.

But there is a distant buzzing.

It is continuous. And it is growing.

Tom paces the floor before distracting himself with the wig. He places it on the head of the model.

The hair is long, straight and dark brown with a neat fringe.

'God, Shatner,' he says loudly in an effort to drown out the buzzing. 'You look more like a woman now than you ever have.'

He checks his phone. Five to seven.

The restaurant is booked for eight, for his next date from the agency, Rebecca.

Tom's clothes are lined up on his neighbours' bed, his slate-grey trousers, light grey jumper and blue shirt. Tom doesn't own a tie. Ever since his elastic-band tie in school he has never had a cause to wear one. On occasion, since he joined the dating agency, the notion of a tie has crept into his head but he fears it may add a formal element to the date or may offer an impression that isn't really true. Besides, he has read somewhere that wearing a tie too tightly around the neck can increase the risk of glaucoma in men. The odds just aren't worth the risk for him. It would have to be a very special date to get him to wear a tie.

'God, Rebecca is such an interesting name,' Tom sits down in front of the model. 'Swahili is it? Yes, I knew that.' He motions his hands back and forth as if he is using cutlery. 'I'd like to say that you are looking particularly beautiful this evening.'

He moves his left hand to his mouth and pretends to chew a piece of food while he scans the model. He has sewed the yellow dress at the rear and it sits much better on the model. The wig really adds a feminine quality too. The arms are still peculiar-looking and the face is unappealing but he is getting there.

'I love your eyes, Rebecca,' Tom says. 'They are certainly one of your best qualities. While we're on the subject, did you know,' Tom retrieves his notebook and flicks through until he comes to a page with the word 'eyes' as a heading, a list of facts underneath. 'Did you know that there is no scientific evidence to prove that sitting too close to the television harms your eyes? Yes,' he slaps his knee and pretends to laugh. 'I know. Neither did I. And did you know,' he glances at the notebook again, 'that the human eye weighs about twenty-eight grammes and there are little creatures that live on your eyelashes which feed off your skin?'

Bzzzzzz

He frowns, shakes his head.

'No,' he mutters and begins to scribble out the last fact. 'That's a bit like that whole nit thing.' He looks up at the model again.

Bzzzzzzz

'Yes Rebecca, did you know that the number-one cause of blindness in the US is diabetes? Did you know that, Rebecca? Did you? Did you?' He stands up suddenly and moves to the sink. 'Jesus, this is a waste of time Shatner, a complete waste of time. I'm reading shite from a notebook about things that nobody seems to want to know about except me. My watch is still missing. My perfect date has the face of a man and my hands are red.' He holds them up. 'Red fuckin' hands Shatner. Jesus Christ.'

Bzzzzzz

He moves to the window and rests his head against the glass.

The buzzing seems to loop toward him.

'Red fuckin' hands,' he mumbles.

From this vantage point Tom can see the entrance to the apartments across the street and the row of balconies nearest to the entrance. A woman appears on one of the balconies.

Tom raises his head quickly.

The buzzing stops suddenly.

'Shit,' he says and pushes himself away from the window.

He hurries into the centre of the room.

'Where are they Shatner?' He scans the area around him. 'The binoculars?'

He spots them next to the phone and scrambles across and hauls them by the strap.

He returns to the window.

The woman is hanging clothes on a line. A T-shirt conceals most of her frame but Tom can still make out her bony arms. When she steps to the side he has a better view, blurred slightly but good enough for him to understand that it is certainly her, the grey-eyed woman.

He counts the number of windows below hers and calculates that she is on the sixth floor.

He makes a note of this in his notebook.

'Would you believe that, Shatner?' he says and scratches his chin with a red finger.

Tom meets his date in a restaurant in Drumcondra. There are dull edges to the room and a badly painted Romanesque mural on the wall. Each seating area sits in a pale, misty arc of light. Tom has arranged the table so the seat faces the door and the water jug and condiments in some way hide his dyed hands.

Tom drinks too much wine.

By the time the mains appear, chicken linguini for him and steak well-done for her, Tom is drunk. It is that drunkenness that comes with trying to conceal drunkenness, the awkward, self-conscious type of drunkenness. His pose is one of stiffness in the chair, his expression forced to one of blankness in an effort to hide the effect of the drink. All this makes him feel more drunk.

It enhances his natural clumsiness and he is so self-conscious that he hardly tastes the food. He is surprised when she orders another bottle of wine.

It's going well, he thinks. Or is it? It must be.

She knocks a small round potato from her plate and it rolls across the table. The lack of comical reaction makes Tom think that she is as drunk as he is.

'I don't even want to be here,' she says, out of the blue, as if she is sharing a piece of a conversation which up to that point had been between her and her alone.

Tom's mouth is full so he can't reply. He doesn't really have a response in any case.

'It's my friend from work. She's worried about me,' she drags out the word 'worried' so it contains elements of irony and sarcasm. 'She should focus on her own relationship, if you know what I mean.' She smiles. The wine has stained her teeth. 'No offence or anything but why would I sign up to a dating agency? Seriously. Why?'

She glides her open hand downwards, from chest-height to midriff, to emphasise what she has to offer and Tom recalls one of those shows he watched as a kid, those game shows like *The Price Is Right* where some scantily clad woman would stand in front of a large washing machine and do exactly the same type of action.

She takes the napkin from her lap and rolls it up.

'I know that there are certain types of people that need dating agencies and she must think I'm one of them.' The knuckles on the hand which grips the napkin whiten momentarily. 'Am I completely wrong? Have I been deluding myself? Be honest here. Am I one of those people?'

Tom takes a mouthful of wine. He keeps the glass tilted at his mouth even when he has finished drinking. She continues to stare at him.

'I don't think you are,' he says when he has eventually put the glass down.

'I didn't think I was,' she picks up the knife and fork and attacks her dinner again.

She has little square teeth like a terrier, Yorkshire or Jack Russell, Tom hasn't decided yet.

'So what's your story? How long are you signed up with the dating agency?'

'A few months.'

'Yeah,' her sight moves from Tom to the right of the table.

'I was on my way home and I thought,' he shrugs his shoulders, 'why not give it a go.'

'Yeah,' she sighs as a waiter with tight trousers walks past.

'It's hard to get out and meet people sometimes, ye know?' Tom says.

'Yeah,' she turns back to Tom. 'It's a complete waste of time all right. You don't seem like the others I've gone on dates with though.'

Tom raises his eyebrows.

'You're all-right-looking for one. Not that I'm into you,' she holds her hands up. 'I want to be honest there. I don't fancy you.'

Tom is unable to meet her gaze.

'You don't mind, do you?' she asks. 'It's nothing personal. Ye know, it's just my opinion.'

'No, I don't mind. I'm grand.'

'You don't look grand,' she says.

'No really. I'm grand. You're just being honest.'

Tom forces himself to eat another forkful of pasta. There is a quiet lull in the conversation. Tom breaks it with a question.

'Do you think that most people are honest?' he asks.

She shrugs and slurps back a large mouthful of wine.

'Would you say there is a way of telling if they are?'

'What's the point?' she asks. 'Honesty makes people miserable.' She picks up the stray potato and takes a bite. 'Can you think of one time when being honest has ever worked out in a positive way?'

He frowns and scratches his head for a moment. 'I don't know.'

She holds the potato a couple of inches from her face, her mouth open to reveal those little white teeth. 'You see? I told you. Dishonesty, you'll see a hell of a lot more of that in your life than honesty.'

'I don't know about that,' Tom says. 'People have morals.'

'Morals,' her voice rises. 'What kind of a person are you?'

'There has to be balance,' Tom says. 'It makes sense. Things work because of a good system. If you introduce a negative it has to be swallowed up by a positive. That's mathematics.'

'You're talking about yin and yang.' She quickly pours herself a glass of wine. It almost reaches the rim. She moves her legs to the side of the table, crosses them. She rocks her foot up and down rapidly. 'Fuck yin and yang.'

Jack Russell, Tom thinks.

The dessert menu arrives. It steals her attention. He is silent while she reads the menu over and over and makes grunts of indecision and small hopeful noises when she comes across something agreeable. When the waiter approaches the table she orders a black coffee and a slice of chocolate cake.

'I suppose I'm being a bit harsh,' she says. 'Some people are honest. They're usually the people who are cleaning up when the dishonest have finished their dinner.' Her hands drop to the table. 'Are you taking notes?' she asks.

'A few,' Tom shows her his notebook.

'Why? What for? What happened to your hands?' She leans

forward, excited. 'That looks like the dye the banks put on money boxes. Are you a robber?'

'No, of course not.'

'Have you robbed a bank?' she inches towards him and knocks the remainder of a glass of wine over the table.

'No, it's just hair dye.'

'Oh,' she exhales as she leans back. 'Hair dye. Great.'

The waiter returns with the chocolate cake and places it on the table, turns swiftly and leaves.

'I hate when they do that,' she complains when he is gone. 'I want my coffee at the same time as my cake. That's the whole point in ordering the two of them together.'

'Yeah,' Tom says.

'What's wrong with you?'

'Nothing.'

'Why are you transcribing our conversation?'

'I'm just doing some research. A kind of scientific survey.'

'Science is a load of crap,' she says.

She rotates her plate a number of times, anticlockwise, stopping when she finds an angle she likes. She then takes her spoon and skims a tiny piece from the edge of the cake and brings it to her mouth. She rests the spoon in her mouth for a few seconds before removing it clean. She slowly returns to the cake and scoops another tiny amount. She continues this act of methodical enjoyment, unaware of his gaze or of anything else around her, gradually working her way along the outer edge of the dessert before moving inwards.

Tom still has a full glass of wine. His head is a bit light, his stomach a bit sick. He chooses to drink water over wine.

'Of course, for that yin and yang stuff to work everything in the universe would have to agree on what is good and what is bad,' she mumbles, examining her spoon. She turns it over, studies the concave side before swiftly licking it. 'I mean, what one person deems honest might not necessarily be honest for another.'

'The truth is the truth,' Tom says.

'The truth is what you believe.'

She quickly finishes off her cake.

Her handbag rings.

She lifts it onto the table, a fat, purple bag which resembles a ruffled pillow. She clumsily clacks the catch open and spends the next twenty seconds or so rummaging inside before locating her phone.

'Yeah,' she answers.

Someone on the other end talks. To Tom, the voice sounds like a long groan. She grunts a couple of times before twisting away from the table slightly.

'What? Now?' She arches her thin neck. She has the look of one of those antelopes that Tom often sees on TV, the moment when they catch the scent of a lion, that initial confused moment which precedes the instinctive urge to run. 'Thanks for the short notice. No, really, I mean it, thanks for completely fucking up my evening.' She hangs up, returns the phone to her bag. 'Look, I have to go,' she takes her coat from the back of her chair, bends her arm behind her a couple of times before successfully finding the gap for the sleeve. 'That was my husband. He wants to see me about something.'

'You're married?' Tom asks.

'Sometimes,' she says and offers a crooked grin. She fastens her bag. 'Don't worry, this doesn't count as an affair or anything. Some kind of yang crap isn't going to come back and haunt you. You can rest easy tonight,' she closes her coat. 'Sayonara.' The high heel of her left shoe angles precariously to the side as she wobbles from the restaurant.

Tom is left with an uncomfortable awareness of the empty space across from him and the realisation that she has not left any money.

He's not sure about honesty but kindness, he thinks, is going half on the bill.

Tom takes the bus home. He rests his head on the window so his nose is partially flattened against the glass and the engine vibrates through his skull and rattles his teeth. There are pretty women at bus stops along the way but he is in no mood to analyse their features. He closes his eyes for a rest and when he opens them again he is almost at his stop.

He leaves the bus.

The breeze feels nice on his face. He wishes it would spin him up into the air and carry him to some other place, a faraway place. Japan maybe, a land where the women smile at strangers.

Tom stops.

There are two people talking outside his building. A woman and a man, Maureen Hill and that policeman that stopped him when he was out with his camera, Garda Harry.

Why are they talking to each other?

Is it something to do with him?

Tom kneels down at the edge of a laneway and pretends to tie his shoelace.

He stays that way until Harry walks away from the building.

Maureen Hill has a piece of paper in her hand. She looks from the paper to Harry as he departs. Back to the piece of paper before plodding through the doors and into the building.

Chapter 16

Tom's grandfather would collect things from the side of the road. He would stop the truck at skips and go through the contents, keeping whatever he considered to be worth keeping. He retrieved a couple of half-decent wooden stools and a three-legged table in Malahide. In Blanchardstown he discovered an old atlas of the world, the pages yellow and rippled from damp. He found a painting in Swords, this ugly portrait of a gargantuan woman wearing a plain black dress. To Tom, she looked like the mother of a boy who had attended the same primary school as he did, Norma Gillespie. So Tom named the picture just that, Norma.

Norma was covered in greenish grime when they found her, so Tom's grandfather cleaned the surface using a Jiffy cloth and a bowl of watered-down bleach. It was impossible to tell if the colours of the painting were diluted after this as they had never seen it in its original state but the cleaning mixture did leave long, sprawling marks along the wooden frame and white streaks at the edges of the painting. His grandfather was convinced it was worth money so he wrapped it carefully in a sheet and kept it safe behind the driver's seat in the front cab. When drunk sometimes he would take this portrait out and examine it. In a way it became a symbol of the life he could be living.

One time, Tom asked him why he didn't just hang the painting up in the back of the horsebox. 'Because then I wouldn't see it any more,' he replied and slowly wrapped the painting in the sheet.

For two weeks they moved from one side of Dublin to the next, his grandfather drinking his way through the insurance cheque. Tom would potter about each town on his own, checking out the shops with very little interaction with anyone else. He would chain-smoke in sheltered spots or find a secluded area of greenery and sit for hours with only himself for company. His grandfather wasn't immune to the depressed quality of the trip. He pulled the truck close to a ditch one evening after they had been on the road for about half an hour. He sat facing forward for a time without speaking. Tom stared at the dash. He knew that something was on his grandfather's mind but he didn't want to have to deal with another problem. Just as he didn't want his grandfather to ever utter the truth about this business of travelling around Dublin in a horsebox as if they were somehow trying to outrun the grief. Everything had changed but through their silence Tom still clung on to the hope that they were getting back to some essence of normality. Even in madness he was trying to find some footing. He didn't need his grandfather openly admitting that there was no point to it. He needed that hope.

'I miss her,' his grandfather eventually spoke, continuing to look straight ahead.

Tom reddened with embarrassment. He could have said that he missed her too, that it is a normal thing to miss someone who has died. But he didn't. He said nothing. And after a short period of silence his grandfather climbed out of the cab, found a gap in the growth that hugged the edge of the road and disappeared into a field, out of Tom's sight. The radio crackled midway between two bands. Tom listened to that static until his grandfather returned.

Some days later, his grandfather, obviously stressed by how quickly his money was dwindling, decided it was wasteful to be moving around Dublin in a truck without earning some money out of it. He got chatting to a builder in a pub in Santry who explained that the merchants were always looking for trucks to deliver to building sites and private houses. He explained that Tom's grandfather just needed to turn up at the builder merchants when they were handing out the dockets in the morning and the lads in the warehouse would load his truck. Tom's grandfather thought this was a great idea. So he set about cutting the rear off the box on the back of the truck.

He got a loan of an industrial-type saw. Tom couldn't take his eyes off him when he was using it, waiting for the slip of a hand and the loss of a limb. His grandfather removed the whole flat piece at the rear of the box. He then cut the piece in two and reaffixed the rear using large hinges to create two doors. Due to a slight misalignment the doors were difficult to close and there were gaps along the join that allowed cold air to enter freely.

When he turned up with the makeshift delivery truck at the builder merchants they refused to load the truck, warning Tom's grandfather that it was a danger to other road users and to anyone in the truck.

'Your granda's off his head,' one of the warehouse lads had said to Tom. 'Really off his head.'

'He's going through a bad time,' Tom said.

'Going through a mad time more like it.'

His grandfather was getting worse. He would wake at night. Tom would hear the creaking steps on the wooden floor, feel the cool draft of air as he opened the door. He wasn't sure where his grandfather went on those nights. Tom would imagine him hunched over, trudging through field after field or standing rigid in the darkness, staring up at the stars, waiting for a sign maybe, something that might show him the way to go. Tom would doze when he was gone and wake to the sound of the door opening on his return and the scent of the world outside which he carried on his clothes.

Late July brought the hard rain. It was unrelenting. It exposed the fact that the truck was less waterproof than it used to be. The water got in through gaps at the upper edges of the makeshift doors. It ran along the dips in the planks, up to the beds. The mattresses acted as sponges. Things became squelchy and the nights became cold. They were forced to sleep in the front cab, which was slightly less draughty and damp but very cramped. Tom soon realised that there is a difference between mental depression and physical depression.

One night his grandfather came up with a plan. He told Tom that there was an opportunity to make some extra cash while they moved from one spot to the next by knocking into houses and asking the tenants if they needed any rubbish disposed of. He gave a rough figure of what to charge, something from five to twenty pounds, depending on the load. When Tom asked what constitutes a five-pound load his grandfather held both arms out and said, 'About this much.'

They would split up, his grandfather taking one street, Tom taking one beside. People weren't interested in their new business venture. Tom got used to suspicious eyes peering from partially opened doors or the shadow of figures behind net curtains. Tom stopped knocking, preferring instead to find some dry spot and smoke a cigarette.

They received the odd job, disposing of a fridge, old battered cooker, mainly dilapidated kitchen appliances. They wouldn't go far with the load. His grandfather would take the back roads, find somewhere big enough to park the truck and just dump the appliance in the nearest field. He didn't believe there was anything wrong with this. To him there was nowhere in Dublin that wasn't a dump.

A few days into their venture and his grandfather arrived back to the truck with a wide-eyed, excited expression. He had picked up a job from someone he'd met in a pub, a big job this time, one that would earn a hundred pounds. By this stage there was nowhere in the truck that didn't feel wet, even the air had the capability to relieve thirst. Tom was grateful for the excuse to move around. The job was in a large back garden, piles of discarded household objects and rubbish, dented paint tins, rotting wood. They got stuck in. Everything was soaked from the rain and everything stank. Balls of woodlice squirmed under the items at ground level and Tom's fingers regularly felt the ooze of slugs crushed on the underside of the object he was lifting.

They shoved their own furniture in the back as close to the cab as they could, laid a sheet of clear plastic on the deck and then piled the rubbish onto this sheet until the truck brimmed. Tom was miserable. His hands were slimy, his clothes wet and dirty. Even his insides felt spongy, his chest and his head. He continuously had this vision of a bath, water covered in bubbles and a yellow rubber duck bobbing up and down.

They drove in silence, the rain beating on the roof of the cab, spraying from the windscreen with each long arc of the wipers. They stopped at a trampled area of grass on a back road. When Tom attempted to get out of the cab his grandfather told him to stay put. He then altered the catch on the seat so it reclined, rocked side to side on the seat until he found a comfortable position and closed his eyes. He would stay in that position until darkness fell.

The roads seemed smaller in the blackness of night. The corners of the world seemed to move towards you. The thumping of branches against the cab surprised Tom and he would whip his head to the side every time. It was difficult for Tom to get his bearings. It seemed as if they might drive off the edge of the world at any moment and just fall for eternity. His grandfather seemed to know where he was going though. The Bedford curved from one sign-less road to the next, crisscrossing lighted, busier junctions before returning to the blackness.

Tom saw the wooden sign lit up in the distance. It was only then that he realised where they were.

'We have to be really quick about this,' his grandfather said as they entered the car park of the hotel next to the cemetery. He spun the vehicle so the rear end of the Bedford was facing the hotel and reversed right up to the door. He was out of the cab quickly and he had swung the back door open by the time Tom caught up with him. His grandfather heaved at the rubbish until it toppled in the direction of the hotel door. He then began to kick it off the back. Tom climbed onto the rear and helped. They pushed and pulled so that the large objects slid from the base. Tom laughed when his grandfather booted a kettle right off the back.

It was infectious.

His grandfather laughed too and in the next moment they were struggling to get anything done, they were laughing so much.

'Someone's coming!' his grandfather suddenly shouted.

He ordered Tom to keep dumping while he ran to the front. By now most of the rubbish was off the truck and blocking the hotel entrance. Tom could see a woman on the opposite side, her hands raised to the sides of her head, her mouth a large circle of surprise. The truck began to pull away from the building. Tom had just enough time to heave a small portable television off the back.

Rock and roll, he thought in his head. And then he was saying it. 'Rock and roll! Rock and fuckin' roll!'

Chapter 17

Tom has too much time to think.

He has been standing next to the window in his neighbours' bed-sit for over an hour now hoping to catch the grey-eyed woman leaving her apartment. The strap of the binoculars pinches the skin on his neck. His legs feel tight and the base of his back aches.

Memories ebb and flow, his grandfather's swollen, stained hands, his grandmother's plot, the Bedford, so vivid he can almost smell the dankness of its interior. There is one with Sarah McCarthy. They were on the roller-coaster ride in a makeshift fairground, a fairground which arrived on the outskirts of her home town on a Thursday and disappeared three days later, leaving only flattened grass and the odd wisp of litter stuck in the trees along the ditch beside.

Sarah had placed her hand on his knee as the cart began to rattle around the small track and for a time Tom was aware of nothing else except that hand, the heat that seemed to envelope his whole thigh, the gentle weight that intensified with each passing second.

For that short ride nothing else existed. Not the crackling atmosphere. Not the hoots and jeers and the lights and the movement. Not the men who ran the rides with their earrings and scars and strong sinewy arms.

Just them.

Tom and Sarah.

Alone together.

And it was only when she lifted her hand that the warped music returned and the air from the motor fan on the ride became a heat against his face and brought the smell of oil and candyfloss and popcorn. And the next instant he was standing with unsteady legs and climbing from the cart and those men who ran the rides were collecting tickets again, moving about the rides like ghosts, hooking safety lines across the openings of bowl-shaped cabs or the cages of the big wheel. Everything was as it had been before.

It saddens him, the idea that memories like these are so rare and fleeting. It seems as if most of his life has been spent patiently waiting for something to happen. And he thinks how strange it is that in replacing his idle patience with the act of searching for Sarah it somehow feels as if she is further away from him than at any time before.

He can't think of what direction to go in from here. He can only think of memories. And he can only imagine the emotions of that time, emotions that may have been formed from real events or might merely have been formed from hope.

He needs to do something constructive.

He needs a distraction.

He opens his notebook, taps his pen rhythmically against the counter and tries to picture the woman from the nightclub, the blonde woman. Perhaps a sketch might jog Fiona's memory, cause some spark of recognition that might lead to the watch. Because maybe if he sorted out the issue with the watch his mind would open up to new ways of finding Sarah.

It is worth a try.

His drawing skills are limited, picked up in primary school, encouraged by his fifth-class teacher Mr Evans, a pleasant man who seemed to consist of 60 percent hair, 20 percent jumper, 10 percent cords and the rest a mixture of wrinkles, spectacles and chalk dust. He had been a builder in a previous life, living over in England in the sixties and seventies before returning to education. He would often refer to the building of a house when educating the children, stating things that contained only a mild hint of sense in them.

'You can't build a wall without a foundation, O'Reilly. It would be good to remember that, son, before you go and stick chewing gum in someone else's hair.'

He believed in a combination of art and music to get the best out of the children and he encouraged creativity through drawing.

'You should always start with the nose,' he once told Tom. 'It doesn't matter how big or small. Sometimes the more bizarre it is the funnier the character will turn out.'

Tom remembers this as he draws a nose for the woman, a kind of lower-case 'n', the kind of nose that the snooty characters had in the comics. He draws the eyes next, two circles with dots in the centre. He spends a moment considering which type of mouth would best convey her features. One small add-on can change the whole expression of the face. A small mouth will match, the slightest trace of a smile, a hidden kind of smile, the type that makes you think that the owner knows a lot more than they are letting on.

Tom was never that skilful at drawing hair but he tries his best. He stands back when he's finished and takes the drawing in. It is terrible, cartoonish and amateurish. He tears it from the notepad, scrunches it into a ball and throws it into the bin.

He tries again, numerous times, but the result never matches the image in his head. Still he continues, keeping an eye on the apartment entrance all the while. He's not sure how long ticks by, another hour, an hour and a half. Eventually a man appears at the entrance to the apartment block, the partner of the grey-eyed woman. His dark hair is still to the side, shirt buttoned to the top, his blue V-neck jumper replaced with a green one. He is engaged in a mellow stroll, hands deep in trouser pockets and a slow rolling of shoulders, down the street and away from the building.

Tom wastes little time.

He swaps the binoculars for the camera and exits the bed-sit.

Down the stairs two at a time and outside, sucking in cold air, feet slapping the road, up to the apartment entrance, only to find the door locked.

He stands to the side and taps his foot rapidly.

A minute passes. It feels like longer. He nervously checks the street for any sign of the woman's partner returning. Two minutes of a wait and there is movement from within. A tall, lean man approaches, a gym bag in his hand, seemingly large enough to hold a tread-mill. Tom pretends to play with the camera until the door swings open. He stops the door from closing with his foot and enters.

The hall floor is beige tiles, the walls painted a cool blue, cone-shaped lights draped from the smooth, white ceiling. There is a lift to the left of the entrance, stippled, silver metal doors which give Tom's reflection an expressionist look to it. Tom doesn't like lifts. He opts for the stairs, jogging at first. Each floor is a double set of steps and by the third floor his chest feels like it is being crushed from the outside and his legs are resisting the challenge.

Tom slows. His movement becomes part walk and part pull as

he uses the handrail for support. There is a sign on each level, the corresponding floor number in yellow against a black background. It is with some relief that he reaches number six. A door leads onto a corridor, grey speckled carpet, the lift entrance nearest to the stairs and a series of apartment doors further along.

Tom stops and thinks. When he had last spotted the grey-eyed woman she was on the balcony at the side nearest the exit. Tom closes his eyes and envisages the location of his own building in relation to these apartments. He works out where the main door would be from this position and figures that her apartment must be the first one on his right-hand side.

The door is white, the number fifty-five in gold digits near the top.

He knocks with a double-rap and readies his camera for a quick shot.

He waits.

There is no answer.

He knocks again. A bit louder this time.

He hears the muffled thump of movement behind the door.

Ready.

Tom places his finger on the button of the camera.

Steady.

His breathing is quick, short breaths.

Ping.

A noise disturbs his preparation. It comes from his right and is quickly followed by a clatter as the lift doors open.

Shit.

Tom inhales sharply, holds his breath.

Don't be her partner. Don't be her partner.

A man exits the lift.

Shit. Shit. Shit.

It is him, the partner, reading a newspaper as he walks.

Tom's instinct is to run.

Where do these corridors lead?

Shit.

A chain rattles against the inside of the door of the apartment. It is followed by a clunking sound and the door opens to reveal a man, sideburns, pompadour hairstyle, big white teeth, clean-shaven. He wears jeans and a white vest. He gives Tom the thumbs-up.

It's the Fonz from *Happy Days*, Tom thinks.

What the hell is the Fonz doing in her apartment?

Aaaaaaay Mrs C. Get me the fuck out of here.

'Let me guess,' the man says. 'Cats.'

Tom isn't sure how to answer. He merely nods his head and the Fonz ducks back into the apartment. Tom moves his frame so he has his back to the man approaching from the lift.

His footsteps are a low steady beat on the carpet.

Closer.

To Tom's position.

Past him from the rear.

There is intense pressure in Tom's lungs. He is afraid to breathe out.

But he has to.

Breathe. Breathe, you fool. Breathe.

He does. It is audible and for one horrible moment Tom thinks the man is going to angle his frame around to have a good look at him.

Instead, his footsteps take him away from Tom and away from the opened apartment door.

He stops at the next door up, retrieves his key from his pocket and clumsily unlocks his door while trying to maintain his sight on the newspaper.

Christ, the wrong apartment.

The Fonz appears again. He holds a wooden box in his arms.

'There's only two left,' he says and directs Tom's attention to two kittens in the box. 'Which one do you want?'

'No,' Tom says. 'I don't want a kitten.'

'What's wrong with them?'

'There's nothing wrong,' Tom stammers.

'Do you want a kitten or not?' The Fonz's voice is loud. Too loud.

Tom is aware of the second man. He has not entered his apartment yet. He must be looking at us right now, Tom thinks, probably wondering where he recognises the man with the camera from.

I have to get out of here.

'I'll take that one,' Tom says and points to a brown cat with a white patch on its back.

The Fonz takes the cat out and hands it to him. Its underbelly is warm and squidgy in Tom's hand. Like holding a cooked ham, he thinks.

'Take good care of him now,' the Fonz says and closes the door.

Tom holds the cat as far away from his body as possible.

The cat stares at him. One of its eyes is weeping. It lifts a paw outward. Tom hears the Fonz's voice in his head.

Aaaaaay.

Tom knows that cats predominately land on their feet when they plummet, that they were once worshipped in Egypt, that they are devoured in certain parts of Asia and that they spend a lot of time sleeping. But none of these facts are particularly practical when taking care of a cat, he thinks. And besides, he doesn't want to own a cat. They are too independent and erratic for his liking. He can barely control his own life without taking on the responsibility of another.

Tom leaves the kitten in a cardboard box in his bed-sit and makes his way to the Manhattan Hotel. For most of the bus journey he is bombarded with the image of the cat clawing its way from the box, scratching his furniture to bits, its eye weeping all over the place. On a number of occasions he stands to get off the bus but each time he convinces himself to stay put. It is only temporary, he thinks, only until he finds an owner.

Fiona is at reception in the hotel.

'First things first,' Tom says when he reaches the counter. 'How do you feel about cats?'

'I don't mind them,' she says. 'We had one in our house when I was a kid.'

'So you'd know how to take care of one.'

'Yeah, I guess so.'

'Good, because I haven't got a clue about domestic cats. I'm not even sure what type of cat it is. Does it matter what type it is? Do you treat them the same?'

'I don't think it matters that much.'

'Grand. It's only a tiny thing so it shouldn't take up too much space in your place.'

'Wait,' she stops him. 'What are you talking about?'

'It's in a box in my bed-sit at the moment, on a blanket. You can keep the blanket if you like. If I'm being honest I don't really want it back. I'm sure the thing is soiling it as we speak.'

'I don't want a cat.'

'You said you like cats.'

'I said I don't mind them. You can find someone else to give the cat to.'

'Who?'

'Not me,' she says. 'The thing would drive Harold mad.'

'Harold is your partner?'

She begins to laugh. It causes the skin around her eyes to crinkle.

'Harold is my rat,' she eventually replies.

'You have a pet rat?'

'Yeah.'

'Fair enough,' Tom mumbles.

'What's wrong with that?'

'I didn't say anything.'

'Rats are great pets. They're very clean, a lot cleaner than cats and dogs.'

'I get it. You're happy with Harold.'

'Yes.'

'You don't want any more pets.'

'No, just me and Harold,' she nods her head slowly, stares at the desk, her eyes glazing over. 'Just me and Harold,' she repeats.

When Fiona looks up again her hand moves quickly to her brow.

'Shit, here's Barry,' she says. 'He's been told that you've been harassing staff.'

'I haven't harassed anyone,' Tom says and turns.

Barry approaches the desk. And Tom has this picture of the man swinging on a thick line, smashing his way through the ruins of a wall. A wrecking ball, he thinks, his heavy spherical shape, his dark uniform, his solid-looking mass, the man is designed for demolishing and crushing.

'Let me guess,' he says when he spots Tom. 'It's about the watch.'

Tom tenses. His gaze moves to the floor.

'Here, take mine,' Barry pretends to remove his watch from his thick wrist. 'Please. Then you might leave us alone.'

'You think I want to be here?' Tom says. 'I've better things to be doing with my time.'

'What could be better than pissing us off every five seconds?'

Tom shakes his head. He turns to Fiona but she looks away. He looks to the revolving door and then to the doors of a lift, which are opening.

A woman is exiting the lift.

Tom's heart suddenly quickens. His palms sweat.

'That's her,' his voice is low, barely audible. 'That's the woman.'

She pushes a trolley and wears a uniform, white blouse and dark trousers, the same uniform that Fiona is wearing. 'That's her,' Tom points. 'That's the woman.'

She works here. She actually works here.

He feels a surge of blood to his head.

It drives him to walk. 'Where are you off to, son?' Barry follows.

'That's the woman from the nightclub,' Tom says and pushes his legs to move quickly.

He feels charged, a buzzing electricity in his hands and arms.

He needs to talk to her. Just for a minute.

Barry walks quickly at his side.

'I want you to move back to the counter, son,' he says.

'But it's definitely her.'

'I've had enough of this,' Barry says. 'You're going to have to leave.'

He blocks Tom's pathway with his bulk.

'I just want to talk to her for a minute,' Tom pleads.

The security guard's hand is a weight on Tom's upper arm. It clamps tightly when he tries to pull away.

'Just for a minute,' Tom says.

'Out,' Barry orders.

Tom exhales. He looks upwards, to the ceiling tiles and the vents, the square dusty speaker above the lift. A warbling, hissing tune emanates from it. No, not a hiss, Tom thinks. More like a buzzing.

Bzzz

Tom angles his frame so he is looking past the security guard. 'You were in the nightclub last Friday,' he says loudly to the woman. 'Do you remember a man with a watch at the bar?'

The blonde steps backward and begins to squeeze her left hand with her right.

Barry grips Tom's other arm so he is directly in front of him, face to face.

Barry's mouth is moving but Tom doesn't hear his words. He only hears the buzzing, the quick, rapid pulse of wings.

He scrunches his eyes closed.

Not now.

Bzzz

Please!

Tom opens his eyes.

'I just want to ask her,' he says and tries to shove past the security guard. 'Were you talking to my friend Karl?' he shouts. 'Have you got my watch? I need to know.'

Tom's arm is suddenly twisted behind him and pulled upwards. The pain is sudden and intense. 'Please,' he says through gritted teeth. 'I just want to ask her about the watch.'

He is dragged toward the exit.

'Have you seen the watch?' he shouts. 'Please. Have you seen the watch?'

From his awkward position Tom catches sight of the reception desk briefly.

And Fiona.

She has her hands up to her face.

She is pale, worried.

Chapter 18

Rossboyne was a damp town just beyond Dublin. It was bumpy fields with random groups of ashen sheep in the distance. Even in August it was all hazy rain and varying shades of grey. And to Tom, it was lavender. He tasted it as soon as he stepped from the cab of the truck. And then he couldn't stop tasting it, in the water, in the milk, in his breakfast cereal, in the scones that Mrs Ryan made from her kitchen in the rear of the local bar, the car park of which the truck would sit in for weeks after they arrived, the lounge of which his grandfather would spend the majority of his time in. It was an L-shaped pub, Ryan's bar, with square, classroom type tables, straight-backed hard benches and a long counter. It was located next to a garden centre, a troop of angry-looking gnomes guarding the entrance. His grandfather fell in love with the quaintness of the place, the relaxed attitude. And the pint of course. How could Tom ever forget how much his grandfather loved the pint in that bar? He was certainly never shy about announcing his love for it.

Tom would go for walks in Rossboyne, long walks on roads that seemed as if they were nothing more than hardened clay. The crows would watch his movements with their beady black eyes and they would aim their beaks at him and caw loudly. It seemed to vibrate through his body, that sound, and the abruptness of its disappearance to the seemingly endless fields would make him feel small. The lack of cars got to him too, the quietness reminding him of a Sunday morning in the city. A perpetual Sunday morning, the sleepy, silent time that people rarely think about and are only too happy to ignore.

One of these walks took him away from his normal route. He had been in the place a couple of days. The clouds were low and ominous, the air heavy. A storm was brewing. The dramatic background gave an unreal quality to objects, especially the man-made objects, like the houses in the distance, clumped together, council-type houses with drab, grey pebbledash fronts and short gardens. There were about twelve of them surrounding a green area and behind them were more bumpy fields. Tom eyed each one he passed. The lower windows on the houses were stained with green grime, the curtains gathered behind. Moss partially carpeted the pathways. A dog barked from one of the rear gardens, single barks. The pause between each one was long and filled with a lonely silence.

Beyond the houses a thick-headed cow watched Tom's approach, slowly rotating its jaw in a chewing motion. The road veered to the left and brought him to detached houses separated by scraggy hedges and wild ditches. Most had some form of stone pillar at the front, decorated differently, perched concrete eagles, orbs or acorns. Unkempt hawthorn bulged onto the roadway in parts, with barely enough room for a car to get past. Tom came across a man at the end of a section of hawthorn. He was skinny and grey, a balding head and an unshaven face. He appeared to be hiding. Tom followed his gaze as he walked. The upper windows of the house beside were slender and without curtains. A woman stood at one of these windows. She was facing in the opposite direction, her naked back in view and the upper part of her behind. Her skin was so white it was almost luminous, smooth and clear. She shifted her angle slightly and Tom caught sight of the side of her left breast. He couldn't take his eyes off her. He was a moth to a flame.

The movement of the man beside him broke his attention, scurrying down the road without looking back once. When Tom returned his sight to the window the woman was facing him, shielded by a towel. She was middle-aged, the sootiness of her roots contrasting with the straw-coloured ends. She had full cheeks and a wide nose that reminded Tom of a boxer. She was a woman that Tom wouldn't have given a second look before that moment but now that he had seen her naked she was different to any other middle-aged woman he had ever seen.

'What are you doing down there?' she shouted, pushing the upstairs window open further.

Tom looked to the ground while he explained he was just out for a walk.

'Well walk then,' she ordered.

And Tom hurried on, caught in a heightened state of confusion, his mind unable to focus on one single thought. He came to the peak of a large hill and discovered that the town stretched for another two miles, a collection of roofs, a spire and at least two more pubs in view.

The storm erupted soon after and he found shelter near one of the pubs. The raindrops were plump and the wind was intimidating. Tom huddled in the doorway of the pub waiting for the worst of it to end.

Tom would sometimes have these daydreams where he felt compacted, as if he was a solid entity, like a wooden block or a round stone. Everything made sense in this daydream. It was as if he could feel his inner core as much as he could feel the world around him. There was security in this daydream, a feeling of completeness and connectivity. When Tom saw the woman naked at that window he could sense this completeness in her. He was compelled to touch every inch of her body, grip his hands around her thighs and just hold them there, rest his fingers on her wrist and feel the beat of her heart, cup his hands at her breasts, lay his hands on her back. He didn't even want her to respond. He just wanted to feel the completeness of her body, the solidness of her form.

Each flash of the sky flared the image of the pale woman into his head, always the same view of her, always facing away from him. For some reason that image was more exciting than if she had been bearing all in front of him. He did not have the words to explain his attraction, nor did he have the understanding to comment on the artistry of the arc of light and shadow which played on her form. There was a part of him which yearned to speak to her, a part of him which wondered if she was even aware of her appeal.

After the rain abated he walked in a spell for a time and this spell only lifted as the heaviness in the atmosphere lifted. The wetter his feet became the more he began to wonder if he had just imagined the woman at the window. The spell was completely broken when he saw the horsebox in the distance, the sun glistening on its cold wet surface.

Some days later and Tom found a stream about a mile from Ryan's bar. He kept his distance from it, merely staring into the water, listening to the continuous gurgle in an almost trancelike state. At the time Tom was enduring these irrational fears of the physical world about him, becoming afraid to touch off anything, afraid to interact, even afraid of the insects. He began to dread their tiny pinch on his skin and he would regularly swipe his hands along his neck to ensure there was nothing crawling there. His grandfather noticed this. It was just another tic to comment on, like his habit of stretching his jaw from side to side and his habit of squeezing his eyes shut like a tight blink, sometimes when he was concentrating and sometimes when he was talking to his grandfather.

Tom barely noticed any of his own little mannerisms, only really feeling negative effects when he tried to stop them. The finger-tapping was the one which he tried to control the most, probably because his hands were constantly in his line of sight or maybe because his hands were the part of his body that he assumed he had most control over. Whenever Tom would tap the tip of his left thumb against the tip of a finger on his left hand, he would be compelled to tap his thumb against all the fingers of that hand. And then he would be compelled to do the same with his right hand. In an effort to control it he would frequently try to prevent his right hand from following his left.

The prevention led to a strange, almost thirst-like sensation. It also brought on a deeply superstitious reaction, as if the impending action was a weight over his head and somehow, inexplicably, a part of his mind believed something utterly terrible was going to happen if he didn't carry it out. Not just to himself but to the whole world, something incredible, as if time was going to halt or the world was going to shift on its axis, plunging everyone from the planet into a dark abyss. Or death. If he didn't tap the tips of the fingers of his hand he was sure that death would visit him. He was aware of how unreasonable it was but eventually the pressure would prove too much and his will would fold and he would tap the tips of the other fingers.

Gradually, as Tom visited the stream more he began to question why he was tiptoeing around the town. Just because he didn't talk to people didn't mean that he wasn't here and just because he didn't touch off things didn't mean that it wasn't happening, this journey, this ordeal. He pushed himself to clear a section of the overgrowth next to the stream with a chunky fallen branch. For a time he felt as if he was waking from a deep sleep. As if he was opening his eyes for the first time in an age. It wouldn't last but for now he could sit with his legs over the embankment and listen to the stream as if he was part of it.

And he felt he could breathe.

And dream.

'Catch anything?'

Tom had been visiting the stream for over a week when he was asked this. He arched his head behind and found himself looking at the woman from the window. Her hair was tied back in a pony-tail and she had light make-up on, her lips soft-looking and her cheeks pink.

Tom wondered if she remembered him.

'You wouldn't catch much in that water. There's a plastics fac-tory down the way. Here, push over,' she said and sat so their shoulders met even though there was plenty of room beside.

'What are you doing down here on your own?' she asked. 'A young man like yourself should be around his friends.'

'I don't know,' Tom shrugged. 'I just come here.'

'It's nice to have a bit of time to yourself. And here's me ruin-ing it on you,' she laughed, paused, stared at Tom. 'You can smile you know. I'm not going to bite your head off or anything.'

Tom forced a smile and rubbed his wrist nervously.

'Mary,' she said and held her hand out.

Tom took her hand. It felt fragile and cold.

'Tom Stacey,' he said.

She smiled.

'I used to go down to the quarry when I was about your age,' she laughed and shook her head. 'I know what you're thinking. This old woman could never be my age. But I was. Once. And I'm not that old, really. To you I probably am. But I'm not.' She plucked a long stem of grass from the embankment and pulled it straight. 'You been down to the quarry?'

'No, not yet.'

'You should go.' She ran her fingers along the piece of grass.

Tom had this sudden image of her at the window and instantly felt uncomfortable with it. He brought his shoulders forward and folded his arms.

'You've no friends around here?'

Tom nodded, looked away quickly, to the water, to the random bubbles and the wavering movement of plants in the murky depths.

'It's funny, don't you think, the main reason your friends are your friends is because you were brought up together. I mean, if you can make friends with the people who live beside you then you should be able to make friends with anyone, no matter where you go. Yeah?'

He nodded.

'Don't see many of the girls I used to pal with any more,' she says. 'Don't see any of them really. Things change I guess.'

She carefully tore the blade of grass in two, vertically. She plaited them together absently.

'How long are you staying in town?' she asked.

'Not sure.'

'You might be here a while?'

'Maybe.'

'Well that's a good thing, isn't it?'

'I don't know,' he said.

'It'll give you plenty of time to make friends. Sure it'll give us plenty of time to get to know each other in any case.'

She placed her hand on his thigh and looked at him for an amount of time that made Tom feel uncomfortable. Eventually she stood and left Tom and the stream behind her.

Chapter 19

It is evening.

Angela rings Tom and invites him up to her house.

He accepts, believing it to be in relation to the watch. When he arrives she is alone in the house. The radio crackles in the kitchen, low and stripped of the bass. An open bottle of wine sits on the kitchen table, half empty, a glass beside. Angela's face is made-up. Her perfume is a mellow hint of berries which sharpens when she crosses her smooth legs or fixes her short black skirt. Her top is low-cut and her bracelets and bangles clack when she reaches for her glass.

She is beautiful.

She pulls her chair close to Tom when he sits and she pats him on the knee whenever he speaks.

'Forget about the watch,' she says when he asks.

Don't worry about the kids or the time or him, Karl? Karl who?

'Do you know where I haven't been in ages,' she pings the rim of her empty wineglass with her fingernail. 'The cinema. Let's go to the cinema.'

'What, right now?' Tom asks.

'Come on,' she grabs his arm and pulls him up. 'Why not?'

It takes them thirty minutes to make what would usually be a fifteen-minute walk. She totters on her high heels, stops to remove a small stone which has invaded her footwear at one point, insists on checking out the properties for sale in the window of an estate agent's along the way. She complains about the tightness of her bra and the distance of the walk. As they near the cinema she links arms with him for support. Her skin is soft and warm.

In the cinema Tom insists on sitting beside the aisle. Since the only aisle seats available are near the front they sit close to the screen, their heads angled upward. The place smells of mild disinfectant and body odour. Angela continuously nudges him during the trailers and adds a little comment on each one, mostly predicting how good or bad she thinks the related film will be.

Tom refuses to share the giant popcorn which she has awkwardly balanced on her legs. He prefers to keep his hands on his lap. Popcorn rains from the massive cardboard bucket every time she dunks her hand in, and the noise which accompanies each slurp from her large cola container reminds him of the times the plughole becomes blocked in his kitchen sink.

The film is bad, not bad enough to be entertaining in an accidently comic way, but bad enough to irritate. About midway into the film he feels the weight of her left leg against his leg and pretty soon her body weight shifts toward him. Tom wonders if it is the comfort of a familiar environment which causes her to do this. He considers how many times she has come to this place with Karl. In the darkness of the cinema she may believe that it is Karl and not Tom who sits beside her now.

And maybe that's what she wants.

Maybe that's why she has chosen to go to the cinema. In here nothing has changed for her. In here she is watching a film with her husband.

Tom squeezes his knees gently and tries to forget about the

warmth of her at his side. He thinks about the receptionist in the Manhattan, about how worried she looked as he was dragged from the hotel. It twists in his stomach, this thought, and he squeezes his knees tightly with his fingers until the pain distracts him.

When the film is over they stroll to a fast-food restaurant at the end of the cinema car park and buy burgers and fries. This is the hour of the drunken eaters. They slump over small circular tables, slowly rolling food in their mouths, staring off into the distance with vacant, cow-like expressions. There is a jumble of staff behind the counter, beautiful young men and women, purring foreign lilts and exotic faces, lumpy green caps and pea-green uniforms. They repeat their questions to the swaying customers.

What drink would you like with that? Large or small? Eat here or takeaway?

Angela holds her burger with two hands. She has been holding it for a good two minutes now without taking a bite. A large slice of tomato edges outward with every movement of her arms.

'Do you think I'm good-looking?' she asks him.

'I'd say you're an eight,' Tom says as he picks fries from a cardboard container.

'Eight out of ten?' she sounds surprised. 'That good?'

'No, your body shape is an eight.'

'My body?'

'Yes, your body is shaped like an eight.'

'That doesn't sound very good. Is that good?'

'That depends on what your preference is.'

'What do you think Tom? Do you think that having a body like an eight is good?'

'Yes,' Tom shoves a handful of fries into his mouth to hide his embarrassment.

'What about my face?' She smiles.

'It's very symmetrical.'

'Thanks,' she laughs. 'And yours is very oval.'

'Symmetrical is good.'

'Yeah?'

'I read about this research carried out where a group of people were shown a bunch of different photographs of other people. In these photographs the faces were altered so that the symmetry was reduced.'

'How?'

'Computer graphics. They widened the mouths on some or made the eyes smaller. It made the faces more asymmetrical.'

'Asymmetrical?'

'More unbalanced.'

'Like this,' she places her hands on her cheeks and contorts her face.

'Kind of,' Tom smiles. 'They discovered that people have a tendency to assign negative traits to people with asymmetrical faces.'

'Like what?'

'Like they expected that the people with asymmetrical faces would be less agreeable and less conscientious than people with symmetrical faces.'

'That's crazy.'

'It is,' Tom rolls one of his fries in salt.

Angela crosses her legs and stares out the window in silence for a time. Tom watches her, like he did when she would sing in the choir.

'You have lines under your eyes,' he eventually breaks the silence.

'Thank you very much,' she frowns.

'No, it's a good thing,' Tom says 'Faces like yours need to have a flaw.'

'What do you mean by faces like mine?' she asks.

'Faces that are almost perfect,' Tom says and takes a bite of his burger.

Angela is quiet on the walk home, more interested in dreaming than talking. She stares up to the sky at times. Tom looks upward, takes in a depth of colour diluted by street-lamps and wishes he could see what she is seeing.

She links him at one point and keeps that link when they reach the house. He follows her inside without being asked and they unlink in the kitchen but sit on chairs on the same side of the table. She looks at him for a time and Tom becomes uneasy. He fidgets with the sleeve of his jumper.

'Have you heard from Karl?' he asks. 'He hasn't been in work.'

'Nothing of any note,' she opens the clip which holds her hair in place and throws it onto the table. 'He can disappear for all I care.'

She stands and pulls at the middle of three drawers to the left of the sink, removes a hairbrush and runs it through her hair in short, almost violent strokes.

'I don't want to think about him,' she says.

She returns the hairbrush to the drawer, moves to a high cupboard and removes a bottle of red wine. She uncorks the bottle using a sleek, black corkscrew, fills two glasses with wine and sits beside Tom.

Tom crosses his legs and turns his body away from her slightly.

He begins to imagine this room on a school morning, the energy in the place. He pictures Angela bumping around the kitchen, the kids tormenting each other, the noise and the movement. It becomes a pressure in his temples, this image. And he feels a tightness across his shoulders and a lurching in his stomach. He sips the wine and his mouth feels syrupy, to the point that when he speaks his tongue sticks to his pallet.

Angela looks tired now. Her eyelids are low and her limbs are loose. She moves to lean against him but he stands and walks over to the window. The street is lit up nicely, beautifully uniform, lined with rowan trees of equal height and width. The pathways are clean and the gardens are all enclosed with the same type of wall, solidly chunky, painted white, flat on the top. The garden is grey cobblestones in a circular design, small bobble-shaped shrubs along the blood-red borders at the side. This is a nice part of town.

Tom remembers he would cycle down this way with the lads before his grandmother passed away and pick berries from the rowan trees. Karl was part of the group. He would call the locals posh and he liked to flick the berries at their parked cars. But there were times when he'd shield his eyes from the sun with a hand and scan the area as a ship's captain would when approaching land. 'Imagine living here,' he would say. And he would get onto his bike then and remain quiet as they returned to their side of the town.

Tom senses Angela behind him. He turns around slowly and she places a hand on his hip. Her head is tilted to the side and she stares at his face.

Beauty can be intoxicating, he thinks.

She brings her face closer to his and Tom stoops slightly.

She shuts her eyes.

Her beautiful face fills his sight.

Her hair brushes his forehead gently.

Tom closes his eyes.

This sudden image of a woman fills the blackness.

She is holding her hands up to her mouth. She is concerned.

'Sorry,' he pulls his head back suddenly.

Her eyebrows dip in confusion. She takes a step backwards.

'I can't,' Tom says.

Her cheeks colour. She blinks once and then slaps him on the cheek.

The pain is a sharp sting followed by a dull ache.

Tom places his palm on his cheek.

'I'm sorry,' he says.

'Get out of here,' she moves to the table and to the wine.

'It's just with Karl and all,' Tom tries to explain.

'Get out,' she repeats and with shaking hands she fills her wine glass.

Chapter 20

Tom got to talking to a local lad in Rossboyne.

His name was Colm Daly. His father delivered the gas cylinders to most of the pubs in the county. If their father's hernia was acting up Colm and his brother J.P. would lend a hand. Colm asked Tom for a cigarette when delivering to Ryan's bar. By the time the cigarette was gone Tom had been invited up to his house.

Colm was the more handsome of the two brothers, his hair a shady red, cut short, his face hard angles which gave him a rough, masculine appearance beyond his years. He played bass guitar in a punk band called Modified Starch, named after one of the ingredients of Bird's Custard Powder. He said they were going to be called Hydrogenated Vegetable Oil but there was a problem fitting the name on the posters. He loved to smoke hash. There were small black-framed holes in most of his tops from pieces of hot hash burning through the material. The floor was littered with flecks of tobacco and ripped and emptied cigarettes. Multicoloured lighters were strewn on the bed and floor and any other flat surface in close proximity, all semi-transparent and all nearing the end of the gas levels.

Colm could function relatively well when smoking hash. He mostly made sense when he spoke and it never seemed to dull his intelligence. Looking back Tom realised that Colm was an extremely intelligent individual. But intelligence isn't always enough. What people need is motivation. And his motivation was getting high.

J.P. was the younger of the pair, terrible acne on his neck and forehead and the type of face that was wide and flat, almost rubbery in appearance. He had long ginger hair, shaped and gelled so it framed his face like a marmalade-coloured helmet. He would spend a lot of time lying on his bed strumming his guitar, all the while moaning about how crap his town was.

Tom began to spend a lot of time up in their house. Their mother seemed to like him. She was a lady with skin withered from smoking, who wore an illusory frumpiness due to her fondness for baggy jumpers and ill-fitting blouses. She would highlight Tom's quiet behaviour to J.P. as an example of how he should be behaving. Sometimes Tom would catch her smiling at him with what seemed to be mild curiosity.

Their father reminded Tom of a character from an *Eagle* or *Warlord* annual, one of those comic strips which involved soldiers returning from the trenches in the Great War, wide-eyed, hair dishevelled and dark shadows at their cheeks. He shuffled about the place nodding and grunting when asked a question, afraid to make eye-contact. Tom would later see this expression on other people throughout his life, usually when they had become crippled by the responsibility of parenthood. It was as if they were forever awaiting some form of doom to descend on them and their family, as if they were not living in the present but were living ten, fifteen, even twenty years away in some cases, in a time when their children are old enough to fend for themselves and they could finally relax.

Sometimes when Tom visited their house he would find their

father in an upside-down position in the sitting room. Mr Daly suffered from a hernia. The whole idea of it made Tom feel ill, the notion that the man's insides were trying to escape to the outside through a tear in the stomach lining. The doctor had advised Mr Daly that due to the fact that it was a low tear he might find some relief in sitting upside-down. Tom would walk into their sitting room at times and find Mr Daly's nether regions at eye level, the man with his head on the floor and his arms anchored on both sides. The days when he was wearing only a pair of pants were the hardest ones to forget.

Their sister Patricia was twelve years old, a young twelve, a shaggy-haired thin girl who would bound about the place looking for missing hairclips or socks or any number of clothes items that she had worn on some random day for some random occasion which she expected her mother to have remembered. Tom didn't envy the fact that they had siblings and he didn't. Their relationship just seemed to be one long brawl. Their mother, after reading some tip in a women's magazine, carried a little bell around with her. She would walk up behind the kids when they were arguing and rattle the bell continuously until they'd stop. Her husband would cringe if he was near, each jingle sending him one step closer to the breaking point. Tom wasn't sure that he could have survived an environment with such fierce competition. What happens to people who don't compete in an environment like that? Are they just forgotten about? Is the weaker side of the world littered with the fallout of those sibling relationships? At least if you are on your own you can claim that you had nobody to learn from. If you have siblings you can merely admit that you were the one who lost.

Tom and J.P. were quite similar in their social and physical attributes, which meant they had experienced a lot of the same things growing up: the humiliation at being picked last for the football teams, the depression of being ignored by most girls and the bitterness of being outside the many clubs or societies that other kids were part of. They were more dreamers. They would sit around, smoking cigarettes, listening to punk and alternative music, waiting for the world to change in their favour. J.P. was frustrated with life, mostly about the fact that there were so many women on the planet and he wasn't with any of them. If a couple of nice girls ever walked past when they were out he would encourage Tom to follow, offering a running commentary on their physiques and which one he was going to let Tom have.

'They're mad for it,' he'd say. 'All women are mad for it.'

He never plucked up the courage to say anything to the girls, even though he knew most of them from school. And if they ever came over to talk, J.P. would stare at the ground and then act sulky afterwards as if his shyness was somehow their fault. In Tom's mind they only seemed to use J.P. as a vessel to get to his brother in any case. They paid little attention to Tom, apart from early on when the knowledge that he was from Dublin created some mild interest. On a number of occasions they commented on his tics. He overheard one of the girls refer to him as 'Blinky' once and he knew that this was what they were calling him behind his back.

There was one girl who was the exception to the rule though. She was a cousin of the lads and she wasn't like the other girls.

She always had time for Tom.

He met her two weeks into his stay in Rossboyne.

'This is Sarah,' J.P. had said in a tone that didn't come close to the fanfare she deserved. 'She's my cousin.'

'Hey there,' Tom waved quickly before bowing his head and shoving one hand deep into his pocket.

'Sarah McCarthy,' she offered her hand and smiled, a smile that he would come to see every time he closed his eyes, the smile of someone who seemed genuinely pleased to know him.

Chapter 21

Mr Grundy is happy to see Tom. He displays this happiness by perching a pink wafer biscuit on the saucer beside Tom's cup of tea.

'There's plenty more where that came from,' he nods to the biscuit and winks.

Tom thanks him and sips his tea.

'So what's in the box?' Mr Grundy asks.

The scratching of claws against cardboard hasn't stopped since Tom entered.

'A cat,' Tom says. 'He's a good one too.'

'Give us a look,' Mr Grundy moves over to the box and Tom lifts the flap at the top. 'What makes him a good cat?'

'What usually makes a good cat?' Tom asks.

'If they're clever, I guess. And friendly.'

'He's all of those things.'

Mr Grundy laughs. 'Looks like a cheeky chappie to me,' he picks the cat up and holds him head-high so they are face to face. 'Oh yeah, he's a cheeky chappie by the looks of him. Frank Grundy knows a cheeky cat when he sees one.'

He places the cat on the ground and teases him with the sleeve of his coat. The cat swipes at the material.

'Do you want him?' Tom asks.

Mr Grundy doesn't reply immediately. He gently pats the kitten on either side of its face. The kitten playfully rolls on its back and swipes its paws at Mr Grundy's hands.

'Why?' he eventually asks.

'I don't want him.'

Mr Grundy picks the cat up and brings him close to his chest. The cat curls up against the heat.

'Is that all?'

'I don't know,' Tom shrugs. 'I guess I thought you might like a bit of company.'

Mr Grundy walks to the window and looks out. The cat seems happy in his arms.

'You're a good lad,' he eventually mutters and walks towards the door. 'I better get this fella a blanket to sleep on.' He moves into the hall and clumps upstairs.

Mr Grundy returns a few minutes later minus the kitten.

'Asleep,' he says and nods in the direction of the room upstairs. He sits down and sips on his tea.

'What happened to your face?' he asks Tom.

'A woman slapped me.'

'Ah Jaysus, Ted Grundy knows all about getting slapped by women. Sure there wasn't a day that went by where I wasn't getting slapped in the face by a woman. I'd have to ask them to slap the other side sometimes, just to even it out.'

Tom nods without smiling.

'What happened, son?'

'It's complicated.'

'The only place where it's ever complicated is in there,' Mr Grundy taps his head. 'You remember that.'

Tom leans back on the chair and places his two hands on top of his head.

'I guess I'm just tired, ye know. It's this business with the agency. It's taking up so much of my time. I don't know why I started it.'

'Do ye know something,' Mr Grundy points at Tom. 'You sound like an Indian without a horse, do you know that?'

'I don't get you,' Tom shakes his head.

'You sound like an Indian without a horse,' Mr Grundy repeats.

'I don't know what that means.'

'Sure I'm telling you what it means if you'd wait for two seconds.' He takes his mug in two hands and sips it, keeps it in front of him as he speaks. 'All right, picture the scene. It's North America, fifteen-hundreds. Horses haven't been introduced to the Indians yet but they still have to catch bison in order to survive. Can you imagine how fast a bison can run?'

'I'd say about thirty-five or forty kilometres an hour.'

'Is that a guess?'

'I think I remember seeing it on a documentary about bison.'

'You ever seen one about Indians?'

'There's not that many documentaries about Indians.'

'You're right. There's plenty of programmes about murderers. Christ, you can't turn the television on without being harassed by a murderer. And do you know what I've noticed. It's always the same fella doing the voiceovers, ye know, the kind of voice that used to be on chocolate ads. When have bloody chocolate ads been replaced with murder? I just don't get it at all.' He takes a sip of tea, looks up. 'What were you saying?'

'Indians,' Tom says.

'Yes. Indians. Without horses. All right, this is the deal. They could catch the bison two ways. They could try to catch a beast moving at forty kilometres an hour on foot or they could try the Piskin method.'

Tom shakes his head to indicate that he has never heard of it.

'This is where the Indians built a V-shape out of branches and rocks and big old tree trunks, about a mile long. Then they'd lure the bison in, trapping them in the end of the V-shape. They could pick them off at will after that.' He places his cup on the small table beside. 'You see, Tom. You're running around, chasing these woman that are too fast to catch. You should be just waiting for them to come to you.'

'What makes you think they'll come to me?'

'Because that's the way the world works, Tom. The right one will come to you. That's if they haven't already been.' Mr Grundy looks to the photo of his wife on the mantelpiece.

Tom finishes his tea and places the mug on the table.

'I have to go,' he says.

Mr Grundy walks him to the door.

'Does he have a name?' he asks. 'The cat?'

'No.'

'Any ideas?'

Tom shakes his head.

'I suppose it doesn't matter with cats,' Mr Grundy says. 'The damned things never come when you call them in any case.'

Tom can't sleep. He sits in his neighbours' bed-sit, a series of cuttings on the table, different facial characteristics taken from magazines and copies of his photographs. He thinks of police shows, of how composite production techniques are used to create an image of a face in an effort to find a criminal. He has discovered how easy it is for errors to occur. The alignment of the mouth, a slight difference in the eyes or the nose, and the face takes on a completely different likeness. He recalls once reading about how a military veteran in the US with no record or previous trouble with the law was convicted of raping and murdering a nine-year-old girl and sentenced to death sometime in the early eighties. The sole piece of evidence tying him to the crime was his likeness to a composite face which the police released to the public. He had been placed in a photo line-up and witnesses identified him as the murderer.

Nine years later, DNA implicated the real murderer. He looked nothing like the composite which was released to the public. So the real murderer looked nothing like the composite but the innocent man did. It shows that there are more complexities to the art of recognition than people truly understand. There are in-built instincts and traits which cause attraction and identification and which affect how one person would be deemed more trustworthy than another, more kind, more suited to be a partner.

Tom scans the images and wonders what effect his face has on others, negatively or positively. Evolutionary psychologists claim there are biological reasons for attraction and there are cues that people see in faces which indicate how good a partner they will be.

'What does my face say about me?' he asks aloud. 'Are there no cues in my face? Am I cue-less Shatner?'

Tom carefully selects the features for his ideal partner from the cuttings, full lips, a thin pointed nose, grey-blue eyes which he has taken from a photograph of a model, not as striking as the eyes of the woman from the apartment across the way but close enough. He places them on a sheet of paper. They look odd on the page like this, he thinks, like the kind of image a serial killer might send to the police as a warning, the type with headline cuttings too. The simplest of statements can look ominous with this technique.

#
I Like Cheese

Tom accidently bumps off the sheet and the eyes slide upwards. It gives the face a kind of fearful expression. He instantly thinks of Fiona, of how frightened she looked when he was being thrown out of the hotel.

A weak buzzing infiltrates his head.

He stands and walks around the room, humming in an effort to counteract the sound.

It doesn't work.

'I can't take this much longer Shatner,' he says and massages his temples.

He decides to go for a walk to clear his head.

Tom sees Fiona in the people he passes, her sadness in their bowed heads and her worry in their hunch against the rain. The cold seems to blend with his bones. It is uncomfortable and painful but it helps him to feel that he is part of something real, something bigger than himself and bigger than the problems which have a stranglehold over him. When he nears the hotel his feet are heavy, his body tired.

And his mind awakens to the buzzing again.

Bzzz Bzzz

How long can he go on like this?

He feels as if he's cracking up.

Will they hear the crack when you break Tom?

There aren't many people up this end of the city. The weather and the night have driven most of them indoors. The noise of the raindrops is constant.

He stops outside the hotel. There is a sensor on the automatic revolving doors. It causes them to spin slowly. There are reflections in the glass. His reflection appears intermittently, hands in pockets, pale face, staring forwards.

Disappears and reappears.

His face.

His frown.

Eventually the door stops.

After a time Tom begins to wonder if he is even there, in that spot.

He doesn't enter the hotel. He thinks about Fiona.

The door begins to revolve again as he walks away.

Chapter 22

Sarah's mother passed away when she was ten.

She lived on a farm with her father, a couple of miles from Ryan's bar, a low-ceilinged, ancient place that was cold and dark and cluttered.

Her father kept cows. That's the way he would say it.

'I keep cows,' like they were nothing more than a bunch of pansies in the backyard and not the livelihood of the family.

Sarah would completely ignore her father, everything he said, all the questions he aimed at her. And there were a lot of questions. It seemed as if the more she ignored him the more he wanted to find out. It is a gift, Tom thought, to be able to ignore that huge bulk of a man. Thinking back, Tom supposes there was a kind of pretence to the questions on her father's part, like it was a game being played out, ask and be ignored, vocalise concern but never actually do anything to relieve this concern. Take a turn and wait for the next.

He drove a Lada Samara, her father, a white vehicle with a hard interior and a frame which reminded Tom of a building block on wheels. He drank too much, tending to go directly to the pub on dropping her off and returning home that evening in a drunken state, with or without Sarah depending on whether she could get a lift from her uncle later that night.

She would cook her father's dinner in the mornings before he left for the pub and he would eat it when he returned in the evenings, sometimes.

'I just throw things into the food,' she told Tom. 'Anything that's on the floor really. I put some bleach in once. He wasn't even affected. He's made of iron my Daddy is. Everything about him is iron.'

They had been hanging around for a couple of weeks when Colm got his hands on a second-hand car, an old Ford Escort with an engine that sounded like a distressed man screaming when put into third gear and a body so rusted and dented it seemed as if it had been chewed up and spat out. After this, Sarah began to hang around with them every day. This suited Tom. He was addicted to her by that stage.

Tom liked to show off when in her company and it thrilled him when she laughed at his antics. He also had this incessant urge to give her things, often drifting into daydreams relating to this, imagining himself wooing her with a massive bunch of roses or inviting her onboard a luxury jet.

Yes baby, this is mine. Let's go for a ride.

She mentioned that she liked the Smiths one time. In an effort to impress her Tom went on the hunt for information on the band. There was a library six towns over and a bus departed for that town twice daily, eight in the morning and three in the afternoon. Tom caught the morning bus and gazed dreamily at varying shades of green as the bus grumbled through identical town after town. He imagined wowing her with his knowledge.

The Smiths, yes of course I know the Smiths.

My favourite album? Why, the first one of course. The one with that song, you know, the one about a glove, the one that you like too.

Tom almost missed his stop and had to shout to the driver to let him out. The driver pulled over, leaving barely enough room for Tom to squeeze between the bushes at the side of the road and the bus. He tore the sleeve of his jacket and scratched his hand.

There were no books about the Smiths in the library but Tom found one about the history of rock and roll and one about Cliff Richard. He read a few chapters from the history of rock and roll while a plump, suspicious librarian eyed him over her circular glasses. He didn't bother with the Cliff Richard one.

Later that evening they went with Colm as he was, in his words, 'seeing a man about a dog'. He was always seeing a man about a dog. It was his way of saying that he was going somewhere that was nobody's business. More often than not it was to sell cannabis to some friends.

'See a man about a dog' or 'I don't give a monkey's uncle', he had plenty of phrases that he would use in a joking manner when stoned, imitating some of the people he would meet while delivering the gas with his father. And he'd often use them in the wrong context, repeat the phrase over and over until it made little sense. Tom and Sarah would sometimes join in the joke. But not that evening. No, that evening Tom was in the back seat of the car with Sarah, trying to squeeze all he had learned from *The History of Rock and Roll* into the conversation. Eventually Sarah stopped him and questioned why he was telling her all about Buddy Holly's plane-crash in 1959.

'Have you read a book about this or something?' she asked.

When he admitted that he had read a book about it she laughed so hard that she curled into a ball in the back seat. She used the window to support her head and her hair clung to the condensation.

'That's mad,' she squealed. 'You're mad.'

And Tom felt this immense warmth in his chest and he

thought that he had never been happier than he was at that moment and he thought how Sarah was the most beautiful girl he had ever met.

In every single way.

Tom couldn't stand to be in that horsebox on his own in the evenings. His new friendships had made being alone even more lonely. So he would join his grandfather in Ryan's bar the odd evening. Tom found his grandfather different in Rossboyne, more animated. He would slap men on the back and grab women by their waists and try to dance with them.

'Come on woman!' he'd shout. 'Barman, play some music.'

This frightened Tom more than his quietness.

In some ways his grandfather became a stranger in Rossboyne.

One evening he sat down next to Tom and began to tell him a story about some kid that had hurt himself on their estate a number of years before.

'I brought him to the hospital on me bike,' his grandfather said. 'I remember it as clear as day. There was this small woman at the front desk and I marched right up to her and told her that the boy had stood on a nail. She said that there was a system and that I'd have to wait across the hall.' His eyebrows dipped as he recalled. 'My grandson, that's what she called him. And I put her straight. I told her that he wasn't anything to do with me, that he belonged to the woman down the road, ye know the fat one, the one that's mad about her garden.'

'Mrs Murray?'

'Yeah, that's the one,' he took his pouch of tobacco from the table and began to roll a cigarette. He smiled. 'He needs a member of his family with him, she says. A guardian or something. So I says that a guardian won't fix the lad's foot. She made the boy show her his foot then. There was this circle of damp on the sock where the nail had gone through. He peeled off his sock and there was all this green gunk around the wound.'

'Green?'

'Green,' he nodded seriously. 'Your woman asked me why I was only after bringing the boy in. I says that all I knew was that the lad had stood on a nail. And it wasn't one of mine, I says. I'm not the type of person who leaves nails around for young boys to just come along and stand on. I was asked by his mother to bring him to the hospital. Sure if I'd of known there was going to be wild allegations flying around I'd have probably told her to ask someone else. The woman said that the boy had been going around all day with an infection and that he might have gangrene or something and that he could have a fever. She ran off then to get a nurse.'

Tom's grandfather placed the cigarette in his mouth, fluidly flicked a match against the side of the box and brought the flame toward his face. After a couple of drags he leaned forward.

'That's green-foot, I said to the boy. You ever heard of the green-foot, Tom?' he asked.

'No,' Tom said.

'Neither did I but ye should have seen the face of him,' he laughed. 'The poor fella hugged his foot closer to his body and I told him that his foot was starting to rot. I nudged him in the ribs with me elbow though, ye know, to let him know that I was only messing and I said that if these fools don't sort it out quickly they'll have to cut it off. Jesus, he was as pale as anything by the time the nurse arrived.' He scratched the hair on his chin for a moment. It crunched against his fingernails. The smile left his face then. 'It got me thinking how people can pick up on things all wrong, ye know, people that don't know ye. Do you get me?'

'Yeah,' Tom nodded.

'I was trying to help the boy and he didn't get me at all. I don't know, sometimes ye can just make things worse by talking. Sometimes you're better off saying nothing.'

He finished the cigarette and stubbed it out on the floor with his heel.

'I didn't have to talk to her, your Nan. She just knew,' he gripped the top of his glass between thumb and forefinger and twirled it gently. 'We didn't have to talk about things, feelings and all that kind of shite. We're not that kind of people. And she just knew.' He stopped playing with the glass and stared Tom in the face. 'You know, don't you, that we're not that kind?'

Tom nodded.

'It's nothing bad. We're just not that kind of people,' he said and went to the bar to get another pint.

Tom was in the pub again a number of evenings later. She was in the lounge, the woman from the window, Mary. She was seated at a stool at the corner of the bar, a glass of stout in front of her. She would chat to the people who entered and when she did this Tom would glance in her direction, taking advantage of her distractions.

His grandfather was joking around. People were giving him sheets of paper and buying him drinks. Apparently he had told the punters that he was terminally ill and that he had a photographic memory. He was offering to memorise people's messages and relay them to lost relatives in heaven.

'Praise the Lord,' he was shouting. 'Praise the Damn Lord.'

Mary came over to Tom's table at one point, a glass of cola in one hand, a stout in the other.

'Hello there, stranger,' she smiled. 'I haven't seen you in a while.'

Tom nervously brought his hands below the table and tucked them under his thighs on the seat. He bowed his head, pushed his shoulders forward as if trying to shrink from view.

She took the stool opposite him and placed the stout and cola on the table.

'Got you this.'

He looked from the cola to the bar. The barman was watching them, his sight moving from one to the other before resting on a glass which he was drying with a cloth.

'I know I shouldn't be buying you fizzy drinks,' she said. 'Bad for your teeth and all that. But it's nice to have a treat now and again.'

She pushed the drink in front of him and rested her hand on his lower arm.

'We're all allowed to be bold sometimes,' she said and urged him to drink it.

Tom removed his hands from under him, gripped the glass tightly and brought it to his lips. His hand shook, causing the ice to rattle loudly against the sides.

'I noticed that you've made a few friends,' she said. 'The Daly brothers are a little bit older than you, aren't they?'

'A little bit,' Tom muttered.

She leaned forward, turned her head so the people beside couldn't hear.

'You mind yourself with them now. Especially that older fella. He has a mean streak in him. I don't know the girl so much. Sharon, is it?'

'Sarah,' Tom corrected.

'Sarah. Yeah, she seems a nice enough sort. She isn't shy that one though, sure she's not? Comes a long way to hang out with you lot, this Sarah one, doesn't she?'

Tom stayed quiet.

'Yeah,' she sipped on her stout, licked her lips slowly. 'What happened to your hand?' She nodded to scratches above his wrist.

'I just caught it on some brambles.'

She took his hand in hers and brought it towards her body.

'Make sure it doesn't get infected now. Keep it clean, won't you?'

'Yeah,' Tom said.

'You promise?'

Tom nodded quickly.

She brought his hand close to her chest.

'Sure, I'll look after you in any case, won't I?'

Tom felt her breasts against the back of his hand. He tensed, sweat breaking out on his forehead. The image of her in the window blinked into his head, her naked form, the paleness of her skin.

He inhaled deeply and only exhaled when she finally released his hand.

'I have to head,' he said quickly, his voice breaking slightly.

'What about your drink?'

Tom picked up the glass and drank, the ice weighing against his upper lip, the chill of the drink hurting his teeth.

'I'll see you around so,' she said as Tom stood and hurried from the bar.

Chapter 23

She has finished at nine for the last two nights. She creeps from the nightclub end of the hotel, head lowered so the longer hair at the back of her head falls around her face. She stops at the pathway to the left of the exit, lights a cigarette, her free palm moving to her cheek. Frequently she changes the leg she leans on. When she does this her hips move in the opposite direction and she swaps the hand which holds the cigarette and she switches the palm which goes to her cheek. She has the look of someone who has enduring worries.

For some reason Tom thinks of her as trapped. He pictures a caged bird when he sees her.

On both nights the car has arrived at the Manhattan a few minutes after nine. She takes a series of quick drags when it parks and flicks the butt of the cigarette onto the roadway, climbs into the car.

Tonight it is raining.

Tom waits for her. He wears his heavy coat, the one which he bought in a flea market three years ago, retrieved from a rack of second-hand leather jackets and vintage cardigans that smelled of must and were peppered with dust. It is overly heavy for the mild night but the collar is large enough to partially conceal his face. He wears a hat, the one which he found in the bag of wigs. It smells of washing powder and softener now. The peak is ironed straight but Tom still has flashes of an image, the hat sitting in the end of the bag of wigs. And when he does, he scratches the place where the hat meets his scalp and imagines a crawling sensation in his hair.

Ticka-ticka-ticka

Tom blinks against the droplets of rain and watches the changing of the traffic lights. He enjoys the consistency of the timing, the regular routine.

Green on the major road, the light hazy in the rain.

To amber. To red. Green again.

The traffic moves off slowly. Almost lazily.

Amber. Red. Pedestrian lights turn green but there is nobody waiting to cross.

Tom thinks of this sequence continuing all night, changing when there is nobody around. The steadiness of it gives him a warm sensation in his stomach.

He hears footsteps behind him, a dampened clacking sound on the wet footpath.

She appears at his left, rolls her thumb across a turquoise-coloured lighter and brings the flame up to a cigarette between her lips. She blows smoke from her nose.

Tom moves towards her. The way she turns to the side slightly alerts Tom to the fact that she is aware of his presence.

'I need to ask you a couple of questions,' Tom says softly.

He maintains a respectable distance.

Her eyes widen and Tom raises both hands in a show of peace. He even takes a step backwards.

'It'll only take a second,' he says.

'My husband will be here in a minute,' her tone is faltering.

'Just a couple of questions,' Tom says. 'Please.'

'You better not touch me,' she warns.

'I just want to ask you about the watch.'

'Leave me alone,' she takes a deep drag on the cigarette and aims her sight to the road.

'I know he showed you the watch,' Tom says and takes a step closer to her. 'I saw the two of you talking.'

'You didn't see anything,' she hisses and looks at him sharply. Her eyes partially close. 'What did you see?'

'I saw the two of you at the bar. He showed you the watch.'

'Jesus Christ,' she looks to the heavens. 'Why won't you just leave it?'

'And then I saw the two of you go out to the corridor.'

'What do you want?' her voice rises and she waves her hands in frustration.

'I just want the watch.'

'That fuckin' watch,' she throws the cigarette onto the ground and crushes it with her heel. 'It's not even worth anything. It's a piece of crap.'

'How do you know it's not worth anything? You've seen the watch, haven't you? It was you in the bar, wasn't it?'

She shakes her head slowly. 'If my husband sees you talking to me he'll kill you.'

'Please, just let me know if you've seen the watch.'

'Why?'

'Please,' Tom places both hands together and his coat opens.

Her eyes widen and she retreats. 'What are you up to?'

Tom follows her gaze to the camera around his neck.

'Have you been taking pictures of us?' she asks. 'What are you taking pictures of?'

'Nothing,' Tom shakes his head. 'I just want to know about the watch.'

'I knew you were trouble.' She points at Tom. Her hand shakes. She turns and begins to walk away from him.

Tom follows her.

'Did he show you the watch in the nightclub?' he asks.

'Christ,' she turns. 'Yes. He showed me the watch. He showed me some stupid trick with it. Now piss off.'

'Then what?'

'Then what? What do you want, the details? What is it you really want?'

'What happened to the watch?'

'Here's my husband. Just leave it,' her words are urgent.

Tom spots the car at the traffic lights. The pedestrian light is green.

'Jesus. Fuck off,' she says. 'Please.'

'What happened to the watch?' Tom asks.

She begins to walk in the direction of the car.

'Please. Don't follow me. You don't understand what he'll do to me. He'll kill me.'

Tom takes one step towards her.

'Where is it?' he asks.

'Jesus. He has it beside the bed. Please. Don't come up to the car. I'll get him to leave it at reception for you.'

'Who has? Your husband?'

'Who do you think?' She talks through the corner of her mouth.

'Who?'

She throws one last glance in his direction.

'Karl has it. Fuckin' Karl, that's who.'

The car pulls up to the pathway and the door opens. She jumps in and leans across the seat, kisses the driver. His face is obscure in the dim light but Tom senses that the driver is looking directly at him. Tom doesn't look away. He watches the car drive off and he hears the buzzing in the distance.

It is moving towards him.

Quickly.

Chapter 24

The elderly woman who sells Tom the flowers has creased skin and a faint moustache. She is wrapped in a plain white shawl and squints as she speaks. Tom imagines she sees stories in all her customers' purchases, affairs in the roses, friendship in the daffodils, sympathy in the chrysanthemums or apologies in the lilies. Perhaps she dreams that someone will buy flowers for her someday, whisk her away from the dreary street, away from cobbles splattered with rotten fruit and the stench of dead fish and cigarette smoke.

'For someone nice I hope,' she says as Tom pays for the flowers.

'Yes,' Tom pauses, thinks about it for a moment. 'For someone very nice.'

Tom brings the flowers up to head-height as he enters the Manhattan even though there is no sign of Barry the security man. Fiona smiles at the approaching flowers.

The smile disappears when Tom sticks his head out from behind.

'Ah Jesus Tom,' she says softly. 'I can't take any more drama. I haven't got the energy.'

'I just want to give you these,' Tom says. 'To say sorry and stuff.'

She exhales loudly. 'Tom. You have to go.'

'Take these, will you?' He moves the flowers closer.

'Tom,' she draws out his name.

'I know that things got out of control. If Barry had listened we could have sorted it out. I spoke to her last night, you know, the blonde woman. She said she was going to leave the watch at reception for me.'

'Tom,' Fiona sighs loudly. 'There's no watch here for you.'

'There has to be,' Tom leans on the counter and scans the desk. 'But there's not.'

'She told me it would be here.'

'Jesus Tom,' Fiona shoves the A4 diary aside. 'Have a look for yourself if you don't believe me.' She lifts a pile of papers up. 'It's not here. It's gone,' Tom. I'm sorry but you have to forget about it and stop hassling the people who work here.'

'There it is,' Tom points to his watch. It is next to a tray of invoices to the right of the desk.

Fiona picks it up, her face drawn in confusion.

'I told you,' he says. 'Here, I'll swap you.'

Tom hands over the flowers and she slowly hands over the watch.

He cleans the face with his sleeve, small circles in an anti-clockwise motion.

'Jesus, I'm sorry Tom,' she says softly. 'I didn't see it there.' She rubs her upper arm absently. 'I don't know what to say.'

'It never left the hotel,' Tom says and examines the back of the watch and the strap.

'Maria had stolen it?'

'Maria?'

'The blonde woman. The woman you spoke to.'

'Not really. Karl had it. And she knew that Karl had it. He's staying in one of the rooms I think.'

She dwells on this information for a moment, her mouth

open, eyebrows raised.

'Maria's married,' she says.

'So is Karl.'

'This sounds complicated.'

'It always is.'

'Jesus, Tom. I'm really sorry.'

'Don't worry about it.'

'I know but,' she shakes her head, casts her eyes downwards. 'You know what I mean.'

'It's grand,' Tom straps the watch to his wrist. He brings it to his ear and feels the small vibration of the hand moving.

'I'll let Barry know about the watch,' her tone is serious. 'Clear things up and all.'

'Good,' Tom says.

'Sorry, Tom,' she apologises again.

'Fiona,' Tom stares at the ground and bites his lip for a moment. He plays with his sleeve nervously.

'Yeah?'

'Do you know anything about Indians?' he asks.

'Not really,' she shakes her head.

Tom inhales deeply, holds it in for a couple of seconds. When he exhales, the words flow out of him, quickly.

'Before they had horses they'd catch bison with a trap.'

She nods.

'And women are a bit like these bison, ye know. I don't mean that they look like bison. What I mean is that you can't really catch them by running after them so you set a trap.'

'I don't like where this is going Tom.'

Tom laughs. 'No,' he says. 'What I mean is that instead of running after women you should wait for them to come to you. Does that make any sense?'

'A bit, I suppose. At a push. What are you getting at Tom?'

'This is a bit embarrassing really.'

'What is?'

'This business of trying to ask someone out.'

'Oh no, Tom. I'm sorry,' her hand moves to her mouth.

'That's okay,' Tom says quickly.

'I really shouldn't,' she says.

'No, that's grand Fiona,' Tom holds his hands up. 'I'm sorry. I'm just chancing my arm.'

'I'm sorry Tom. It's just bad timing at my end.'

'No, that's okay. I understand,' Tom inches backwards towards the revolving door. 'I should never have asked.'

'Tom wait,' she calls after him.

'No, it's okay. Really, it is.'

'Tom,' she laughs.

'What?'

'Jesus, you'll have me as mad as you.' She looks to the side, smiles and shrugs. 'I'll give you a ring,' she says.

'Yeah?'

'Yes.'

'Are you sure?'

'You want me to change my mind?'

'No. No. Give me your number and I'll give you a ring sometime.'

'I'll ring you Tom.'

'Okay, fair enough. I'll give you my number.'

'I have your number. Everybody in this place has your number.'

'I'll write it down in any case.'

He writes the number on a page in his notebook, rips it out and hands it to her.

'Thanks for the flowers,' she says.

'That's all right,' he says. 'They weren't that expensive.'

He walks away from the counter, turns before the exit. 'Thanks,' he says.

She gives him a little wave and looks at the number on the page. She covers her eyes with her left hand and shakes her head, smiling all the while.

Tom leaves through the revolving door.

He crosses the street and stands in the shade of a massive grey building, boarded windows and a wooden sign displaying the name of a property company.

His legs shake and his thoughts feel untamed. They kick about his head wildly, spark and run and jump.

He should be happy.

But he is nervous and unsure of himself. There have been dates with the agency but this is the first time he has asked someone out since that incident in work.

He needs to calm down.

He rubs his hands together and breathes quickly.

Calm down.

Calm down.

He closes his eyes.

And a cold breeze catches him unawares.

The way it hits him, the way it causes the nerves to stand on his legs and back, the way the darkness of the shadow engulfs him and the droplets of rain fall from the grating above, it takes him away from the now and for one horrible instant he is back in that beat-up old horsebox and there is a gift in his hands, wrapped in brown paper, tied with a string. His name is written on the front, neatly in pen, the writing of a woman.

His heart is beating quickly.

Fear?

Excitement?

The brown paper gives way to softness underneath when he presses his fingers against it.

And Tom is untying the string, a fat, weaved type of string. And he finds a jumper inside. Knitted or bought, he isn't sure. It is red and heavy. And there is a note, written in the same handwriting as the parcel.

> *To Tom,*
> *For those cold nights.*
> *Love,*
> *Mary xxx*

Mary from the pub. Mary from the stream. Naked Mary.

Tom recalls the confusion of that time, how he wasn't sure what the woman had wanted from him.

He stands in the cold shadow for a moment.

Unknown to himself he is squeezing his eyes tightly at regular intervals.

Chapter 25

Tom has one eye on his phone for the next few days. He hears phantom ringing whenever he is surrounded by excessive noise. He splashes from the shower at times or flees from the rumbling whoosh of a kettle only to discover that his phone is still quiet and nobody has rung. In a way his life becomes quieter. He keeps the volume of the radio and television low. When reading, his bed-sit is silent.

Sometimes an unpleasant feeling drops into the pit of his stomach, a sensation like falling from a height. When this happens he grabs his phone and ensures that the battery has sufficient charge to make it through the day, or he pats his pocket until he feels the shape of the device through the material of his trousers. He charges the phone whenever he gets the chance and when leaving for work he carries the charger with him.

Although the phone call is a dominant force over these days he still spends a lot of time in his neighbours' place and uses the model as a distraction. He buys polymer clay from an arts and crafts shop and begins to construct the nose using the ideal characteristic cuttings as a template. The size of the nose quickly becomes a problem. It is supposed to be proportional to the ideal face but William Shatner's face isn't the ideal face.

'It's just not happening Shatner,' he says as he holds a rough prototype of the nose up to the model's face. 'I'm sorry but your head is going to have to go.'

Tom journeys to the city centre, to shops and department stores, on the hunt for a damaged mannequin. His search brings him to a large clothes shop along the quays, brisk staff and dazzling lights, pop music loud enough to crack the healthiest of thought-processes, a window display with birdcages, bonsai trees and gold sheets of fabric. The shop assistant is a young girl. She wears the type of clothes that the store sells, eighties' style, long T-shirt with a leopard-print design, leggings, her hair big, blonde and puffy. She is the type who makes a face when forced to interact with people over twenty-five, the kind of face that someone might make if they have found something disgusting stuck to their shoe.

'What for?' she asks.

'It's for art,' Tom lies.

'You're an artist?' She raises her left eyebrow ever so slightly at this news.

'Yes. I am an artist,' he says. And then he repeats it so as to convince himself of the lie. 'I *am* an artist.'

'There might be a couple in the storeroom,' she says.

'I just need the head,' Tom says.

'Why didn't you say that?' She rolls her eyes. 'We've loads of those. Dave breaks them off the damaged mannequins all the time. He uses the head as a football when he's on his lunch break.'

She disappears through a set of double doors at the rear of the shop and soon returns with a head. There is little detail to it, hollow, a few scuff marks near the ear, but it is in good condition.

Tom thanks her and returns to his neighbour's place.

He opens a beer and takes a swig before gnashing away at

Shatner's neck with a hacksaw. When he has finished he places the head in a clear plastic bag and rests it on the table. He wedges a piece of wood in the hollow mannequin head and uses a dowel screw to attach it to Shatner's body. The join is a bit messy but he will easily be able to conceal it with a neck scarf, he thinks.

Tom shoves his hands into his pockets for a minute and stares at the head on the table.

Alas, poor Yorick!

He decides that the trauma of cutting his friend's head off warrants a break from the model. He drinks more beer and stares out the large window of his neighbours' bed-sit.

He doesn't receive any phone calls.

The following day, Tom returns to his neighbours' bed-sit and to the model. He replicates the dimensions of the mannequin's face on a sheet of paper. He sketches a rough shape of the nose on this page, holds it up to the mannequin's head for a moment, offers a disappointed grunt before retrieving another page and repeating the process. This time he reduces the width of the nose. He holds the head next to the page, looks from one to the next a number of times before shaking his head and repeating the process. Thirty-one pages later and he is satisfied with the dimensions of the nose.

Using modelling clay, he sets to work shaping the nose. It takes him over an hour to create his first draft. Luckily, the notch for a nose on the mannequin's head is smaller than his ideal nose so he will not have to cut it off. Instead he presses the back of the modelling-clay nose onto the notch. He figures that the extended shape will help keep the new nose in place when he glues it later. The modelling clay goes out of shape slightly when he presses it and he spends the next ten minutes rectifying this. He then removes the nose and bakes it. When he takes it out of the oven he notices that there is a crack on the right-hand side of the clay. Tom has to start the process all over again.

'Jesus Christ, Shatner,' Tom talks to the head in the bag. 'This is going to drive me insane.'

At half one in the morning Tom has a new nose.

He is happy with it.

He wraps it in newspaper and puts it on the table.

As time moves on without a phone call Tom's urge to ring Fiona grows.

But he doesn't ring her. Nor does he go anywhere near the hotel.

He isn't a stupid man. A bit eccentric maybe, he thinks. But he has enough sense to realise that if Fiona sees him at the hotel the possibility of a date will disappear.

He has to control himself.

Bzzz

'Control' might not be the best word, he thinks.

He has to be patient.

He has to be an Indian without a horse.

He dedicates time to the ears. As the better part of each ear will be concealed by the wig, Tom doesn't go into too much detail. While they are baking he rings up a pizza-delivery service using a number retrieved from a television advert. His call is answered by a man with a heavy Dublin accent who keeps referring to him as 'Bud'. Tom doesn't order a pizza but he does ask if the man could ring him back so he can confirm that his phone is still working.

'You're having a laugh, Bud,' the man refuses.

He hangs up.

'Some people, Shatner,' Tom says and shakes his head.

Tom paints the model.

He makes a large batch of paint, mostly white with a small

part yellow and a splash of red. He mixes and adds until he has a suitable skin colour. He paints the head of the mannequin and the arms and hands of the waxwork model. It dries darker on the model than it does on the head so he adds extra white and repaints the arms and hands. He paints the nose and the ears. They need two coats. He leaves them to dry on newspaper beside the open window and lays some jewellery next to the ears and the nose, a bracelet and a couple of bangles that he bought in a charity shop.

Tom adds a bit of red to the cheeks of the mannequin. He thinks about Fiona while he does this. He worries that he may have given her the wrong number or that she may have lost the number. Perhaps there is something wrong with her phone?

Underneath the apprehension there is a heavier dragging feeling in his gut. It tells him the real truth. She is not going to ring.

Tom cuts the iris and pupil parts from the ideal-eye magazine photograph and sticks them to the eyes of the mannequin head. He glues the nose and ears to the model. He cleans up the paint and brushes and places them in a box. He sweeps and dumps the collected rubbish into a black refuse sack along with the earlier drafts of his noses, other clay parts and debris from his activities. He ties a tight double knot in the top.

Tom is about to leave his neighbours' bed-sit when he remembers the lips.

'How could I have forgotten the lips?' he says to Shatner. 'The lips are a key element of the face.'

They shouldn't take too long to do, he thinks, and retrieves the red paint from the box, and a brush. He pours some of the red paint into a container and slowly begins to colour the lips.

'This will make the lips seem fuller, Shatner,' he says. 'And that's important.'

He uses small dabs and moves slowly, careful not to go outside the lines of the lips.

'Full lips make a face seem young and healthy. Evolutionary psychologists believe that the colour of the lips also offer an indication of fertility.' He regurgitates information he has read in a cosmetic journal. 'Full lips are developed by,' he pauses, searches his memory for a few seconds before continuing, 'oestrogen. And the more oestrogen a woman has the more fertile she is. I suppose that makes you think doesn't it? So many men don't want to be tied down with kids. They don't want to be putting any buns in the oven, if you know what I mean. So really they should be going for women with the lowest levels of oestrogen. I don't know, maybe women with excessive muscles.'

He takes extra care at the corners of the lips.

'Physically strong women.' He moves across and dabs at the upper edge. 'With a full beard maybe.' He steps back to examine the lips.

They look well.

He pulls the mannequin forward and tilts it across the counter so the head is closer to the open window, in the hope that the glue and paint will dry quicker.

There is a sudden knocking at the door.

It develops into successive light tapping.

'Hello, is it okay to come in?' It is Maureen Hill from downstairs.

Shit.

Tom hurries to the black refuse sack to get rid of the red paint and the brush.

Don't push the door.

Please!

The refuse sack is tied with a knot, so Tom grabs the plastic bag which contains William Shatner's head and throws the paint in. He carries both bags to the door.

'Hello?' Mrs Hill calls again.

'Hang on, just a minute.'

Tom raises the black bag to chest height and uses it to obscure the view of the bed-sit as he squeezes out the door. 'Just cleaning up a bit,' he says and awkwardly closes the door behind him.

'Are they back?' she asks.

'Who?'

'The Walters.'

'No, they're still away.'

'Oh sorry, I thought I heard you talking to someone.'

'Must have been the radio or something.'

'When are they due back?'

'Wednesday, I think.'

'Grand,' she says.

'Grand,' Tom agrees.

She pinches her lower lip.

'I've been thinking,' she says. 'And I don't know how you feel about it but, well, I was thinking that maybe you shouldn't say anything to them about me being in their place. Just in case they get the wrong idea.'

'I suppose,' Tom motions forward slightly. He just wants to get out of there. He hates holding rubbish. This image keeps flashing into his head, the rubbish bag nestled neatly in the metal bin in his bed-sit. And he imagines the sound of the lid closing.

Clunk.

'We both know it was an innocent mix-up,' she says. 'I'd hate for them to get the wrong idea.'

Tom nods.

'I wouldn't say that we're best friends,' she says. 'But I've known the Walters for years and I always stop to talk to Mrs Walters. She's a very nice woman. So,' she leans forward, 'maybe we'll just keep it to ourselves. What do you think?'

'That sounds grand,' Tom says.

Clunk.

She exhales dramatically.

'Oh, thank God we've sorted that little problem out. You worry about these things, don't you?'

'You do,' Tom steps forward.

'When did you say they'd be back?'

'Wednesday.'

'Wednesday.' She folds her arms. 'From,' she frowns, 'where was it again?'

Tom closes his eyes briefly. He tries to recall the place. All he can think of is the bin.

Clunk.

'I have to head inside,' he says. 'Put this stuff away.'

'Of course,' she smiles and nods, looks to the black plastic bag and then to the bag with William Shatner's head in it. His features are obscured slightly by the material of the bag but the outline is still visible, as is the red paint which streaks the face.

Maureen Hill's eyes widen. She pales instantly and turns as quickly as her magnitude will allow.

'Grimsby,' Tom remembers.

She doesn't acknowledge him. She rocks towards the stairs, almost tripping at one point in the panic of her departure.

'Grimsby,' he calls after her once more before moving to his own bed-sit.

Chapter 26

One of the evenings Mary was accompanied by a man, tall if he wasn't so stooped over, and handsome if it wasn't for his pained expression. His arms were long and bent awkwardly at the elbows, his hands curled inwards as if collapsing in on themselves. He wore an old suit of crumpled black material and he reminded Tom of a spider.

Tom would later find out that he was Mary's husband and that he suffered from chronic arthritis.

The couple sat at a table in Ryan's bar, side by side facing the same point on the wall. They didn't turn to each other once and they didn't speak. After a time, Mary left him and made her way around the bar. She wore a flimsy dress, the type which ended above the knee and hinted at what lay underneath with every movement of her hips or legs. Her hair was tied up on her head, revealing the paleness of the skin at her neck. The women in the bar reacted differently to Mary than the men. They had little time for her. They offered blunt, unsmiling greetings and immediately found distractions to prevent a conversation following. The men would watch her though, bouncing on heels, shouting witty lines and straightening their backs. And she would lay a hand on their upper arms when talking to them, press against them as she laughed, play with her hair when listening.

She made her way towards a group which contained Tom's grandfather and he tried to move her on with a couple of curt lines. He was in a drinking mood that evening. As he had been for the last couple of evenings. The boyish joviality which had come on him in Rossboyne was gradually evaporating to reveal his true self.

'I want to borrow your grandson,' Mary said and winked at Tom. 'I've a few jobs that need doing.'

'You'll have him worked to the bone Mary,' a member of the group shouted, his chin slimy with spit and drink, a toupee rotting on his head.

'I'm a hard boss,' Mary folded her arms. 'I'll get the boy up and about no bother.'

She moved closer to Tom. 'Ten sharp tomorrow,' she said. 'And don't be late or you'll be a sorry boy.'

The group cheered and whooped at this.

Tom's grandfather moved to the bar to get another drink. He had started on the whiskey by that stage.

Tom left the bar early that evening but he would wake during the night to find his grandfather crying. Tom had never seen his grandfather cry before. Even at his grandmother's funeral the man had kept an unwavering hold on his emotions, merely nodding and grunting at the offered hands and condolences.

'She's gone,' he muttered. 'Don't you understand?' He swayed near the door of the horsebox, rummaging in his pockets. 'She's gone.'

Tom remained still and quiet, hoping the darkness would conceal the fact that he was awake.

'Where's me keys?' His grandfather staggered forward. 'I need them.'

He sat down on the floor of the horsebox, muttering to himself. The next moment he was asleep.

Tom climbed from his bunk and removed his grandfather's boots. He placed a blanket over him and gently tilted his head so he was facing to the side.

When Tom woke the next morning he lay as still as he could, tense, listening.

He only relaxed when he could make out the steady sound of the old man breathing.

The dirt of the windows diluted the morning light and gave the kitchen a muddy quality. Mary was next to the cooker, her hair wild, a blonde halo of frizz surrounding it. She had no make-up on and she was lacking the smiling, carefree nature that she usually had in the bar. There was a greyness and lifelessness to her skin which made Tom think of dry, crumbling leaves.

She has aged, Tom thought. In a single night the woman had become old.

The kitchen smelled of grease and the air was warm from cooking. A pot sat on the hob with a dirty silver base and blackened interior rim, the slow plop of bubbling porridge coming from inside. There was a vase on the table, flowers drooping over the side, petals stained brown on the surface. There were net curtains on the window, dead flies and insects caught in the threads. The place had a poverty that Tom had not expected, the way the wallpaper was peeling at the upper edges, the way the bulb hung naked from the ceiling and the dark tiles on the floor were chipped and cracked.

It was an unloved room, a divorced and neglected type of room.

Mary scooped a splodge of porridge into a white bowl.

'Eat up,' she said and left.

Her footsteps were loud on stairs without carpet. The echo of her clumping feet dampened as she moved from stairs to landing. Tom listened carefully and tried to imagine the layout of the house. He played with the sleeve of his jumper. He was nervous and the smell of the porridge was turning his stomach slightly. A deep voice sank through the upper floorboards to his position at the table. Tom's heart raced suddenly. It was her husband.

A low thumping sound soon followed, then the noise of something heavy sliding across the floor.

Tom's imagination ran wild.

He pictured the man dragging his wife from the room, his spider-like arms flipping her into the air and rolling her in fine silver strands.

Round and round.

Up and down.

Covering her body and legs and moving towards her face, faster and faster, spinning until her whole frame was shrouded in layers and she resembled a butterfly in the pupa stage.

I will be next, Tom thought. He will hear the click of spider legs scuttling down those wooden steps. He will see the crooked shadow grow tall on the wall. He will spy the black hairy body through a crack in the door. And soon, he will be covered, trapped and suffocated, devoured in this dusty building.

Tom listened carefully for more movement.

For a time it was quiet upstairs.

Then the steps began again. Her steps.

Each time he detected her near the stairs his heart would give a slight jolt and the tempo would increase.

Rumpa-thump.

Rumpa-thump.

He wasn't sure what work she had planned for him. There was no end of things that needed to be done. But he prayed it would be a job in the garden, cleaning the windows or pulling the weeds.

Perhaps her husband would watch while he worked, he thought.

Perhaps they would both watch him, size him up, figure him out.

Rumpa-thump.

Rumpa-thump.

What if he wasn't here for work? What if she wanted him here for something else?

She moved down the stairs.

Tom sat upright and taut. The support of the chair was hard against his back. He folded his arms and tapped his foot rapidly until she appeared at the door.

She was still unsmiling.

Was this the same woman he had seen naked at the window?

'He's asleep,' she said and walked over to the hob. She stirred the porridge. 'You make sure you don't disturb him with your noise, won't you?'

Tom was quiet. He nibbled on the inside of his bottom lip.

Mary turned from the hob.

'Sure you won't?' she repeated, louder.

'I'll be as quiet as I can.'

Her face darkened and she approached the table.

'You're not eating your porridge,' she stood with hands on hips. 'What's wrong?'

'I'm not hungry,' Tom inched to the edge of his chair.

'But you've always liked porridge.'

'What?' Tom said softly.

'Eat your porridge,' she ordered and returned to the pot.

She turned off the gas, slopped some porridge into a bowl and sat down next to him. She took a spoonful from the bowl, blew on it before shoving it into her mouth. The spoon clacked against her teeth as she brought it out.

Tom held the spoon above his own bowl. The mixture was grey and lumpy. It no longer steamed as hers did. He dipped the spoon in, gathered a small amount and brought it upwards.

'What do you want me to do?' Tom asked quietly.

She arched an eyebrow.

'About what?'

'What work do you need me for?'

'I'll ask your father what needs doing,' she said and stirred the porridge in her bowl, blowing on it at the same time.

'My grandfather,' Tom corrected.

'What are you talking about?' she snapped. She glanced down at his bowl. 'Eat your porridge.'

Tom nervously played with the porridge. He was aware of the perspiration on his brow and the sharp sting under his armpits, the trickle of sweat down his side.

She stopped stirring and looked at his bowl again.

'Why aren't you eating your porridge William?' Her anger brought colour to her cheeks.

Tom dropped the spoon. It slowly submerged in the porridge mixture. He pushed his chair back without looking at her and stood.

'William,' she said. 'What are you doing?'

Tom briskly walked through the kitchen door and into the hall.

Rumpa-thump.

Rumpa-thump.

'Answer me William,' her voice grew louder. 'William!' she shouted. 'Don't walk away from me.'

Tom opened the front door. He felt the blood pumping in his head, a coldness across his back, the looseness of his shaking hands.

'William,' she called after him. 'Don't you walk away from your mother.'

Tom stepped outside the house and when he felt the cool air on his face he ran from the garden. He ran until his heart seemed to rattle in his neck and head, until his lungs felt like flames in his chest.

Chapter 27

Garda Harry is at the door to Tom's bed-sit.

His chest rises and falls rapidly, his nostrils flare with the pressure of each exhalation.

As if he has been running, Tom thinks, and steps aside so he can enter.

He strides to the opposite end of the bed-sit, turns and scans the room, his eyes frequently returning to Tom. The light overhead accentuates the sweat on his face and there is stiffness to his movements as if he is encumbered with limited flexibility.

It is the pose of someone who is tense.

The pose of someone who is expecting something to happen.

Tom's camera is on the counter and Harry picks it up and rotates it in his hands carelessly.

'What do you want?' Tom asks.

'This is a digital camera, isn't it?'

'Yeah.'

'Where's your printer?'

'I just print photos off in the library.'

'Where are the photos you printed off?' He slaps the camera roughly against the counter.

'Hey,' Tom steps towards him.

'Stay where you are.'

'What?' Tom stops. 'Why? What's this about?'

Harry raises his palm to indicate that he is waiting on an answer.

'I cut them up,' Tom squeezes the fingers of his left hand nervously.

Harry frowns. 'Why?'

'I didn't need the whole photograph.'

'Why not?'

'I just needed pieces of them.'

Harry thinks about this for a moment. His eyebrows dip and he looks at Tom's hands.

'Where are the cuttings?'

'Most of them went out with the rubbish. They're probably still in the bin downstairs. I'll get them for you if you want,' Tom moves in the direction of the door.

'Stay where you are,' Harry snaps loudly, the tendons in his neck standing out.

'What's going on here?' Tom asks.

'You tell me Stacey,' he takes a step towards Tom.

'I don't know what you want,' Tom's chest tightens. His hand moves to his forehead, his fingers tremor. 'What do you want?'

'Jesus, Stacey.'

'What?' Tom says quietly.

'Where are the photos?' Harry drops the camera.

The cracking sound seems to fill the space long after it has landed.

Tom stoops and reaches for the camera.

'Get back,' Harry warns.

Tom ignores him. He grabs the camera, kneels and begins to collect the broken pieces which are scattered around.

'Get up Stacey.' Harry's hand moves under his coat. When his hand comes into view again he is clutching a baton.

'Get up,' he says.

Tom rises.

'Get over there,' he nods to the far wall of the bed-sit.

'It's wrecked,' Tom holds the camera towards the policeman.

Harry brings the baton forward quickly, hitting Tom on his left shoulder. Tom loses his footing and falls backwards. It is an undignified fall, the type that seems as if it is happening in slow motion. He lands painfully on his behind and twists his arm slightly in the effort of protecting his head. It is only when he is in a seated position that a sudden rush of fear envelops him.

'You stay there,' Harry says.

Tom's instinct is to run.

He tries to stand but his movement is sluggish and he is pushed back down.

'I said stay,' Harry hisses through gritted teeth.

Tom holds an awkward position for a moment, his arms bearing his weight so he feels his pulse hammering through his palms. Gradually Tom eases himself to a seated position and Harry begins to walk around the room.

'Where are the fuckin' things?' he says.

He moves to Tom's chair, the one which faces the small window. He violently shoves it forward. There is a snapping sound.

Tom feels a dipping in his chest, a curling arc of dismay.

A groan follows that arc.

My chair.

Harry glances at him quickly before moving to a bookcase at the back of the room. He straightens his arm and runs it along the books so they thump to the floor. He hunkers to the floor and begins to shake the books. A bookmark falls from one. He lifts it up quickly and inspects it before flicking it away. It spirals in the air and lands at Tom's feet.

'I know about you groping that woman in work, Stacey. I know plenty about you.'

Tom shakes his head and closes his eyes.

Harry moves to the cupboards, roughly scoops the contents to the side so they crash onto the floor, tins, glass spice jars that crack and splinter. A plastic airtight container bounces from the counter, the lid popping open and sticks of spaghetti spilling onto the floor. They crunch under Harry's feet as he moves to another cupboard.

Pieces of food are kicked under the fridge and the oven.

How am I going to get them out of there?

How am I going to clean this place?

A low hum begins to emerge from the questions in his head. It moves as a drill would, boring towards him, growing louder with each second.

It's not a drill, he thinks. Of course it's not a drill.

It is a bee.

That damned bee.

Tom covers his ears with his hands but the buzzing continues. He increases the pressure, pressing his palms against his ears.

Harry is beside the opened fridge, his head ducked inside. He scoops things from the fridge and throws them to the floor, cheese, eggs, milk, a glass jar of sauce, the wetness of the contents transforming the sound of breakage into a dull splat. The sauce spreads like paint, splashes his feet, flecks the wall.

Bzzzzz

Tom blinks his eyes tightly. He struggles to his feet.

The pain in his head glows and intensifies with any sudden movement.

Harry has his arms inside the fridge as if he's trying to climb in.

Bzzzzz

Tom slowly walks to the door and to a sweeping brush that leans against the wall.

This room, he thinks. I have to clean this room.

His left foot slides out on the sauce, so quickly that his thigh muscle sings sharply and he almost loses his balance. He steadies himself and continues on.

There is glass underfoot.

It crunches with each step and alerts the policeman.

Harry is quick. He is beside Tom in an instant and swinging his right fist. It connects with the top of Tom's crown. Tom falls, the momentum pushing his head back so it strikes the edge of the door.

There is this feeling of dullness, a moment like wakening in the darkness of night.

His sight soon sprinkles with dots of shadow and light. The pain follows, like water rushing into a space. Tom's hand moves to the point where the door has struck. There is heat and stickiness in his hair. He looks at his hand and it is covered in blood.

'You stay where you are,' Harry points at him. 'Fuckin' pervert.' He moves closer to Tom.

'Where's all your stuff? Your photos, where do you keep them?'

Tom doesn't answer. The buzzing has become a looping sound, the way a plane will spin and crash in those old war films, the engine sound changing as if he was right there watching it, somehow sitting on a cloud in the stratosphere.

The Doppler effect, Tom thinks. That's what it's called, isn't it?

The darkness pulls at him. It is a weight at the base of his crown.

The policeman taps his foot against Tom's shin.

'Come on, where's all your stuff?'

'It's a change in the waves,' Tom mumbles, his eyes blinking rapidly with the effort of keeping them open. 'Depending on where your position is.'

'What?' Harry is confused.

'The way the noise of a car sounds higher when approaching you and lower when moving away from you.'

'What are you talking about?'

Tom closes his eyes and sees an image of the bee riding the waves, up and down on the looping line, wings buzzing furiously.

The sight is so ridiculous. He feels like vomiting and laughing at the same time.

'What the fuck are you playing at?' Harry shouts.

Tom feels his shirt tightening around his neck, feels the ground move away from him.

He opens his eyes and sees Harry's face coming closer to his.

The pain that suddenly courses through his head is so fierce that it causes his eyes to roll upward, his legs to go limp momentarily.

The policeman supports his weight.

'You think this is funny?' He pushes Tom against the wall.

Tom groans loudly, his hands moving to his head.

'I'm not leaving until I find something. You understand that.' He moves away from Tom. 'It's not so funny now, is it?'

Tom is weak. He bends forward and places his hands on his thighs for support.

'What were you buying women's clothes for?' Harry is beside his chest of drawers. He takes each one of Tom's drawers out and upends them. 'I know you have some in here.'

'I don't have them any more,' Tom mumbles.

Harry stops suddenly. 'Where are they?'

'I gave them to her.'

'To who?' His eyes widen.

'Shatner,' he mutters. 'I gave them to Shatner.'

'Who is Shatner?'

'The model.'

'Where is she?'

'In the bed-sit.'

'Jesus Christ, Stacey. You think I won't find something?' he storms back to the kitchen area. 'I know there's something. Even if I don't find it now I'll be back. You'll slip up, wherever you're hiding your fuckin—' he kicks the counter, the noise vibrating loudly in the small bed-sit '—photos. Or the women's fuckin' clothes,' he kicks out at the bin.

It falls over, the lid opening.

An object falls out, wrapped in a clear plastic bag. It rolls a couple of metres before hitting a wall. Red is the dominant colour inside, but as the bag settles the shape of a nose can be made out. And eyes, dark colours behind the opaque covering.

'Jesus Christ,' Harry takes a step backwards. 'Jesus fuckin' Christ.'

Tom slumps to the ground. The world is spinning too quickly now, the lights are streaks of brightness. He tries to stand but the pain is unbearable.

He sinks. His sight is blackness.

Words reach him, panicked words rattling down the phone.

'Yes, that's what I said. A fuckin' head. A real fuckin' human head.'

Chapter 28

His grandfather slouched against the side of the horsebox, cleaning the face of a watch with his sleeve.

'You should have this,' he croaked, held the watch by the strap and rocked it back and forth in front of Tom.

'I'm okay,' Tom pushed his hair back with his fingers. He harshly brushed the front of his jumper with his open palm, quickly checked the flies on his trousers.

He was nervous.

He had been invited to a party, a friend of Sarah's. And tonight was the night he was going to make his move. Time was getting away from him. They wouldn't be staying in Rossboyne much longer, he knew that, not now that his grandfather's mood had darkened again. Besides, this business with Mary was an emotional complication that he couldn't deal with. He was terrified he'd meet her every time he left the horsebox. He had asked Colm for some advice and received an open-mouthed expression and an astonished reply.

'Mad Mary?' he shouted. 'What the hell are you doing around her? Jesus Christ.'

Tom asked why she was called Mad Mary and Colm took a long drag on his cigarette and lay back on his bed.

'Because she's fuckin' mad,' the smoke poured from his nostrils and formed a cloud above his face. 'Why the hell else would she be called that?'

Tom felt his hope sink even further at this.

Tom's grandfather staggered over to a candle which sat on a saucer next to Tom. He held the watch up and tilted it so the glass front reflected a circle of light.

'Look at it. It's a good one,' he said. The smell of drink on him had a sour quality. 'I want you to have it.'

'I'm heading out,' Tom said flatly.

'Where?'

'To a party.'

'You'll be back late?'

'Probably. Don't know.'

He offered Tom the watch again.

'Thanks,' Tom took the watch to keep him quiet, strapped it to his wrist and made his way to the door. Behind him he heard the sound of a metal ring being pulled and the fizzing of drink rushing towards the opening.

'That's a good watch,' his grandfather said.

Tom looked back once to see his grandfather unwrapping the portrait of Norma. Tom knew his grandfather would just stare at that painting for the rest of the evening, until he was too drunk to keep his eyes open or to raise his head.

The party was on in one of the council-type houses on the opposite side of town, Clara Dunne's. She was a skinny girl with bright pink hair. She wore excessive eye make-up and black lace dresses, whispered when speaking and had an unhealthy obsession with death and death-related topics. Tom thought about Sarah as he made his way there, about how he was going to get her alone, how he was going to explain his feelings, and the consequences if she felt the same. He imagined himself living in the neighbouring town, the one with the library, close enough to see Sarah but far enough away from the delusional Mary. He wouldn't need much money to survive.

Jesus, sure they were surviving on little as it was.

Besides, poverty would be a worthwhile embrace if he was to be with Sarah.

A gang of people opened the door to him, cheering and whooping. He was swallowed up and propelled into the house, to a hall littered with bottles and cans.

Everybody was drunk already. Sarah and Clara wore matching checked shirts but, in Tom's mind, Sarah looked infinitely more beautiful. They had finished off most of a litre bottle of vodka, drinking it from cone-shaped glasses with little umbrellas on the side. They squealed when they saw Tom and hugged him tightly. But they were like newspapers blowing in the breeze, moving from one place to the next, wrapping around different people at the party and staying wrapped until they were shaken off.

Clara insisted that they listen to the Doors but Colm didn't like the Doors and refused to put them on. Clara and Sarah disappeared for ten minutes and when they returned there were streaks of black down Clara's face from crying. She looked at Colm through slitted eyes until he changed his mind. The pair instantly brightened when his will caved and he put on a Doors tape. The girls began leaping around the place like lunatics.

J.P. was drunk and angry, perched in the corner of the sitting room on a puffy orange armchair, chain-smoking and drinking wine from the bottle.

'I have some news,' he said when Tom approached him. 'Some good news and some bad news.'

Tom sat down beside him and opened a can of beer. He was

unsure of himself, nervous about the chaos of the place, the unpredictable nature of the people.

'The good news is that I'm drunk,' he swigged on the bottle for dramatic effect. 'The bad news is that I'm going to be a father.'

Tom waited for the punchline.

It didn't come.

He was stunned. For Tom, sex had always been a peripheral goal, kind of like becoming an astronaut or a pirate. He knew it was possible but he never actually believed it was going to happen to him. It had certainly happened for J.P.

J.P. went on to explain how he had met this girl at one of Colm's gigs. Some fat girl, he had said. She had a tie-dyed T-shirt and a green streak in her fringe. She was older than him, shared a house with a gang of punks.

'Doing it for the dads!' J.P. shouted and took another swig of wine.

As the night wore on J.P. kept referring to Jack Kerouac's *On the Road*, his favourite book, a book that he liked to carry around with him, tucked in the inside pocket of his forest-green army jacket. He would often take it out and read some lines for Tom, and Tom would wonder if J.P. believed the book had been written especially for him, an agenda for his future, the plan his life was supposed to take.

J.P. hated the idea that this plan was being taken away from him, of parenthood being thrust upon him. It was everyone's fault except his and he vocalised this loudly from the orange chair. Some years later Tom would think about J.P.'s attitude and in his own way he would relate to it. Like J.P., he also wished that his life had ripened slowly and naturally and not been bluntly altered by unexpected events. Tom would consider how differently he would have developed with the slow introduction of challenges, imagine a world where he had time to regretfully wave goodbye to each stage of his life. He supposed that the difference between himself and J.P. was that, whereas Tom mourned the life he was given, J.P. mourned the life he would never have. To him parenthood was accepting a type of imprisonment, where he would be partially controlled by someone else, but worse still it would be a willing imprisonment, as if he was enrolling himself into some torturous asylum.

Tom struggled to finish the can of beer. It seemed to churn in his gut. He inhaled deeply in an effort to get rid of the feeling of nausea before moving into the kitchen. It was quieter in there. He sat at the edge of a small group of girls who were having a serious conversation about the benefits of red wine.

Sarah appeared at the doorway.

'Found you,' she said. Her voice was uncharacteristically high. She slinked her way towards him, drawing her head to the side and nibbling on her index finger.

Her eyes were partially closed.

Tom tried to smile but his nerves merely caused his mouth to tremble slightly.

The sickness in his stomach grew as she got closer. He sat up straight and placed his hands on his thighs for support.

Sarah stooped forward when she reached him and without pausing moved to kiss him.

Tom kissed her back but he was too aware of his stomach to enjoy it. And the kiss tasted bitter too, cigarettes and alcohol and strong perfume. The longer it went on the more bitter the kiss tasted until eventually he had to pull his head away. He turned to the side and vomited.

When he was finished he was aware that talk in the room had stopped. His sight was blurred but he knew they were all looking at him.

Tom heard the voice then.

It was her voice.

Mary's voice.

It was coming from the hall. She called for her son.

'William!' she shouted. 'William!'

Tom closed his eyes and wished himself somewhere else.

Chapter 29

The detectives arrive.

The scene is hazy and surreal. There are strangers in his bedsit, in his home, shouting and brandishing guns. There is a rolling pain in his head and the pull of the darkness, a pull that he has to fight constantly. The room is a complete mess. And in some terrible way it is this mess that keeps him semi-coherent, the fear that these strangers are going to alter something else in his place which separates him from unconsciousness.

He sees the scene like he is watching a damaged reel in action. There are moments of black and moments where people seem to move too slowly or where voices sound stretched. It isn't long before a detective realises it is only the head of a waxwork dummy in a bag on the floor.

It's the weight, Tom thinks. That's the giveaway. A human head will weigh much more than a waxwork head. He recalls this programme he once saw, a kids' programme centred on the human body. They asked how a person could weigh a human head.

There was a brief cartoon of a man with his head resting on a weighing-scale and then a presenter appeared. He was bald on top, with long hair at the sides and back, the type of person who makes Tom think of vegetarianism and foraging and signs with the words 'Save the Squirrels' written in fat red paint strokes.

'Impossible and easy,' he had said. And Tom thought how it is impossible for something to be both impossible and easy but the presenter went on to back up this statement. Impossible, in that you would have to remove the head and weigh it at the exact time it comes off, before everything starts to spill out.

Easy, in that the human head and brain is predominantly made of water so if you dunk your head in a body of water and work out the weight of the displaced water the result will be pretty much the same as the weight of your head.

Tom imagines doing just this, lowering his head into a body of water. But the water is warm and black, so black that it would seem as if he was headless if viewed from the side.

And the warmth is soothing.

And Tom is soon thinking of nothing but the warm, black water.

Until he feels something tugging at his arms.

And he hears voices in the hall.

Tones of disbelief.

Maureen Hill is mentioned a couple of times and a reference to someone being a fuckin' idiot. The words 'deep shit' are also used.

Tom is heaved upward, supported as he moves downstairs and outside.

He is in a police car.

The rear is filthy and the driver revs the engine harshly at traffic lights.

They stop at a hospital, St Andrews.

Tom is seen to immediately by a nurse with a lilt to her accent. She speaks to him as if he is a child and Tom likes this. He can't remember the last time someone has shown him concern. She cleans the wound with strong, confident pressure. The cut only needs paper stitches but he is advised to rest and to avoid tasks that need excessive levels of concentration. Tom wishes he could do that. He wishes he could turn his brain off. He wishes he could avoid looking at the tray of hospital equipment next to the bed, wishes he could stop mentally rearranging the position of items so they would sit on the tray more neatly.

She lays a hand on his arm before he goes. And Tom feels the heat of her hand long after she raises it again.

The same policeman drives him back to his building.

Garda Harry is still in his bed-sit. He wears a T-shirt and jeans and he is in the process of shifting dirt from the dustpan into the bin. He stops when he sees Tom and rests the dustpan on the counter.

'I'd like to say that on behalf of myself and the force I apologise for my actions,' he says without emotion. 'I was acting in the interest of public safety. And I made a mistake. I'll put everything back in order as a gesture of goodwill.'

Tom half-expects Harry to stick a 'yours sincerely' at the end of his apology.

'You know where everything goes?' Tom asks.

'I have a good idea.'

'I'll show you,' Tom says.

Harry scowls, composes himself quickly and nods.

'First, you can remove that dustpan from the counter and clean underneath,' Tom says and moves around the bed-sit.

The spaghetti is gone from the floor, the glass shards cleared and the splashes of sauce cleaned. His chair has already been set the right way up and Tom checks it for damage. There is a thin crack where the left hind leg is screwed to the base. It should be okay though. Tom tells him where to position it and Harry follows the instructions.

'Left a bit,' Tom directs. 'No, the front bit left, toward the window. A bit more.'

Harry's face reddens with every order.

'I think it needs to be forward a bit more,' Tom moves to the side. 'Yes, that's it. Push it forward a couple of inches.'

'Christ,' Harry huffs. His movement is slow, like a reluctant teenager, Tom thinks.

When Tom is happy with the position he tests the chair.

'No, it's not there yet.' Tom stands. 'Move it to the left a bit more.'

'All right, you've had your fun,' Harry says. 'The chair is perfect where it is. What have I to do next?'

'But it's not perfect,' Tom stands behind the chair and stretches his arm outward. 'The chair has to be facing the window exactly.'

He directs his hand sideways.

'But it has to be ahead of the door. I don't want to be able to see any part of the door when I'm sitting down. But I also don't want to have the picture in direct line with my eyes,' he points to his picture of Elvis which hangs on the wall. 'It has to be far enough forward,' Tom sits, 'so that I can see the upper shelf across the way but not the tip of the objects on the shelf below. And when I sit forward I should be able to see a tiny section of the bulb that is hanging in that room over there. No,' he stands. 'It's not right. It's not right at all.'

Tom moves the chair ever so slightly to the right. He sits down and angles his hand in the direction of the door. He remains this way for a few seconds before standing. He then alters the angle of the chair ever so slightly clockwise.

The policeman leans against the wall. He smiles to himself and shakes his head. His eyes are glassy with humour. He checks his watch. It is eight thirty-one. When he checks it a second time it is eight forty and Tom is still working on the position of the chair. The humour has gone from Harry's face. He has an expression of disbelief. It soon softens to one of pity.

'How long have you been like this?' he asks.

Tom doesn't answer. He is lying flat on the ground, tipping the chair to the left in movements so small that the policeman can't see any difference.

'Look, Stacey,' Harry walks closer. 'Tom Stacey. Tom,' he repeats loudly.

Tom looks up. His brow wrinkles.

'This isn't going to work, Tom. I'll never be able to get the place the way you want it.'

Tom glances to the chair as the policeman speaks, as if it is the policeman who is the distraction.

'Is there anything else I can do instead?' Harry asks. 'Tom. Is there anything else I can do?'

Tom stands.

'No, that's okay.'

The policeman walks to the door and opens it, stands next to it massaging his palm. He frowns.

'Just give me a shout when you're finished and we can sort some other way of making up for the,' he pauses, 'the misunderstanding.'

Harry begins to close the door.

'Hang on,' Tom says suddenly.

The policeman stops and raises his eyebrows questioningly.

'You know how to find people, don't you?'

'Yeah,' Harry drags out his answer.

'I'm looking for someone.'

'Who?'

'A woman.'

'We don't do things like that down in the station.'

'All I want is an email address.'

The policeman looks at the chair for a moment, the solitary position in front of the window, the small window that looks out onto the side of a building.

'I don't know,' he eventually says. 'It's not for anything weird, is it?'

Tom is tired, too tired to finish sorting out his bed-sit.

He doesn't want to spend the night surrounded by this mess. There are too many problems upsetting the balance of the room; the scratches and the marks for one, the fact that all his appliances and furniture have been disturbed. It is like looking at a dislocated joint, he thinks, the same features but set at the wrong angle.

It feels as if it is not his any more.

Someone has come in and has taken that away from him.

He can't face staying in the bed-sit tonight.

A part of him feels that the bed-sit may never feel the same again.

Tom changes into his stripy pyjamas. It is a lumbered change, an effort to push his foot through the twisted leg of the trousers, the buttoning of the shirt taking an excessive amount of time. He washes two painkillers down before grabbing a duvet, a couple of blankets and a pillow.

He trudges to his neighbour's place.

His feet feel heavy. His legs feel distant, more detached than usual.

It is the bang on the head, he tells himself. The bang on the head is making him feel like this. That impact would have caused his brain-process to disrupt, a kind of scrambling of his thoughts for a moment. And his brain is now in the process of trying to return to normal.

Rebooting.

That's a nice way of looking at it.

Tom pushes open the door to his neighbour's place. He barely hears the usual squeak that accompanies the swinging of the door. There is a haze around his sight and when he tries to catch the edge of that haze it moves with the movement of his eyes.

He is unaware of the blankets dragging in the dust behind him.

Just as he is unaware of the figure who stands against the banister rail of the stairs.

The figure sways slightly, watches Tom intently as he moves inside the bed-sit.

Tom pushes the door closed. He doesn't lock it.

For the first time in years he doesn't even bother brushing his teeth.

Tom lays the duvet on the floor first, pulls at each corner until it forms a neat rectangle. He places the blankets over the duvet in the same fashion, folding them backward at the top to make room for the pillow. A cool breeze enters through the open window. It causes the hair on the model to sweep back and forth. It carries the scent of vinegar from the chipper on the street outside. It carries noise too, the engines and the random voices. There is a whoop and a playful scream.

Tom switches off the light and gets under the blankets. He looks to the window. The model is a dark silhouette against weak light outside. Tom wonders if the paint and glue are dry. He wonders if the features will hold together when he brings it to the agency for the first time.

'An adventure, Shatner,' he says, even though Shatner's head is no longer there. 'I'll bring you on an adventure tomorrow.'

There is a flutter in his stomach at this notion, at the prospect of showing his creation off for the first time. Because it is a creation, he thinks. And although he wasn't serious when he said it was art to the girl in the shop, now that the idea of art has been planted in his head he is beginning to feel that there is something artistic about the whole thing. He has created a woman, not a real woman of course, but he has created something that will hopefully lead to a real woman.

He imagines Martha and Anna from the agency in the room with him.

What about Fiona?

'Fiona isn't going to call,' he says.

Sarah?

'Sarah is the past.'

What do you want Tom? Tell us what you want?

'I'll show you what I want,' he closes his eyes and pictures himself placing his form on the desk in the office, the two women nodding appreciatively.

A gauge for humour, why didn't we think of that Martha?

Indeed Anna. Indeed.

Tom pictures himself unzipping a large suit-type bag.

The slow, careful reveal, head first, moving downwards, the grey eyes, the thin nose, the yellow dress against the curves of her body.

Wow!

Sleep pulls at him.

Absolutely wow!

Dragging him under.

The waves are black and they wash over his senses.

He needs sleep. Just a little rest.

The door suddenly crashes open.

'You fucker!' a man shouts.

His footsteps are heavy enough to shake the floorboards.

They move past Tom's position on the floor towards the silhouette at the window.

Chapter 30

Colm and Clara were standing at the front door when Tom walked out to the hall. Clara was gesturing with her hands and explaining that there was nobody called William at the party, in that repetitive, irritating way that drunk people do. Colm was speaking with the mellow tone of someone who believes they are fully in control of the situation.

J.P. staggered in from the sitting room, smiled goofily in Tom's direction and mouthed the words 'Mad Mary'.

Tom walked past him and Mary crossed her arms and shook her head angrily, nodded at his approach.

Tom wished he hadn't come to this party. He wished it was the next day and he was only listening to Sarah's stories of drunkenness, wished he was ignorantly helping her through her hangover. Jesus, he thought, will she even want to talk to me again after the whole vomiting thing?

Tom pushed past Mary at the door.

He needed to be away from her, them, everyone.

He pictured the river briefly, the lull of its gurgle, the meandering calm, the constant movement, the sureness of the direction.

'You all right?' Colm grabbed his arm.

Tom pulled away and walked.

Mary came after him.

'William,' she called. 'Don't you walk away from me.'

Tom upped his pace and so did Mary.

She was at his side, speaking, but Tom barely heard the words. The pitch of her voice rose. Her face was angry.

Tom began to jog, past houses which were dark at that hour.

She ran too, her coat opening. She was wearing an old pair of tracksuit bottoms and a loose-fitting nightshirt. She panted in the effort to keep up.

'William,' she called. 'Get back here William. Please.'

Tom increased his pace.

'William please,' she pleaded. And there was pain in that voice and it cut Tom deeply and his thoughts moved to his grandmother, to a time when he would nestle in beside her on the sofa as she read from a nursery rhyme book.

It didn't seem that long ago.

How had he found himself here? What had happened?

'William,' Mary called

And Tom ran faster.

Wee Willly Winky.

Runs through the town.

Upstairs downstairs

In his nightgown.

Away from the row of council houses, along dark roads.

The trees whispered, seemed to hush each other, warned of his approach.

He pushed his legs as hard as he could and her voice gradually faded into the distance.

He was left with the sound of his shoes patting the road surface.

Tapping on the windows

Crying through the locks.

He could see Ryan's bar in the distance. There was a sole spotlight shining out front. The Bedford was a black bulk in the car park. It was a creature crouching in the night. And it grumbled, a continuous grumble that grew louder as he approached.

Are all the children in bed?

It's past eight o'clock.

His legs slowed.

There was something wrong.

The engine shouldn't be running.

He came to the Bedford from the rear. There was a tube. It was attached to the exhaust. It was snakelike, slinked along the ground at the side of the horsebox, led to the front wheel of the cab and lifted from the earth up to the window, which was open a fraction.

Tom moved around to the driver's side, found a grip at the point where the wood met the cab, hauled himself onto the step and gripped the door handle.

He pulled.

The door opened first time.

He dropped from the step while the door swung open fully.

Tom could see his grandfather's head resting on the steering wheel.

His eyes were closed.

He was dead. Tom knew this immediately.

In some way, Tom would think later, he always knew it was going to end like this. And the weight of this knowledge is something that he would carry for a long time to come.

His grandfather's arm was in a forward position at the side of the steering wheel. His sleeve was caught on the indicator. The weight of it was dragging the indicator downward, causing it to buzz continuously.

Bzzzzz

Like an angry bee.

Bzzzzz

It vibrated in Tom's head.

Bzzzzzz

He wasn't sure how long he was standing in that position. At one stage she appeared, Mary. She looked into the cab and she screamed. And he turned to the scream and she had her hands over her mouth and her eyes were similar to the eyes of a victim in a scary film.

But worse. Because nobody could act out that expression.

Nobody could pretend like that.

He looked back to his grandfather.

And Mary screamed.

And the indicator buzzed.

Chapter 31

A character flashes into Tom's head.

It emerges from his memories of the fairground in Rossboyne.

They had been in the haunted house, a cart slowly creaking its way through a darkened tent, plastic skeletons on the walls, a stuffed dog hanging from the ceiling.

The character had been at the end of the ride, this dummy in a torn suit which shot upright from a horizontal position, only to be knocked back down in the next instant by the cart.

Blink and he was there, blink and he was gone.

This image flashes into Tom's head because for one horrible moment he feels as if he is that character. He springs from the ground just like that dummy, with a force that seems to be completely out of his control. And for a time after he feels as if a hardened substance has filled every inch in his body, tightening the muscles so suddenly that they vibrate momentarily.

He stays like this for what seems like an age.

Unable to move.

Rigid.

With a fear that shows itself as dampness on Tom's forehead, across his crown and down to the base of his back. It flashes in his head, this fear. But a section of Tom's mind still ticks along logically because this part of the brain seems to work independently from the rest, the part that compels his hand to pat the kettle three times after he has used it, the part that makes him continuously return to a door to check if it is locked, the part that prefers lines and squares and likes to package the world into neat little bundles, the part that he hates, that would drive him over the edge if he thought about it too much. But even the act of thinking about it has become part of the compulsion, the act of organising his mind into different compartments. Because by organising his mind into separate compartments, surely this means that it is the compulsion that is now controlling his mind and that it has spread, this madness, this disease, this infection. And that is more frightening than any intruder or attack. If it is spreading, when will it stop? He may end up like some of the unfortunates who have compulsions so bad that they spend hours rolling hand over hand under running water, their brains telling them to go and do something else.

Eat.

Sleep.

Move.

Do something for fuck sake. Just leave the sink and do something.

Anything!

Or he may end up like those who are affected so badly that they can't bear to hug their children for fear of contamination. Or those who are unable to leave their rooms. Or those who spend so much time on their irrational routines that they have no time to do anything else.

That is a fear worse than any, the fear of losing the mind.

And that is what makes Tom brave. Because he knows he is brave.

I am brave.

He is not violent or persuasive. But he is strong. You have to be strong to cope with the thing he has. So he stands and he shouts back at the intruder.

And the intruder does turn slightly, veers to the right, his shoulder rumbling along the wall for a couple of meters.

But it is too late because the intruder is heading right for his model.

And he is smashing against the head of the model.

And the model is falling forward.

And it doesn't stop where Tom is expecting it to stop. And it doesn't stop where the intruder expects it to stop either. Because the intruder immediately throws his hands out in an effort to prevent it from falling any further.

But he is too slow.

The model falls forward, slides across the counter and drops through the open window.

Tom's feet are in motion and he is at the window quickly and his hands move upward, grip his own hair and pull.

He looks down.

She has landed on the roof of one of the extensions attached to the building, face down, her arm at a strange angle.

Tom looks from the model to the intruder.

It is Karl Wallace. He smells of drink and sweat, sways drunken-ly. His eyes are directed towards the model, unblinking. The fingers of his right hand are in his mouth and he is biting down hard.

'What have you done?' Tom shouts. 'Jesus Christ!'

Karl turns towards the voice. He blinks for a time, his fingers still in his mouth. He begins to shake his head slowly, closes his eyes before suddenly gripping the sides of the sink and vomiting. He grunts when he's finished, breathes heavily and then begins to sob.

'What have I done?' he leans against the counter. 'Jesus Christ, what have I done?'

He turns so quickly that he loses his balance and strikes his shoulder against the wall.

'How do I fix this?' He grabs Tom by the collars of his stripy pyjamas. 'You have to tell me Tom. How do I fix this?'

He releases Tom.

'I'm fucked. Fuckin' hell I'm so fuckin' fucked.' Karl slumps to the ground. 'Oh for fuck sake. Oh God.' He covers his face and begins to rock back and forth. 'Oh God.' His words are muffled by his hands. 'I'm fucked.'

He continues this motion for a minute, the sob transforming into a slow whimper.

Tom looks at the model again. It is too far away to calculate the extent of the damage. But he does know of a way to reach the model. There is a door in the basement that leads to a set of cold grey steps, which in turn lead to the roofs of the extensions. On occasion, he has seen Mr Reilly, the landlord, move through that door with a toolbox in one hand and a coffee in the other, always a coffee in the other. He is the type of person who probably needs to have a coffee for every task he does, sips it while contemplating his next move. Tom briefly imagines Mr Reilly sitting naked with a Styrofoam cup in his hand, his wife in bed waiting on him.

Come on honey, hurry up and finish your coffee.

The model is on the third section over. I could reach that, Tom thinks, and he decides he will get the model as soon as Karl leaves.

Karl is silent. He is a closed bundle.

Tom wonders if he has fallen asleep. He flicks on the light and Karl suddenly raises his head, opens his eyes. They are red and watery. His mouth hangs open drunkenly.

'Who was she?' he drawls. 'What was her name?'

'She didn't really have a name,' Tom says.

'What?' The alcohol has resulted in his face taking on extended, exaggerated expressions, the eyebrows raised for longer than they should be, his mouth forming and holding an 'O' shape.

'What?' he repeats.

'I just called her Shatner,' Tom says.

'A fuckin' prostitute,' Karl shouts. 'I should have known.'

'What are you talking about?' Tom asks.

'You,' he points at Tom. His finger wavers in the air while he does it. 'You and a dead prostitute.'

'She's just a model,' Tom says.

'That's what they all say, you fool,' he shakes his head.

'No really. She's not real. She's just a model.'

'What?' He tries to stand quickly. His legs give way and he ends up on his knees. 'You,' he places his hand against the wall and stands slowly. 'You're sick. You really are.' He stumbles towards Tom, staggers to the side for a stretch before hitting the wall. 'You're sick.'

'Stay there,' Tom moves towards the door. 'I'm getting dressed and bringing you home.'

Tom supports Karl as they move through the building, shushes him when he begins to call Tom a sick bastard, tenses when he tries to push him away.

They totter down the main street and Tom watches the traffic lights change and soothes himself with the predictable sequence, a sequence that continues on regardless of the day and regardless of what is happening in people's lives.

'She's left me, ye know,' Karl says at one point, stops and hangs his head. 'And it's all your fault. Why did you have to stick your nose in?'

'I'm sure she'll take you back,' Tom says dryly.

'She won't.'

'She will,' he nods regretfully.

'I love her.'

'Good,' Tom pulls at his sleeve. 'Come on.'

'I can't leave my husband,' Karl imitates a female voice. 'I could never leave my husband.'

Tom stops pulling.

'She was okay before you turned up at the hotel,' Karl raises his head and looks at Tom through bleary eyes. 'You messed it up. You and that fuckin' watch of yours.'

Tom feels the urge to walk away, to just leave Karl here in his drunken state. He thinks of Angela, questions whether she will be better off without him. But it is not his decision to make. He's not sure if he could ever make a decision like that in any case.

'Come on,' he eventually moves on and drags Karl the rest of the way home.

The door to Karl's house opens quickly after Tom knocks. It makes him think that Angela has been awake. He imagines her crouched over the kitchen table, smoking cigarettes and waiting for the phone to ring.

She opens the door fully and makes a noise when she sees him, a deep sigh, the sound of someone releasing a lot of pent-up pressure. She places her arm around Karl and leads him inside. There are words from her, too low for Tom to make out.

They may be encouraging words to her husband or a relieved prayer to God.

Tom isn't sure.

They may even be the words 'thank you'.

Chapter 32

Monday.

It is time for Tom to clean up his neighbours' bed-sit.

Clean up?

No, he thinks. It is time to dismantle the clean lines of his neighbours' bed-sit and clutter up the room. It pains him to do it but it is a necessary evil. The Walters are due back on Wednesday.

Tom sweeps around the furniture and thinks about how he is going to miss the bed-sit. He tries to memorise the layout of the space, mentally absorb the atmosphere so he can carry it around with him long after he leaves. He leans his chin on the sweeping brush and looks through the large window. He will miss this window more than anything else in the bed-sit.

Shatner is slumped on the floor next to the sink in a bad condition and Tom doesn't have time to fully rectify the issues with the model before his meeting with the agency. Nor is he planning to break the appointment.

Because he never breaks appointments.

Unthinkable.

In fact, he will probably arrive five minutes before the agreed time because equally Tom hates to be late. Punctuality is important for him and he believes it is important in a partner too, so important that he has reflected it in his form.

For some it is easy to regard lateness as a nuisance but once time is gone it is gone for good and lateness can have a knock-on effect on the rest of the day. Just say, Tom thinks, the partner he chooses is habitually late. He imagines that all those lost minutes would merely pile up over the years until he becomes completely crippled with the notion of wasted time and unable to focus on anything else in life. No, he thinks, that just wouldn't do.

He sweeps the floor of the kitchen area next to the model. Shatner is no longer the clean, whole specimen she was before the fall. She has lost her legs, a clean break around the midriff. It is possible to balance the upper half on top of the legs but it has an instability that may cause him problems at his meeting with the agency. The right side of the face has caved in. The right arm had snapped off too but he has rectified this problem with a dowel screw. Surprisingly, the nose is still intact. As is the left ear.

Tom decides that he will manoeuvre the wig to hide as much of the bad side as possible and he will angle Shatner away from the women when revealing her. One good thing about the accidental split is that the model fits nicely into two black refuse bags, meaning she is easier to carry.

For every dark cloud, Tom thinks.

Tom begins to return all the photographs on the walls to their original position. His phone rings as he is doing this. It is Garda Harry.

He has an email address.

Tom writes it down in his notebook.

Sarah89@CMmail.ie

He repeats it a number of times to ensure he has it correct. When Garda Harry hangs up Tom places the notebook on the edge of the settee and holds the pages open with his phone so he can see the email address. He glances at the opened notebook frequently as he finishes fixing the photographs. His stomach dances, his head is light. His hands shake as he pulls cushions from the floor and throws them onto chairs.

He stops at one point and stares at the opened notebook, as if some deeper meaning is going to show itself from the address. It is a link, he thinks, to his past and to a part of his life that has been buried in the recess of his head.

Eventually, he returns to the task of untidying the place.

The large cushions for the sofa are still in the corner of the room. He uses both hands to lob them onto the sofa. His phone slides from the top of the notebook and lands on the inner side of the armrest.

Tom surveys the room, his feelings a mixture of nostalgia and compulsion to clean.

The room looks the same as when he first entered, the floor a bit cleaner maybe, he thinks, the sink too. He takes the door off the latch and closes it behind him before the impulse to straighten the cushions becomes unbearable.

It is at the exact moment when the catch locks that he remembers his phone is still inside.

Jesus Christ.

From: Tom_Stacey@glooble.ie
To: Sarah89@CMmail.ie
Subject: Hello

Hello Sarah,

I'm not sure if you remember me. Memory is funny like that. For some, the big events in their lives might be non-events in others. I don't think I'm unforgettable but I have a feeling you might remember me, you know, the same way that you'd remember a certain type of sweet you used to eat as a kid or even one of your toys. Not a doll though. I don't think I'm as memorable as a doll. That's if you played with dolls of course. For all I know you weren't into dolls at all. You could have been into tennis or fancy paper or anything really. But that's not what I'm getting at here, what I'm getting at is that you might remember me. I hung around with you and your two cousins for a bit. My name is Tom Stacey. I lived in the back of horsebox in the car park of Ryan's pub with my granda for a short while. We were pretty close, you and me, in my head at least, but that's all about that memory stuff again and for you it might not have been the case at all. But if it was the case and if you're interested in catching up, I'd love to, meet up even. Maybe?

Let me know what you think,

Take care and talk soon (hopefully)

Tom Stacey

Chapter 33

The contents of Tom's black refuse bags rattle and shift as he walks into the agency. He places them to the right of the door and uses his two hands to control the displacement. When the bags have settled he opens one and feels around until he finds the personal profile reports he has been working on. He closes the bag, stands and places a report in front of each woman. The reports are nicely bound with a neat blue edge and a clear cover on the front.

Tom moves the chair in front of the desks so it is in line with the door, and sits down.

Martha immediately begins to flick through one of the reports while Anna claps her hands together.

'You were taking notes, Tom,' she says.

'Sorry?' Tom is confused.

Anna points to the ledger.

' "He seemed distracted as soon as he got there," ' she reads. ' "About twenty minutes had gone and I noticed he had a notebook. I think he was writing down what I was saying." '

Anna offers him a look of dissatisfaction. 'I'm disappointed, Tom. You can't take notes during a date. Surely you know that by now.'

'She was drunk,' Tom says.

'That's no excuse.'

'And she was married.'

'What?' Anna's voice rises an octave. 'That's impossible.'

'She was,' Tom nods.

'No, no, no,' Anna slides her folder across to Tom. 'You're wrong Tom. You're completely wrong.'

'Her husband rang during the date.'

'That's crazy talk Tom. Look,' she rotates the folder on the desk and points to a tick-box marked 'single'. 'You see that Tom?'

'Maybe she lied.'

'She wouldn't lie. What would she lie for?'

Tom looks across to Martha. She is skimming through the pages, paying little attention to the details. She stops.

'What is this, Tom?' she asks.

'It's to help find a match. It's what we talked about.'

'But it's all nonsense. Animals and loyalty,' she flicks further on. 'Specific details on your sense of humour. A rating scale for levels of interest in hobbies. What are we supposed to do with this?'

'It all makes perfect sense.' Tom sits forward in his chair. 'Pick a section. I'll explain how it makes perfect sense.'

'I'll be honest and tell you right away that it doesn't look like something we can use.'

'Maybe when you read the whole thing,' Tom says.

'Look, Tom,' Martha shakes her head slowly. 'We couldn't give a form like this to the ladies. It's only relevant for you. That would mean the girls would have to fill out two forms, the normal form we use and then,' she makes quotation marks with her fingers, 'the Tom form.'

'What's wrong with that?' Tom asks.

'Then everyone would have to have their own specific form. Everyone would end up filling in hundreds of forms.'

'But they'd have more of a chance of finding their perfect match.'

'It's just not workable.'

'It's workable for me,' Tom stresses. 'It will help me find my match. Surely that's the point of the agency.' He looks to Anna for a reaction.

She merely sticks her bottom lip out sadly, bats her eyelashes and looks to the desk.

'But you asked me what I was looking for. The last time I was in this office. Didn't you?'

'Tom,' Martha's voice is stern.

'Didn't you ask me what I was looking for?' he repeats.

'Tom.'

'This form will tell you.'

'Look Tom,' Martha folds her arms. 'We've been meaning to talk to you about your membership.'

Anna reddens and bows her head.

'I think it's time for honesty on the matter,' Martha continues. 'I don't know Tom. It just seems that you aren't getting what you're after with this agency.'

'But that's why I have that form.'

'We all seem to be of a different opinion as to what a good match is for you. So maybe it would be best if—'

'Hang on,' Tom interrupts. 'I've one more thing to show you.'

'Tom, we need to discuss this,' Martha says loudly.

'It'll only take a minute,' Tom stands.

Martha looks to Anna and aims her hand at Tom and exaggerates her annoyed expression.

Anna shakes her head and shrugs.

Tom quickly drags the bags to the left side of the room. He turns and stands with hands on hips.

'I don't suppose you could both sit over on the far side of the room?' he asks.

They remain silent and remain seated.

'Okay, it's not essential,' Tom nods, hurriedly removes the contents from the bags and begins to assemble the model. He hasn't even finished balancing the upper part onto the bottom part when Martha asks him to leave.

'Hang on,' Tom says and rapidly steadies the model.

Surely if they see her in one piece they'll change their minds, he thinks.

Surely when the dress is covering the legs again they will give him a bit of time.

Surely when the scarf is hiding the gash between head and neck they will calm down and listen to him. Or when the wig is on, when it conceals the fractured and smashed side of the face, surely they will see what he has been trying to do.

But the more he rushes the harder it is to keep the two pieces together.

And Martha has raised her voice. She is demanding that he leave.

Tom stops what he's doing and looks at Martha. Her face is pale and she holds the phone receiver in her hand.

'I'll call the guards Tom!' she shouts.

To Tom, he feels as if he is the only person in the room who is calm and in control. It is like watching a scene in a soap opera, he thinks, witnessing a fictional car crash where all the actors are freaking out and overreacting and he is on his settee slowly shoving popcorn into his mouth.

Anna starts to scream and Tom's cool demeanour is broken.

He decides it would be best to leave the building. He roughly shoves the two parts of Shatner into the bags and crashes out of the room.

'Jesus Christ.'

He takes a deep breath when he gets outside, glances back, half-expecting Martha and Anna to come charging out with pitchforks and burning torches in their hands.

His back and palms sweat. It causes the material of the bags to slip from his grip. The left one drops first, opens to reveal Shatner's head, caved in and scratched and deformed.

Tom has this vision of the model lumbering towards him like the monster in Frankenstein, a deep voice booming around him.

Was I a monster, a blot upon the earth from which all men fled and whom all men disowned?

What was he thinking? He should never have brought her to the agency in this state.

Tom wipes his palm on his trousers and retrieves the bag.

He walks. From one street to the next, the bags swinging with his movement, striking him on the shins at times. Past market stalls and street artists. Tracksuit-wearing young men with grey skin and rattling Styrofoam cups. To an internet café beside a junction in the road.

The place is practically empty. The heating is too high, the air an uncomfortable itchiness on his skin. He takes a seat facing the door, tries to calm down before using the computer.

Calm.

Calm.

His hands shake slightly as his fingers flitter across the keyboard and his breathing is quick as he logs into his email account.

There is only one new email in his account.

It is from a woman.

It is from Sarah McCarthy.

Chapter 34

Wednesday morning.

Tom goes to a department store. He walks up and down the aisle of shirts, reading and rereading the sizes. Each shirt is folded inside clear cellophane so they all appear to be the same size. A staff member approaches him, a young girl in her early to mid twenties, foreign accent, high cheekbones and nice complexion. She offers to help and when he declines she moves to walk away but pauses and smiles.

'I'll measure you if you like,' she says.

And he nods and soon she has a tape measure curled like a belt around his chest. He reddens when she moves up to his neck. This redness doesn't dwindle until minutes after she has left him beside a row of shirts that are his size.

He picks a blue shirt, matches it with a pair of grey trousers and a navy tie with orange zigzags cutting from left to right. He pays for them at a till partially hidden amid piles and racks of clothes. He leaves the shop and swaps the clothes he wears for his new attire in the toilets of a fast-food restaurant two streets over.

'Moonlight Serenade' plays on the speakers set into the ceiling above the sinks and he can't help but think that it is playing for him. He pictures himself outside an apartment block singing this very song to an opened window.

He knows that things are going to work out this time.

He just knows it.

Tom keeps the top button of the shirt closed even though it presses into his Adam's apple, and tries his best to put a decent knot in the tie. She is worth a tie, he thinks. She is worth the risk of glaucoma.

But the tie is a struggle. It is continuously short at the front end, the knot always too tight. He returns it to his bag. As he leaves the shop he considers if he should ask someone to help him tie it, opts against it and soon decides that perhaps a tie isn't that important.

My Sarah doesn't go in for ties and suits and cravats, my Sarah doesn't care for stuffy gatherings of a formal nature. She is a simple girl, my Sarah is, a girl of simple tastes.

Tom gets the 10 AM train to a town near Rossboyne, heads about half a mile east to a small roundabout, takes the first exit, continues straight until he reaches a second roundabout and takes the second exit. According to the directions, if he was driving, it should take him seven minutes to reach the pub.

But he is walking so it takes a lot longer.

Mud from the road-edge stains the hem of his trousers. His shirt catches on wild brambles whenever he is forced to avoid any approaching cars. He bends down to tie his shoelace at one point and leaves a muddy print at the back of his trousers from the foot which trails his bended knee.

Tom reaches the town at eleven thirty, two hours before he is due to meet Sarah.

Ryan's b ar is smaller than he remembers, the interior refurbished with wine-coloured leather seats and a shiny black bar. He buys a pint and sits as close to the door as he can.

The television is on. It shows horse-racing. One race is exactly the same as the next to him.

One thirty comes and goes.

There is no sign of Sarah.

Tom clumsily flips a beer-mat over and over between thumb and forefinger, noticing how his hand shakes when he tries to concentrate on the task. A number of patrons come in for lunch and he stares at each one, his stomach flipping like the beer-mat, his head arched to the side in an effort to see if anyone is trailing behind.

He then gathers all the beer-mats on the table and places them in a neat pile, waits until he is finished his pint before visiting the toilet. He takes his bag and coat with him. The toilets are clean and empty, smell like mild bleach. He hurries when washing his hands for fear of missing her. When he returns there is a couple sitting where he had sat, a child squirming in a high-chair beside, blonde hair and a mouth full of small, square teeth. The child looks at him and Tom looks away immediately. He takes a seat at the bar nearest the door. He is self-conscious in this spot, nervous. He consumes his pint quickly.

Tom begins to think there might be another entrance to this place. He starts to believe he may have missed her. At two fifteen he asks the barman if there is another entrance to the pub.

'Not to the public,' the barman says without looking at him.

The football starts at three.

At three fifteen Tom asks the young girl who is collecting the glasses if there is another entrance to the bar. She tells him that there is not. Tom asks her if she knows if Sarah McCarthy is dropping in. The girl says that she doesn't know a Sarah McCarthy and moves behind the bar.

By four Tom has had his fill of drink. By half four he is walking from the pub.

He stands in the car park for a time and thinks about his

grandfather. There is a blur of feeling when he sees him in his head, a hazy warm glow in the centre surrounded by a weak halo of light. It is the same when he thinks of his grandmother. Tom wonders if this is how everyone he knows will be remembered. Not individual scenes or actions which they have carried out, just a distant glowing warmth, growing if still alive, fading when dead. Until eventually they disappear altogether.

He hasn't thought about his grandfather's death in a long time. It's not that he has avoided it. He has merely compartmentalised it in an area deep within his brain, a box in a basement, dusty and warped. If he opened it now he would probably only find a plain watch and a painting of a fat woman, he thinks.

But still, there must be a hole. How else would the buzzing have escaped from the box?

He hears it now, the indicator stuck in a downward position. And a coldness passes over him that has nothing to do with the breeze at his back. He blinks then and sees her face, Mary. And he imagines what her boy would have looked like before he died. He imagines him with black wavy hair and a smiling, pleasant face. William, a popular twelve-year-old boy, who probably played hurling and fished and liked to skim stones on the stream and dream about where his life would take him before cancer took him instead.

Tom feels pity when he thinks of her now, at her loss.

And certainly at her loneliness.

By seven thirty Tom is on a train heading for Dublin.

As the sky darkens it becomes easy to see the reflection of his fellow travellers in the carriage window. At one point his sight rests on his own reflection. His eyes are sleepy from the drink.

And sad.

He brings his hands up to his neck and unbuttons the top button of his shirt. His frame slumps immediately. He lets out a sigh that causes the man beside him to jerk suddenly and knock the book he is reading onto the floor. It lands at Tom's feet but he doesn't pick it up.

He is just too tired.

Tom is on the chair facing the window in his bed-sit.

It is a small view and in some ways he can't help but think that his life is like this view, the life of most people maybe, how they only sees a tiny fraction of the possibilities this world has to offer and even then these possibilities are too far out of reach for most.

Tom recalls the time he was seeing the psychiatrist. He wanted Tom to go through an obsessive-compulsive inventory to gauge if he suffered from OCD and to figure out how badly his compulsions affected his everyday life. Tom refused. In an effort to convince him, the psychiatrist told him about an extreme case of OCD he had come across, about how a patient in a hospital was so obsessed with cleanliness that they couldn't even bring themselves to use the toilet.

'This isn't uncommon,' he told Tom. 'This is how much these compulsions can take over. They take your time initially, to some extent your sanity, and then they try to take your dignity.'

The doctor's reference has stayed with him long after other advice or recommendations have evaporated from his head. The reason why it has stayed is because Tom has always used it as a sign of hope.

I'm not as bad as that, he would think. I'll never be as bad as that.

There has always been hope. Even during the darkest days of his life. But this experience with the agency and the knock-backs he has had lately, he wonders if he will ever hope again.

He hasn't bothered to check his email yet. He knows that Sarah hasn't been in touch, just as he knows that Fiona hasn't been in touch despite the fact that his phone is still stuck in his neighbours' bed-sit.

He has accepted this.

He has little choice.

Tom hasn't taken the model from the black bag. He will throw it out with the next bin collection. But he has taken Shatner's head from the bin and cleaned him up. The head now sits on the counter, looking at Tom as Tom looks out of his small window. Perhaps Shatner can become a permanent piece of the furniture, Tom thinks. Perhaps he can sit him in a nice vase or maybe even put him in a goldfish bowl. He toys around with the idea of filling the bowl with water and getting a couple of fish to keep Shatner company. But it is a brief idea. Goldfish are just too dirty to manage.

He stands, leaves his bed-sit and walks to the bathroom.

The neighbours are home. He can hear the television through the walls. It is a comedy.

Mr Walters laughs in time with the audience laughter. Tom listens like he has done on so many occasions. But this time he doesn't leave when the cold gets uncomfortable. He gets down on his hunkers and rests his head against the wall.

The minutes tick by.

Music plays to signify the end of the programme and Tom listens as Mr Walters flicks through the channels before stopping at another programme. Again, it is a comedy, American, the jokes come thick and fast and so does the man's laughter.

There is a break for the advertisements, Mrs Walters asking if her husband wants a cup of tea. There is a gurgle in the pipes as the kettle is filled and soon the audience laughter returns.

Tom listens to a brief conversation about a cousin in England and the price of shoes 'across the pond'.

Tom slumps to the floor. He is tired.

One programme to the next.

Channel-hopping and snippets of music and talk and engine roars, football commentators, each sound short and cleanly cut off, like the way Tom would hold his hands over his ears as a kid and release it at quick intervals.

And behind all the noise Tom feels the beat of his heart, steady, filling his head.

And a question forms amid the beats, broken up like the channel-hopping sounds on the television.

'. . . ere . . s . . . t . rin . . . . ming . . .?'

'Where . . . that . . . coming . . . ?'

'. . . is . . . ringing . . . from?'

Where is that ringing coming from? Where is that ringing coming from?

It is his phone.

His phone is ringing. It is in his neighbours' bed-sit. And Mr Walters is shouting.

'Where is it?' he booms. 'Where is the bloody thing?'

The sound increases momentarily before it stops altogether.

'Hello, who is this?' Mr Walters shouts, pauses, shouts again. 'Tom who? I don't know any Tom. Does a Tom own this phone?'

Tom is completely still.

He is afraid to make any noise, afraid to breathe even.

'Who is this?' Mr Walters demands. 'Fiona who?'

Tom feels a lifting sensation in his chest, a rollercoaster-ride sensation.

'Don't you go anywhere, missy,' Mr Walters says. 'I want to know who this phone belongs to. Don't you dare hang up.'

There is a pause.

'They hung up,' Mr Walters says. 'Can you believe this? I knew there was somebody in this place.' His footsteps clump around the room. 'Who do people think they are? Breaking in here and leaving their phones around the place. And cleaning the place up. Jesus Christ, I've never seen the sink so clean. Who would break in and clean a place up? I don't get it. I really don't.' His footsteps stop. 'Fiona. Do you know a Fiona? I don't know anybody called bloody Fiona.'

Tom stands and places his palms against the wall.

He feels like a shaken soda bottle. There are things bubbling inside him, pushing to get out.

He wants to cheer, sing, jump around the place like a madman, do anything but stand in the spot where he stands now.

But he doesn't.

He controls his actions and he closes his eyes and he feels the coolness of the flat wall against his palms.

And he smiles.

Acknowledgements

I'd like to thank all my family and friends for their support, all those who I have worked with in writing groups, everybody in DCU library, the Irish Writers' Centre and the Axis Centre.

A big thanks to Samantha, Gillian and Paul for their encouragement, to Lia Mills for her guidance, Keith Cullen for his literary comment over the years, Miriam Corcoran for her advice, Niamh Boyce for her feedback and Carrie Anderson for her input.

Thank you Faith, for being so brilliant!

Thanks to everybody in Liberties Press, for taking on the book and for being so great to work with.

A special thanks to my Mam and Dad for their unending support. (You are the best.)

Thanks to Mya and Emma for inspiring me.

And, of course, thanks to Sonia for everything. But especially, thanks for always believing in me.